In the vinyl recliner facing the table was a second body. The gunman was nowhere to be seen, but he had done his deed and left behind his mark. On the floor near the recliner was a red scarf and a small .22-caliber revolver.

It was at that moment that I received one of the great shocks of my life, for the unconscious figure in the vinyl recliner was none other than Elvis Presley himself—a man who had been dead for five years.

The
ELVIS
MURDERS
Art Bourgeau

CHARTER BOOKS, NEW YORK

THE ELVIS MURDERS

A Charter Book / published by arrangement with
the author

PRINTING HISTORY
Charter Original / May 1985

ISBN: 0-441-20431-7

Charter Books are published by The Berkley Publishing Group,
200 Madison Avenue, New York, New York 10016.
PRINTED IN THE UNITED STATES OF AMERICA

To Randal "Tex" Cobb, who through the years has shown me that luck is only a problem in distance and timing.

One

 Radio Johnson was the greatest Elvis imitator of them all. Otherwise why would anybody want to kill him? At least those were my thoughts backstage at the Elvis Presley Memorial Tribute near Memphis.

The occasion was the fifth anniversary of Elvis's death. Exactly five years ago, August 16, 1977, on the eve of a ten-city tour, Elvis had died. As far as last days go, it was nothing to brag about. He died with more of a sigh than a roar. Like many entertainers, he had lived a topsy-turvy life, sleeping away the days and prowling away the nights. His last day was no exception.

Following his usual pattern he rose late in the afternoon of August 15, had coffee, visited with his daughter Lisa Marie, and occupied the evening with routine things like a trip to the dentist and a racquet ball game, finally going to bed around the time most people were leaving for work on the morning of August 16, 1977. In the early afternoon he told Ginger Alden, his girl friend, that he was going to his bathroom to read. She went back to sleep. Sometime later she awoke and found his half of the bed still empty, but this didn't alarm her, because he routinely spent long periods of time in the bathroom, closeted away from even the small world of his entourage. She went back to sleep. Later in the afternoon she woke again and became concerned that he was still absent. She checked his bathroom and found him unconscious on the floor. Unable to rouse him, she called for help from Al Strada, one of the entourage, who in turn brought Joe Esposito, another of the entourage. Joe called for an ambulance, and while he waited, he began mouth-to-mouth resuscitation on the lifeless body of Elvis. The ambulance arrived and rushed him to Baptist Memorial Hospital, but it was no use. The King of Rock and Roll was dead.

Like rings on a tree, people tend to mark time with major events. Ask any American over thirty years of age what he was doing when he heard the news of John Kennedy's death, and I'll bet he can tell you, even though the years since number closer to twenty than ten. I was in a high school math class when the principal made the announcement over the loudspeaker. Girls immediately began to cry. I found this strange, since as a president, Kennedy had been very unpopular in the South, but later, after living through the deaths of Robert Kennedy, Martin Luther King, Jr., the Olympic athletes, and a host of others, I came to understand how public figures are a national resource. When someone or something destroys this resource you have every reason to cry.

When I first heard the news of Janis Joplin's death, it was early morning. I was in the shabby bedroom of a shabby little apartment overlooking nothing. There was a girl with me, a sweet, pretty girl who had gotten mixed up with some not-so-pretty people. After they had finished with her, she had gone walking through the streets looking for her baby—a baby that existed only in her mind. When the news of Joplin's death came on the radio, she tried to blink back the tears, but they kept coming until she started to cry like she had lost her best friend. I put my arms around her and tried to say comforting words, but they did no good. Her grief had to run its course. Later, when the crying was done, she said, "Whenever I was alone and afraid, all I had to do was listen to my lady Janis sing, and I knew I had a friend who could understand me."

Elvis's death affected me differently, but it affected me nonetheless. Like millions of others, my heart didn't stop when I heard the news, but I did feel a sense of sadness and oldness with the passing of a legend larger than any one man could carry. For only once in a blue moon comes a man designated to receive the curse of Greatness. Elvis was such a man. He sought, wooed, and seduced the curse like it was a woman, entering freely into its matrimonial bonds for better or worse, till death did part them. And even as they laid poor Elvis in his grave, the Greatness lived on, waiting for the moment when with a sweet, sweet kiss it could turn another frog into a prince—or even a king. And with the passage of five years, there were frogs aplenty.

Dressed in their finery, they all came acourting. They came from every middlesex village and farm, from every wide spot in the road, from every swamp, river, creek, rock, and lily pad imaginable. They came from every big-city bus station, truck stop, drugstore, and way station on their own personal road to oblivion. They came from every place of the night where tired men still dare to dream dreams of greatness, only to see them evaporate with the morning's dawn. These were the people who loved Elvis. These were the people who made him King. And come they did, clad in white jump suits all aglitter with sequins and sunbursts, desperately plunking their magic twangers, hoping to catch the eye of Greatness before the vacant throne vanished.

Greatness took little notice of these little men. But someone else did, and that someone else was a murderer. . . .

> —*Taken from the rough draft of an uncompleted article titled "King of the Five and Dime" by Snake Kirlin for* Ultra Suave *magazine, December, 1982.*

Two

 Several months have passed since I wrote those first few pages of "King of the Five and Dime," but it still remains unfinished. In that period I've started writing a mystery novel and completed two other magazine pieces for *Ultra Suave*, the grungiest men's magazine on the market. But each time I rolled a sheet of paper into the typewriter and tried to finish the story of Radio Johnson and the Elvis Presley Memorial Tribute, the words wouldn't come out.

People in literary circles call that "writer's block" and speak of it only in reverential tones over dry martinis. To the layman it simply means you have dried up on a particular subject, and the words won't come until you find a new way to approach it. This often happens when a writer becomes too closely involved with the people or events he is writing about. That's what happened to me after I accepted the assignment to write a magazine piece on the Elvis Presley Memorial Tribute for *Ultra Suave*.

Those readers who have followed the exploits of my partner, F.T. Zevich, and me through my previous works will undoubtedly shake their heads in wonder and say, "When did Snake Kirlin become a magazine writer? At the end of his last adventure he was leaving town in a beat-up Cadillac convertible. What gives?"

That is certainly a valid question. Unfortunately, while the events that befell us in the period between the close of our last adventure and our introduction to Al Saltzman, publisher of *Ultra Suave*, would make interesting light reading, they do not pertain to our story. I will dispense with them by simply saying they involved Florida, a singing telegram company, a dude ranch, and forty fat ladies. Need I say more?

When the call came about the Elvis Presley Memorial Tribute, we were in Galveston, Texas. It was hot. That was not unusual. Galveston is always hot in August. F.T. says it rained that day, but I don't remember it.

I do remember that F.T. was trying to balance his checkbook and I was watching television when the phone rang. It was Al Saltzman calling from New York.

"Snake, that you?" he yelled. I held the phone away from my ear. To Al, phones were still in the orange-juice-can-and-string stage.

"Yeah, Al, it's me. How's everything in New York?"

"Like the gynecologist said—I'm up to my elbows in work." He paused to give me a chance to respond. I didn't, other than to make a mental note to use that clever piece of repartee the next time I'm the luncheon speaker at the Methodist Ladies' Auxiliary.

With the social amenities out of the way, he got down to business.

"Snake, I have an assignment for you. Do you know where Eldorado, Tennessee, is?"

"Sure. It's a medium-sized town east of Memphis. It's not quite close enough to be a suburb, but it almost is."

"Right. I want you and F.T. to get on up there. He can do the pictures. When you get there I want you to write me a piece on the Elvis Presley Memorial Tribute."

"What's that?" I said.

"It has been five years since Elvis died. In that time it seems like a million Elvis imitators have surfaced, and a whole cult following has grown up around them. All through his career he had a great influence on a lot of singers, but those singers still developed their *own* styles and did their *own* songs. This is different. These people are impersonators. They come out on stage dressed exactly like Elvis, they look like him, and they do his show word for word, and the crowd goes crazy."

"Granted Elvis was a good singer and a bad actor, but I don't see why anyone would want to impersonate him," I said.

"He was more than a singer. He was one of the four most important things to happen in America since World War Two."

I couldn't resist. "What are the other three?"

"Television, atomic energy, and the birth control pill," he said.

"What about the space program?" I countered.

"Hell, Tang and Teflon are the only two good things that have come out of that whole mess," he snorted.

I didn't agree with him, but I let it go. "I understand about the importance of atomic energy and television, but how do you figure the pill and Elvis?" I said.

"The pill is easy. With its invention women became masters of their own destiny for the first time in history. They could now enjoy sex without fear. They could pick and choose when to have their children. They could pursue careers, have multiple lovers, and experience life to whatever level they chose. Before the pill women were no better than serfs tied to the land; the land being their own fertility. With the pill this serfdom was broken and women have now entered a new era."

That was strange talk coming from a man who made his living selling photos of high-priced models holding open the lips to their nether parts for all the world to see.

"What about Elvis?" I said.

"Elvis was the first one to tap the energy of the teen-ager. Kids in the fifties were restless, inhibited, and trapped. Didn't

6

you ever see *Rebel Without a Cause*? Kids were different then. When he came on the scene he changed all that. He released that energy. He gave teen-agers an identity of their own. He made being a teen-ager a separate stage of life, something more than an embarrassing period between puberty and marriage. He made it an identity to be proud of, and the kids worshipped him for it. Without him there could have been no Beatles, no Rolling Stones, no record industry as we know it today—"

"All right, you've convinced me," I interrupted. "Now what is this Elvis Presley Memorial Tribute—some sort of candlelight service in memory of him?"

"Hell, no—it's much better than that. It's a combination of Woodstock and "Queen For a Day." Pyrite Records is throwing a festival to crown the world's greatest Elvis imitator, and the prize is *to be Elvis for one year*! The winner gets a mansion like Graceland, the cars, the girls, the money, a recording contract, and a tour. This thing is for real, and it's big. Whoever wins it is going to get millions. I want you to get over there and report on it."

It sounded interesting, so I accepted. We haggled some about price. As usual Al wanted to pay me far more than I thought the piece was worth, but publishers are like that.

It took two more phone calls and three days of our refusing to budge before the money arrived.

We used the waiting period profitably. I read every biography of Elvis carried by the local bookstore, and F.T. continued to try to balance his checkbook. By the time the money arrived I felt I had a pretty good handle on Elvis, but F.T. was no closer to balancing his checkbook than before. We took the money and headed for the bank.

The bank was a squat little affair made of stone, smoked glass, and plastic plants. The parking lot had yellow diagonal stripes indicating where you should park. I maneuvered the Caddy in such a way as to take up three spaces reserved for handicapped people.

It was early and the bank was nearly empty. The old guard took one look at us, swallowed hard, and reached for his gun.

I couldn't blame him. We were a pretty sight. Both of us were well over six feet tall. I weighed about two thirty, and even though I was starting to go to seed I could still see my belt buckle when I thought to hold my belly in. F.T. weighed about two fifty and had enough scars to make you think he'd lost an argument with a Pioneer chain saw. He was sporting a very dapper mustache, and I had grown a beard that itched like hell. We were both wearing sunglasses. F.T. didn't need his; I did.

F.T. headed right for the bullpen where the officers sit making paper clip chains all the livelong day. He marched past the secretaries without so much as a glance in their direction and sat down in one of the chairs in front of the manager's desk. I sat in the other one. I could tell we were dealing with a man with corporate power. The chairs are a dead giveaway. If he's a climber, he will have two visitor's chairs in front of the desk. If he's a lackey, he will only have one and it will be beside the desk.

The man behind the desk had the cookie-cutter, part-on-the-left-side sameness that bank managers have the world over. Bankers like to call this image "solidity," but blandness is a better word for it. Bankers are a McDonald's hamburger in three-piece wash-and-wear.

F.T. produced his records and went on the attack immediately. Financial negotiations are often subtle in nature, but F.T. is more than diplomat enough for the job. After delicately maneuvering the conversation to the right moment, he picked up the manager's five-pound glass ashtray and smashed it against the wall.

The old guard again reached for his gun, but I waved him off. I appreciated his kindness, but we didn't need any help. The man behind the desk was ready to negotiate. It only took a few more minutes before he realized those little rascals who work deep in the bowels of the bank had moved the decimal point on our last deposit one place to the left and had shorted us a considerable sum. The problem solved, we closed our account, and the cashier brought us a nice fat stack of twenties.

The guard took us to the vault and went through the two-key routine to open our safe-deposit box. There wasn't much in it except an emergency fifth of Uncle Jake's Sipping Whiskey, a .38-caliber revolver, and several leather boxes like those jewelry comes in.

The old guard took one look at them and said, "Are those what I think they are?"

F.T. said, "Yeah."

"Could I see them?" he said in a small quiet voice.

F.T. handed them to him. His old hands shook as he removed the rubber band that kept the stack together and began to open them with great respect for their contents. The first two or three were Purple Hearts, beautiful with the purple ribbon and the heart with George Washington's head in the center. The next couple I didn't recognize because they were Vietnamese decorations. Then came the Silver Star. And then the last box—the Navy Cross and F.T.'s recon wings.

Tears came to the old man's eyes as he fingered the ribbons. In a voice barely above a whisper, and so shaky I almost didn't understand him, he said, "I lost my youngest over there."

F.T. put his hand on the old man's shoulder and said, "I'm sorry."

The old man wanted to talk about it, but he didn't know how to start, so he just said, "Was it hot over there?"

"Hotter than the andirons of hell," said F.T.

We waited for more, but that was all there was. The rest was too locked up inside to come out except as tears. We collected our stuff and left him there.

Outside, the manager was waiting for us. He was all smiles and apologies.

"Mr. Zevich, I'm very sorry for the problem you've had. I don't want you to think this is how our bank normally operates. My assistant tells me that it was all just a problem with the computer, and by way of apology we'd like you to have a little gift to make up for all your trouble."

With that he thrust a Waring blender into F.T.'s hands.

"Normally," he continued, "we only give these for increased deposits, but this time I think we can make an exception."

F.T. cradled it like a baby, and we headed outside for the Caddy.

Armed, oiled, and bankrolled, we were on the road again. I pointed the nose of the Caddy toward Memphis and left Galveston in a cloud of burned rubber and muffler smoke.

We made it past at least three exits before it was time to gas up. While I watched the numbers on the pump run up and the money in our wallets run down, F.T. went next door to the local grocery. I was still checking the oil when he returned with a bag of ice, a fifth of Bacardi rum, and two boxes of strawberries.

Once we were again underway he began to fiddle with the cigarette lighter. Satisfied with the results, he filled the blender with ice, rum, and strawberries.

I was trying to watch him out of the corner of my eye, but the necessities of the road kept distracting me, so I finally asked, "What the hell are you doing?"

"Making us a cocktail, what do you think?"

"Oh," I said and switched cassettes in the tape player. Soon the inside of the car was filled with Tracy Nelson's fabulous voice singing "Down So Low." The tape was just coming to the part that sends chills up and down my spine when F.T. set the blender on the dash and began to push its buttons. Tracy's voice was drowned out in a high-pitched whine as the Waring liquified, purified, rectified, atomized, and in general screwed up television reception for forty miles.

Up ahead of us a Chevy Vega pulled off to the shoulder of the road. Having owned one of the worthless little Detroit handjobs, I knew he was probably having trouble, so I stopped to see if we could help.

I got out and approached the Vega from the driver's side. The window was down and a hand was sticking out with a wallet in it. The driver didn't even look around. "Officer, I know I was speeding, but there's a good explanation—"

I looked around to see what he was talking about. Then I saw it. The blender full of strawberry daiquiris on the dashboard looked just like the old flashing red light.

10

I gave him a severe tongue-lashing about his driving, took twenty dollars for our trouble, and headed back to the Caddy.

It was early evening when we finally neared the festival. The day was still hot, but the shadows were long as the sun moved westward.

Finding the place had been no trouble. It would have been tough to miss it. Every radio station on the dial ran commercials for it, and there were billboards advertising it all the way to Texas. Some of them were funny, some not, but they all had that "South of the Border" quality that eats its way into your brain until you feel like you'll break out in a rash if you don't get popcorn, peanuts, pecan roll, and salt water taffy all at once; and your eyes ache to see the incredible two-headed calf, millions of deadly rattlesnakes in captivity, men wrestling alligators, the giant grizzly bear, and Indian dancing girls.

In Tennessee the billboards took on new heights of sophistication. One had a figure of Elvis in his white jump suit covered in sequins made out of lights that blinked on and off like an obscene Christmas tree. Another had a spastic Elvis strumming a guitar with a motorized arm that made him seem as if he were scratching mechanical crabs. Still another had the RCA Victor dog licking his hand with a red mechanical tongue. But the tackiest of all had a bloated Elvis, clad in robes of white with a large crown on his head, sitting on a throne. In his mechanical hand he held a scepter. As the arm made a lazy sweep, blessing all in sight, a cartoon bubble from his mouth lighted up with the words "All I have I give to you." That one took F.T. by surprise. He sputtered a couple of times before finally saying, "Look what they've done to him. He looks like Liberace doing a goddamned Imperial margarine commercial." There was no rage in his voice, only sadness.

The last couple of miles the traffic was asshole to belly-button, creeping along at a snail's pace, filling the air with exhaust fumes until it shimmered, and my nasal passages felt black from breathing its foulness. Overheated cars had to be inched around. Vendors on foot stalked the line of traffic selling everything from half-melted ice cream cones to day-old newspapers. An old man died while we waited. Four people tried to buy his ticket.

Finally we reached the main gate and continued our slow progress toward the parking lot that served as the campground. There, surrounding the flying-saucer-shaped auditorium, was acre upon acre of gasoline-eaters of all shapes and sizes from old Volkswagen buses decorated with fading flowers and peace symbols, to large station wagons wrapped in imitation wood, to motorcycles, to pickups, to vans, to four-door sedans. They advertised every culture and counterculture the length and breadth of the land, but they all had one thing in common—they had come to have a good time, and they were busy doing just that. F.T. and I were smack dab in the middle of the Elvis Presley Memorial Tailgate Party, and one hell of a party it was.

We put the top up on the Caddy and started to make our way toward the arena to pick up our press credentials. The mood of the crowd was good as they celebrated in peaceful harmony. We stopped for beer with a family from Des Moines, and had fried chicken with another from Shreveport. Everywhere you turned there were lawn chairs, coolers, round, three-legged grills all hot and cooking, and smiles. There were card tables piled high with stuff to sell: pictures, posters, records, scarves, T-shirts, statues, magazines, and jockstraps all adorned with Elvis's image. Teen-agers and adults talked and laughed together. The smell of marijuana mingled with the smell of meat cooking over charcoal, and the noise and happiness caught you up in its tide. It was a Woodstock with beer bellies.

It took about an hour of moving free and easy with the crowd to finally reach the arena, where a guard directed us to a house trailer that operated as the event's command post. As we arrived at the trailer we heard the faint but unmistakable sound of gunfire coming from inside. It was the sound of a small-caliber weapon, probably a .22, not much louder than the crack of a kid's bullwhip, but in the right hands, deadly enough to stop a grizzly in its tracks.

12

Three

The trailer had two entrances: one connected to the rear of the arena by a closed-in ramp that allowed people to come and go without being seen; the other just a normal door.

We opened the door and went in slowly, taking care not to get in the line of fire. We were in the bedroom of the trailer. The bed was rumpled like somebody had recently taken a nap or enjoyed a matinee there. The walls were covered with posters advertising the festival. We crossed the open doorway in a crouch and flattened ourselves against the wall. There was not a sound in the trailer. F.T. cautiously peered around the corner. Drawing no fire, he began a cautious descent down the narrow hall with me bringing up the rear.

The bathroom was on our left. It was empty except for a couple of dirty towels and a toilet kit on the edge of the sink, which a quick glance showed to contain a handful of plastic medicine bottles. On the other side of the hallway was the second bedroom. It was much smaller than the first, and was also rumpled and empty.

The hallway was about the width of a bowling lane, but it seemed twice as long. We held our breath with each step and waited for it to be filled with incoming fire aimed at us. The hallway ended at the living room-kitchen combo, but our entrance was blocked by the body of a man lying in the doorway.

We stepped over him and checked out the room. There was a slight smell of gunpowder in the air. The room was furnished with the usual imitation-this and cheap-that which comes with trailers. The kitchen table had been turned into a desk and was piled high with papers. A couple of open briefcases lay on the floor nearby.

In a vinyl recliner facing the table was a second body. The gunman was nowhere to be seen, but he had done his deed and left behind his mark. On the floor near the recliner was a red scarf and a small .22-caliber revolver. I had no doubt this was the weapon that had been used.

We turned our attention to the man lying in the doorway. He was a middle-aged man with styled hair and half glasses, the kind you associate with lawyers. The kind that allow you to look down your nose at life. Everything about him was designer from head to toe. He wore loafers with little gold buckles and designer jeans. I couldn't tell who had designed them, since he was lying on that part. His designer shirt was made out of a fabric whose name sounds like an African country. The sleeves were rolled up. On one wrist he wore a gold Rolex; on the other, two or three gold bracelets sufficed.

His shirt was unbuttoned halfway down. F.T. opened it the rest of the way to examine the wound. There, high on the chest and to the left of the breastbone, nestled in a patch of graying hair, was a small dark hole.

"Looks bad. From the powder burns I'd say he was shot at very close range. Help me raise him enough to get my hand under his back."

I gently raised his shoulders, and F.T. slid his hand behind the man's back. "The bullet is still in there. There's no exit

14

wound. We have to be doubly careful. It could be lodged against a vital organ.''

F.T. checked his neck for a pulse. "It's very weak, but I'm getting one." He took off his sunglasses and held them under the man's nose. "Breathing is shallow. Chest isn't working too well with that hole in it. See if you can find me a pack of cigarettes.''

On the table was a pack of Marlboros. I handed them to him.

"Now get around here, slip your hands under his back, and lift up slightly. We have to open the wound up a little," he said.

I did as I was told, lifting until his back arched slightly. F.T. took the cellophane off the cigarette pack and began to stuff it into the wound.

"Why are you doing that?" I asked.

"Chest wound," he said. "The most immediate danger is air getting into the chest cavity and collapsing the lungs. He's a goner if that happens. This will at least stop the air. It's a trick we used in Vietnam. While I finish up here, check out the other guy and see how bad he's hit."

It was at that moment that I received one of the great shocks of my life, for the unconscious figure in the vinyl recliner was none other than Elvis Presley himself—a man who had been dead for five years.

F.T. looked over at me and said, "What are you waiting for? Get busy."

When I still didn't move, F.T. finished up and came over to see what was wrong. He took one look at the man in the chair and said, "Christ, he looks just like him, doesn't he?"

Then I felt really stupid. Of course he looked like him. He was supposed to look like him. That's what we were doing here—reporting on a festival of Elvis imitators. But the resemblance was uncanny all the same.

He was dressed in a navy blue jogging suit and sported at least fourteen gold neck chains. I took his pulse while F.T. unzipped the top of his suit to examine the wound.

"How is he?" said F.T.

"I'm no doctor, but his pulse is strong and regular."

The wound was low and in the fleshy part of his right side. "Look at the powder burns," said F.T. "He was shot up close too."

F.T. felt for the exit wound. This time there was one. "The bullet passed through, and there's not much bleeding. He'll be all right. The other guy is our problem. I'm going to keep an eye on him while you go for help."

I took the entrance to the auditorium at a gallop. Backstage was quiet. There was nobody in sight. Just the quietness of a theater at rest. I ran onto the stage and yelled, "Anybody out there?" The only answer was my echo in the empty hall. Nobody appeared to throw me out or even to ask what I was doing there.

I ran down the steps at the end of the stage. I was going too fast and missed the bottom one, landing hard on my right knee. The pain shot up my leg in sharp flashes. It was my bad leg. I struggled to my feet and took a step or two only to collapse again as it gave way under my weight. I half crawled, half dragged myself to the first row of seats and slowly pulled myself up like a skier climbing a ski pole after a fall. There was no leg in it, only arm and chest power. The strain made the sweat pop out on my brow, and my mouth tasted metallic from the strange infusion of chemicals my glands were releasing into a body grown soft from the good life.

I was shaking like a leaf when I finally got to my feet. Gingerly I tested the bad leg. It held my weight this time, but just barely. Using the seats as a crutch I began to slowly make my way up the aisle. The expanse looked like a mile to the exit. I tried to speed things up a little, only to have it go out on me again, and I slipped and smashed my ribs into the edge of a chair. The pain was so sharp that it doubled me over, and for a moment I couldn't get my breath.

The bile rose in my throat until I felt like throwing up. All I could think of were strawberry daiquiris, beer, and fried chicken, and the very thought made things worse. For a moment I went cold—ice cold—as the sweat continued to pour out of a system being sorely tested.

I said a prayer: "Lord, if you'll just let me find a guard without throwing up, I'll start to jog again." That was heavy duty coming from me, considering how much I hate jogging.

The Lord, being the sport He is, let my lunch stay down, but He took His own sweet time about it, and I had to swallow hard a few times to choke back the familiar acid taste. Shaky, sweaty, clammy, I started again, only this time slower. The pain in my leg continued to move up and down at will, making me take short breaths in an effort to control it.

After about ten rows the floor started to slope upward. The concrete floor had just been buffed, making it slick as glass. I fell again about row twenty, but this time I caught myself and didn't hurt my knee, but I did feel a sharp pull in my side where I had banged it earlier.

I started again, but now my progress was even slower. The pain in my side and leg was so constant that I was still taking shallow breaths, which served to make me light-headed. I felt like I was going to pass out, but somehow I made it to the entrance to the auditorium.

A half-dozen careful steps brought me to the outer doors, where I pounded on the glass to get the attention of the two guards standing outside having a smoke. They turned, saw me, and came running. One fumbled with a key ring large enough to unlock every diary, chastity belt, and fishing tackle box in the state. Finally he got the door open.

While they relocked the door, I gestured the way I had come. "Two men in the trailer have been shot! Get an ambulance and a doctor! Call the police!"

They both took off for the trailer, leaving me to my own devices.

As I started back I remembered—F.T. and I were within sight of the trailer when the shots were fired. Nobody had come out of the rear entrance, but the gunman was gone by the time we reached the living room. That meant the gunman was somewhere out there in that empty auditorium, and I was locked in with him.

Four

When you're in snake country you don't try to move too quickly. If you do, you may run upon a rattler before he has a chance to get out of your way. Instead you make a little extra noise to allow for the fact that somewhere out there may be a deaf snake who needs more warning than usual.

That's how I made my way through the auditorium and back to the trailer. Since I'd already covered the auditorium at a snail's pace, I felt sure that he wasn't hiding between the rows of seats. Still, as I limped back down the aisle, I moaned and groaned loudly enough to give him ample opportunity to get out of sight. Bravery is a fine thing as long as it doesn't go hand in hand with stupidity.

The guards had used their radios to call for help, and by the time I reached the trailer, guards were posted at both entrances to keep out unwanted visitors. When the guard at the tunnel entrance saw me limping, he came forward and helped me into the trailer.

"Be careful," I said. "Whoever did the shooting is still in the building. He didn't have a chance to get out the rear door of the trailer before we arrived, and the doors to the auditorium were locked when I got up there, so he has to be in the building somewhere."

"Don't worry," he said. "They don't pay me enough to go in unarmed after somebody who has just shot two people. That's the sheriff's job, and I believe I'll leave that part to him."

"Have you been in touch with him?"

"Yep. Him and the doctor are on their way."

Inside the trailer, F.T. was doing mouth-to-mouth resuscitation on the fellow in the designer rags. When he saw me he stopped for a second and said, "What happened?"

"The knee went out on me. How are you doing?"

"Can you take over here? I need to look at the other guy. They've radioed for the doctor, but you know how thick that crowd is. It'll take him all night to get here."

"You think this mouth-to-mouth is helping him?" I asked.

"No, I think he's dying, but we can't sit here and do nothing."

I hobbled over and knelt beside the fallen man. I tilted his head back, cleared his mouth again, and settled in with a steady rhythm. His mouth tasted of cigarettes, beer, and hurt.

F.T. went to the Elvis imitator and checked his pulse, his pupils, and the wound. "He is doing fine, but we still have to be careful." He went into the bedroom and returned with a blanket which he placed over the wounded man. "The big danger now is shock. Getting shot—even with a flesh wound like this—causes some of the body's systems to malfunction, and the shock can kill you just as dead as the bullet."

He looked around impatiently. "Keep it up. I'm going to see what is keeping that doctor."

I kept up the rhythm in the fight to keep life in an unwilling body. In a few minutes F.T. returned with three men. Two of them carried a stretcher while the third, a man with snow-white hair combed back in a pompadour, knelt next to me and started to check for vital signs on the fallen man. In a moment

19

he said, "Get him on the stretcher and out to the ambulance." With that he turned his attention to the unconscious Elvis imitator. After checking him out he said, "It's not serious, but we'll get him to the hospital too." Looking at F.T. he said, "Where did you learn that trick with the cellophane from the cigarettes?"

"Vietnam," said F.T.

"Figures," he said. From the gruff way he said it I could detect the respect of one professional for another.

F.T. changed the subject. "While they're taking them out, can you look at my partner's knee? It's bad anyway, and he hurt it again when he went for help."

I lowered my trousers, and the doctor looked, probed, twisted, and pinched.

"How is it?" said F.T. We didn't need a doctor for that. I could have told him it hurt like hell and was as wobbly as a three-legged table.

"It's swollen. The ligament is pretty loose, but it'll be all right. I'm going to give you some ice packs and an Ace bandage. I'll show you how to put it on. For now I want you to go in the bedroom, lie down, and put the ice on it. I want you to stay down for the rest of the night. The ice will constrict the blood vessels and slow down the internal bleeding. This will keep down the swelling and the soreness. Tomorrow morning I'll have the boys drop off a set of crutches for you."

F.T. helped me into the smaller middle bedroom. I took off my pants and got into bed, then the doctor wrapped a couple of packs of gelatin that looked like swimming pool water around my knee. I immediately felt a deep freeze start to set in. He took two more and gave them to F.T. "Put these in the freezer until the first two thaw out, then switch them."

"How are you going to get through all this traffic to the hospital?" I asked.

"Standard emergency procedure. We keep a road clear for police use and medical use. When you have this many people, there are always problems that need quick solutions."

After he had gone I said, "Don't you think he was taking a big chance leaving two gunshot victims lying in an ambulance

20

while he looked at a bum knee?''

"Nope," said F.T. "The ambulance left as soon as they got them loaded. The doctor came in his own car."

With the wounded out of the way it was time to deal with the next piece of business: the gunman. As I told F.T. about my walk through the auditorium and the realization that the gunman was locked in, a strange look came over his face. It was the look of the hunter.

F.T. is a man born to bear arms for God, country, woman, or whatever obscure reason men go to faraway places and kill each other. For those men the cause is unimportant. All causes sound good on paper. What has meaning is the comradeship in arms: the laughing, the crying, the fighting, and the dying. Something as natural to those men as childbirth to women. I, on the other hand, have never had any great desire to bear either arms or children.

As he left to round up the guards and deploy them in a suitable military manner, I put my hands behind my head and thought, *In for a penny—in for a pound. F.T. won't leave till that gunman is found.*

It was a silly rhyme that sounded more like a high school cheer than a Shakespearean sonnet, but it accurately summed up the situation. Zevich and Kirlin—adventurers at large— were on the job again. A thought that instantly made me sick to my stomach.

When F.T. returned he took one look at me and said, "You're looking a little green around the gills. What you need is a beer. I'm going to check the refrigerator. We've got time for a quick one before the police arrive."

I'd forgotten all about the police. He was right; they were due, and our experiences with the police had not been pleasant. Along the way we had been fingerprinted by the Tennessee Bureau of Investigation, and if the police ran a check on us, they were going to find us linked with several unsolved murders.

F.T. reappeared with two cold cans of Old Blue. As he popped the tops I said, "What happened with the guards?"

F.T. gave a disgusted snort. "Mutiny in the ranks. Nobody

was willing to go in and flush him out. That's the trouble with these goddamned rent-a-cops—no guts. They just want to stand around and drink beer while they watch the girls in halter tops.''

"What's wrong with that? I've seen many a day that I would have killed for a job like that," I said.

"Me, too. But not now—we've got work to do."

"You can't expect a man who is unarmed, not a deputy, and being paid minimum wage to go out there and risk his life. It doesn't make sense. Sit down and drink your beer. The sheriff will be here shortly."

F.T. paced and grumbled until the sheriff arrived.

Sheriffs normally come in one of three sizes. There is the Richard Widmark size, which is to say a little man who is mean and full of himself. The Gary Cooper size is a fatherly man on the tall and lanky side who is generally only mean enough to get the job done. And the Broderick Crawford size, which is to say a mean fat man.

Our sheriff was cut from the Broderick Crawford mold. He had oily, graying hair, a mustache darker than his hair, and a voice like the Great Gildersleeve.

F.T. took the deputies and him into the living room, where he described what had happened. The sheriff listened quietly while F.T. boiled everything down into clear, concise details. When he got to the part about the gunman still being trapped inside the auditorium, the sheriff sent the deputies out to get the shotguns from the trunk of their car.

Once they were armed they began to search the auditorium. F.T. wanted to go along, but they wouldn't let him, so he had to content himself with pacing the length of the small bedroom over and over while I drank beer and stared at the ceiling.

They were gone a long time, which I took to mean they were doing a thorough search, but they still returned empty-handed.

"What happened?" said F.T.

"He was gone. There was a door open backstage. That's how he got out. We found this near the door," said the sheriff, holding out his hand. In it he held a Halloween mask

22

of the face of Elvis Presley. It was a good likeness, but a creepy one nonetheless.

"You think the shooter was wearing this, Sheriff—" Then I realized I didn't know his name. He filled in the blank for me—"McDuff"—and I finished my question. "—Sheriff McDuff?"

"Until the victims regain consciousness and can tell us what happened, I think we can safely suppose that the gunman wore this mask when he entered the trailer and did the shooting. When he didn't need it anymore he dropped it like he did the gun and the scarf."

"What do you think he did with the scarf?" I asked.

"Probably used it to cover the gun as he moved through the crowd. What easier way to move out there than wearing an Elvis mask and carrying a scarf? There must be at least a thousand people in the parking lot doing exactly the same thing at this moment," he said.

"What about the gun? Isn't that what professional hit men do, use a small-caliber gun and drop it at the scene?" I said.

"I've heard that, but we don't get that many professional hit men around here. Now, if you're finished with your questions, there's a few I'd like to ask. First, what happened to your knee?"

I told him about falling while I was going for help. He raised the sheet and took a look. "It's swelling a little. You'd better keep off it for a day or two. That ice ought to bring it down some. Old injury is it?"

"Football," I said. He nodded in agreement. What I had said wasn't true, but sometimes the shortest distance between two points is a little lie.

"Now, let's start at the beginning again just to make sure I have everything straight," said the sheriff.

I told him how F.T. and I were covering the story for *Ultra Suave*, and how when we arrived we came to pick up our press credentials, heard the shots, and the rest was history. "What do you think the motive was—robbery?" I said.

"Nope," he said. "I think we can rule out robbery. There is quite a bit of cash out there, and both victims were wearing expensive jewelry. Sorta rules out robbery."

"What, then?" I asked.

The sheriff pondered this for a minute before he replied. He handed me a piece of paper and said, "This is it."

I looked at the paper. It was a piece of white notebook paper. On it, written in block printing, were the words THE KING IS DEAD. LONG LIVE THE KING.

When I finished reading it I passed it to F.T. "Where did you find it?" I asked.

"Under the recliner."

"You really think this has something to do with it? It sounds like something out of an Ellery Queen novel."

A frown passed over the sheriff's face. "I think we're dealing with a psycho."

"A psycho—you mean some lunatic who is going around taking shots at whoever he happens to run into?"

"Crazy, yes, but at random, no," said the sheriff. "The note rules it out. Whoever did it had a reason in mind—a crazy reason, but a reason."

"Which brings us to the next point. Who are these two men who were shot?" I asked.

"Preliminary identification seems to indicate the older one is Ace Feldman, the president of the record company that's throwing this festival. The other one appears to be Radio Johnson, the Elvis imitator."

"What do you mean 'appears to be'?" said F.T.

"The older fellow had a wallet. The identification in it said he was Ace Feldman. The other fellow had no wallet, but the hospital thinks it's Radio Johnson. I know both of them by sight, but I haven't been to the hospital yet."

Our conversation was interrupted by a deputy who had a young woman in tow. She had a stunned look on her face.

She appeared to be in her late teens. Her black hair was moderately long, parted in the middle, and layered. She was wearing a fancy cowboy shirt open three buttons from the top, jeans, and a wide belt with a rodeo buckle. She filled out the jeans and shirt nicely with a lean body built for speed.

"The guards just found me. What happened?"

"Who are you?" asked the sheriff.

"I'm Lisa Feldman. My father and I are throwing this show."

He gave her a long look and decided to drop the Broderick Crawford and go for the Burl Ives routine. He put a fatherly hand on her shoulder.

"There was a shooting here this afternoon. Two men were injured. We haven't made a positive identification yet, but one appears to be your father. He was carrying his wallet. The other had no identification, but we think he is an Elvis imitator named Radio Johnson."

"Oh, no!" she cried. She staggered a step or two as if she'd been hit, leaning heavily against the wall. "I didn't know it was them. The guard only said there had been a shooting. Are they . . . dead?" She had some trouble saying the last word. I couldn't blame her.

"No, neither of them is dead. They've been taken to the hospital. We haven't had any word on their condition yet."

With this news a nervous energy seemed to fill her. Wringing her hands she said, "I've got to get over there."

"I'll have a deputy drive you," said the sheriff.

Their exit was interrupted by the sound of the phone. Everybody froze still as a photograph while it rang once, twice, then three times. A voice from the living room called out, "Sheriff, it's for you."

We stayed in our frozen positions, looking at each other but not really seeing each other until the sheriff returned.

"That was the hospital. Radio Johnson is going to be all right. It was just a flesh wound and he's conscious. He'll be fine by tomorrow."

"What about my daddy?" said Lisa.

The sheriff shook his head. "Honey, I'm afraid your daddy slipped away from us. They did everything they could, but he was just hurt too bad."

It took a minute for the gentle way he said it to sink in, then in a voice full of disbelief she said, "My daddy's dead?"

The sheriff nodded his head. "I'm afraid so."

There was a long silence, then she said it again. "He's

dead?'' The sheriff didn't answer. "But he can't be," she said as her eyes filled with tears. "We had lunch together. He can't be dead. Not now, not when all we worked for was coming together. He can't be dead."

Nobody said anything. There was nothing to be said. Words wouldn't change or help anything. She wiped her eyes and took several deep breaths. The first few were ragged, but gradually they became smoother. She looked around as if she were searching for her purse. Failing to find it she said, "I need a cigarette."

None of us had one. Then I remembered the pack on the living room table and mentioned it.

For the first time since she had been in the room Lisa seemed to notice us. While she studied us the sheriff told the deputy, "Get the smokes for her, and bring us each a beer while you're at it."

"Over my dead body," said Lisa. Pointing her finger at me she said to the sheriff, "I'll see you in hell before I'll let you give beer to the men who killed my father."

Five

Grief is a powerful emotion that often causes people to do irrational things, but even that irrationality follows a pattern. Almost every funeral has its array of stock characters. Of these, there are many minor roles, but only four major ones: the Stoic, the Mother Hen, the Drunk, and the Hysteric.

The Stoic is the biggest pain in the ass of the four, for he is the one who always has to "John Wayne" it by sitting dry-eyed and silent, staring into space while he chain-smokes Camels. Rather than sharing his grief with others, he causes them to tiptoe around lest they disturb him.

The Mother Hen is pleasant enough. She is normally a middle-aged woman whose main concern seems to be whether everyone has enough to eat. Hers is by far the nicest role.

The Drunk is self-explanatory except to say that often the Drunk fills two roles: that of the Drunk and that of the Hysteric.

The Hysteric is the one who becomes mean or crazy in grief,

turning on good friends or close relatives and attacking them for no apparent reason as if they were life-long enemies. Old slights—whether real or imagined—assume importance far above their actual worth, and rifts occur that often last a life-time.

Having worked for Willard Surlew at the Y'all Come Back Funeral Home, I was familiar with the roles, so Lisa's choice of the Hysteric didn't surprise me, but it didn't please me either. After all, nobody likes to spend time with your lips glued to those of a dead man, blowing air into him while you try to talk God into changing an irrevocable decision, only to then find yourself accused of murder by the next of kin.

The sheriff held up both hands like he was stopping traffic. "Wait a minute, honey. You've got it all wrong. These fellows didn't kill your father. They're the ones who found him, and it was their quick thinking and first aid that kept him alive as long as he was. In fact the guy in the bed," he said, pointing to me, "hurt his knee going for help. That's what he's doing in bed."

"You mean they aren't the killers . . . ?"

The sheriff assured her to the contrary and introduced us, telling her of our free-lance role for *Ultra Suave*.

A hurt look crossed her face. This girl had more faces than Eve. "I'm sorry. I didn't know. I just assumed they were the killers, and you were holding them." She crossed to the bed. "You hurt your knee going for help?" she said as she raised the sheet. Gazing down at me she said, "It's all swollen."

I was nude under the sheet and tugged at it to cover myself. F.T. and the sheriff smiled at my embarrassment. "You can't walk on that leg," she said.

"I can—"

"But the doctor told him not to," interrupted F.T. "He's supposed to stay in bed until tomorrow."

The deputy returned with the beer and cigarettes. Once Lisa had a cigarette lit, her poise seemed to return.

"You can't be moving around with that knee. Where are you staying?"

"In our car," I said.

"You can't do that. Why don't you stay here tonight? Nobody is using it." Then remembering what had happened, she turned to the sheriff. "That's all right, isn't it?"

"Sure. It sounds like a good idea."

"What about fingerprints? Aren't you going to check the place for prints?" I said.

He shook his head. "You've been watching too many movies. There've been so many people through this trailer, we could find the prints of the shooter and never know it. What I *am* going to do is post a guard at each entrance just to be on the safe side. That brings us to the next point. I hate to bring up business at a time like this, but your father is gone. Who's in charge of the festival?"

"I guess I am," said Lisa. "Daddy and I own the company together. Everybody associated with it works for us."

"I don't mean to rush you, but do you know what you are going to do?" said the sheriff.

She walked to the room's lone window and stood there staring out and smoking. Finally she said, "If Radio can perform, I'm going to go ahead with it. Everything my daddy and I have in the world is tied up in the Elvis project. He would want me to see it through to the end. I won't let him down."

"What does Radio have to do with it?" said the sheriff.

"He's going to win the contest."

The sheriff ran his hand through his hair. "Pardon a country boy's ignorance, but this *is* a contest. How do you know he's going to win it?"

"Because it's rigged, that's how," she said. "When we discovered Radio, we needed a vehicle to get him in front of the public, so we came up with the idea for the festival." She laughed a hard little laugh. "Elvis himself couldn't win this one."

After that declaration Lisa had little more to add. The sheriff took her to the hospital to identify the victims. About an hour later he called. The dead man was her father. The wounded man was Radio Johnson.

F.T. took his camera and went out in the crowd for the article pictures while I lay in bed and thought about Lisa.

She was young. How young was hard to tell. She could have been as young as seventeen or as old as twenty-five. Her youthful, unlined face made me think seventeen was about right, but her poise seemed a bit much for one so young. Also, she smoked, a habit I tended to associate with grown women rather than kids. However, whether she was seventeen or twenty-five didn't diminish the fact that we had stumbled into the middle of the worst day of her life.

When she returned she'd evidently forgotten I was there, because she ran down the hall into the living room and broke down, letting her tears roll.

Like most men, I'm profoundly moved by a woman's tears. In the South some would call it chivalry; in the North some would call it guilt. Whatever the reason, the result is the same. To hear a woman cry makes me feel uncomfortable, so I struggled into my pants and hobbled into the living room.

I sat down beside her on the sofa and reached out for her. She hesitated only long enough to see who it was before she was in my arms like an eight-year-old who had just seen her puppy run over.

Earlier she had shown poise beyond her years, handling the part of the capable, tough businesswoman well, but now that need had temporarily passed, and the pendulum had swung away from the part of her that was a woman and back to the part that was still a little girl.

We sat like that for a time. Me, offering the minimal comfort that a stranger's shoulder can give at a bad time. She, accepting it and making do in the absence of someone with more meaning.

Presently the time for crying passed, and the time for talking about the memories that precipitated the tears began. I listened and added only the minimum amount to keep the flow going.

"I'll miss him," she said in a choked voice. "He was both mother and father to me."

"Where is your mother?"

"I don't know. They split up. Last I heard she was living in California with some muscle-bound instructor from a health club." There was bitterness in her voice, and embarrassment, too.

"Have they been divorced long?" I asked.

"Since I was young," she said. "It was hard for Daddy, raising me and starting a record company too. Somehow he did it. In the beginning we moved around a lot. Daddy was working to help promote small-town shows—mostly country and western—at fairgrounds and racetracks. We lived in a lot of motels. Ate a lot of meals cooked over a hot plate. And chased a lot of rainbows before we bought Pyrite Records and settled down in Memphis. Even after we settled down it was still hard, but by that time I was old enough to help out answering phones, filing, typing. Then later on doing taping and working sessions. That's what I do best—recording. Daddy always said I had the ear in the family. In fact we never had anything that even resembled a hit until I took over in the control room."

"How old were you when you started running record sessions?"

"Fourteen," she said.

"Isn't that a bit young?"

She bristled at that remark. "What does age have to do with it? Tanya Tucker was only twelve when she started recording."

"You like working the control room?" I asked.

"I love it. Making music is my life," she said.

"How did the musicians take to having a girl run the session?"

"That's where Daddy came in. He was good at two things: promotion and keeping them in line. You see, he was a pretty tough old—"

For a moment her memories came too hot and heavy, threatening to engulf her in another wave of tears. She got up from the sofa, lit herself another cigarette, and got me a beer.

When she was once again seated I picked up the thread of the conversation. "So your dad kept them in line—"

"Right," she said. "He didn't allow any funny business. You know how flaky musicians can be with sex, drugs, and

31

things like that. But when I was around, Daddy made sure they were straight. At first they didn't like it, but when their records began to sell, they decided I knew what I was doing."

"Your dad never remarried?"

"Nope. Between me and the record company he never had time."

"If you don't mind me asking, how old are you?"

"Eighteen," she said.

"Just old enough to drink legal and mess around with guys," I said.

She smiled at my feeble attempt at humor. It was a nice thing to see after all the tears.

"Seriously," I said, "do you have a boyfriend or somebody you can call to come be with you through all this?"

She hesitated a moment before answering. "Nope, afraid not. I've never been one for dating much. We spent so much time at the business that I didn't meet anybody, and Daddy would never let me date a musician."

We talked more. She continued to paint a picture of a gruff, tough, loving father and a daughter who adored him. But I didn't have to be a psychiatrist to see there was more to him than met the eye.

There's a reason divorce courts normally award custody of the children to the mother. The reason is she usually does a better job of raising them. If a Southern divorce court gives custody of a child to the father, it is only because the mother is a well-known piece of dog meat.

In Lisa's case her remarks indicated her mother had packed up and run, leaving everyone with no choice about custody, and Ace had had to make the best of a bad situation, which he had tried hard to do. From that trying a strong bond had developed between the two of them. A bond of "it's you and me against the world." That was the good side, the side perceived by a young, loving daughter.

There was another side to the same coin, a darker side she unconsciously told about. It was the story of a man who spent his life as a two-bit con man. A man who married poorly, as con men often do. A man whose wife took off, leaving him saddled with a young daughter and a bleak future. A man who bought or conned his way into the ownership of a broken-down record company, and who flogged himself and his daughter unmercifully in his pursuit of the old American dream.

It was also the story of a child who, as a young girl, assumed the role of wife as well as daughter. Not in the carnal sense, but in the emotional sense. A duality of roles that women seem capable of playing from puberty onward if necessary. And with this assumption it became the story of a girl trapped. A girl with no friends, boyfriends, or fun in the normal way. A girl in some respects old beyond her years, and in other respects still in swaddling clothes saddled with a hard, suspicious, overly protective father.

I questioned her about habits or enemies that could have led to the killings. Again she painted saintly verbal pictures, but this time she included Radio Johnson with her father. Pictures of men without enemies. I couldn't speak for Radio Johnson, but a man like Ace Feldman accumulates a bottom drawer full of enemies mean enough to eat sautéed scorpions.

As the talk began to run down we reached a point where neither of us wanted to be with the other any longer, so I left her in the living room and hobbled back to the bedroom, stretched out, and thought some more about her life.

Baggage, baggage, baggage—the world is full of emotional baggage. If you have parents, you get baggage. If you don't, you get baggage. If they care about you, you get baggage. If they don't care about you, you get baggage. There's no winning, only knowing when to cut your losses. Then there are those like Lisa who never seem to see what's going on. Who never understand the ins and outs of the baggage and breakaway game. Who can't see the forest for the trees. Those are the ones we at times call stupid, and at other times happy.

As show time drew closer, first one and then another popped in to give condolences to Lisa. I paid little attention to them, being totally absorbed in *The Unforgiven*—a great thriller by another of the MacDonalds, only this time it was Patricia instead of Ross, John D., Gregory, or Philip.

However, the sound of raised voices in the living room drew my attention away from the bleak Cape Cod atmosphere and back to the present. The man's voice was hard and mean. I didn't like the things he was saying. Lisa's voice was tight and frightened. I struggled into my pants again and hobbled toward the living room to see what was going on.

I made it to the door without him seeing me. Crossing my arms, I nonchalantly leaned against the wall to keep him from seeing how badly I was limping.

Crossing your arms is an unconscious defensive posture that can get you into a lot of trouble in a fighting situation, because it ties up your hands almost as effectively as a pair of hand-cuffs. I would never have done it if my opponent had been close enough to do anything.

When Lisa saw me her expression went from rabbit-scared to assured self-confidence. The man noticed the change and looked around to see what source it was drawing its power from. He didn't have far to look.

While he was busy giving me the once-over, I returned the favor. He was the spitting image of Elvis—that is if a white jump suit and boots, black hair adorned with enough grease to fry fish, a sneer that looked like a badly repaired harelip, and a nose like a Buick resembled Elvis. From the way he looked at me I could tell it was love at first sight on his part, too.

"Snake, I'd like you to meet Mr. Lorenzo Patuit, one of our Elvis imitators. Mr. Patuit was just leaving," she said in a sweet voice.

He glared at her, and he glared at me. Neither of us melted and ran down into our shoes. As he got to his feet he said to Lisa, "Just remember what I said. I meant every word of it." Somehow the tone of his voice made me think he was not referring to an invitation to Sunday dinner.

His presence, timing, and attitude ran the coincidence meter up to the red line in the suspect department, so I decided to detain him for the sheriff.

As he tried to pass me I stopped him and said, "I believe I've heard of you. That's Patuit as in horse's ass, isn't it?"

He glared at me and tried to push past without saying a
word. I had my body braced with my good leg, so keeping him
at bay was an easy matter.

"You didn't answer my question. That's Patuit as in horse's
ass, right?"

That did it. For the next few seconds the action was sweet.
He made the common mistake of reaching out to grab me with
one hand while he took a swing at me with the other. As his
grabbing hand made contact with my chest, I held it against
me with my left and broke his little finger with my right. F.T.
taught me that trick, and it worked perfectly. Patuit let out a
high-pitched scream that brought the guards running.

He didn't faint. I'll have to give him that. But he did crouch
down and clamp his mangled hand between his legs while he
made unintelligible sounds the likes of which I hope I never
utter. As the guards took him away he was hurting too badly
to voice the usual threats.

Lisa took it badly. The violence of the day had stripped
away her adult veneer as cleanly as cold cream removes grease-
paint from a clown's face, leaving in its place a scared teen-age
girl with nobody to turn to.

I limped over to the couch and sat down. "What happened?" I said.

"As soon as he heard about Daddy's death he dropped by
to see if he could pressure me into throwing the contest in his
favor."

"And—"

"When I wouldn't . . . he threatened me."

"How?" I asked.

"He . . . he threatened . . . to throw acid in my face," she
said as she covered her face with her hands.

I left her alone for a moment before I said, "What happened then?"

"That's when you came in. Do you think he really meant
it?"

"Want the truth?" I said.

"Yes."

35

"I don't know. F.T. knows a lot more about the dark side of human nature than I. He's the one who should have been here."

Since she did not bring it up, I did not go into my theory that Lorenzo Patuit might be the killer.

She put her hand on my arm. "I'm glad you were here. Today seems to be your day to save me."

"And me without a clean suit of armor to my name," I said.

The sheriff came by again before the show. He looked tired. I couldn't blame him. It had been a busy day. He had a couple of questions about Lorenzo Patuit. I answered them and then asked, "Do you think there's enough evidence to book him for the killing?"

"Nope," he said.

"Why not?" I asked.

"Because I just finished questioning Radio Johnson. The killer is a woman."

Six

 That evening the show came and went without me. My throbbing knee, the strain of the day, and the long drive conspired to rob me of my second wind.

Lisa insisted on being backstage throughout the show, so F.T. accompanied her, leaving me alone in the trailer.

I got to a stopping place in my book and decided to take a nap. Even though it was still hot and muggy outside, the air conditioning brought the temperature down to the point that the bedspread felt good as I pulled it up and tucked it under my chin.

Sleep came easy, but I paid for it with a parade of dreams all starring a blond Mae West wearing an Elvis mask. She was dressed in a skintight red sequined dress that cinched her figure into an hourglass that threatened to overflow from the top. She sashayed into the room carrying a scarf in her hand. Concealed under it was a gun. I saw it and tried to yell to warn the other people in the room, but they just laughed. She raised the gun and fired. Blood flowed everywhere like a busted waterbed until everything was covered in its sticky redness, and I felt as if I were drowning.

The sound of the phone woke me. It was morning outside. Lisa was asleep in the lone chair in my room. Curled up as she was in the fetal position, all she needed was her thumb in her mouth to look all of five years old again. As the phone continued to ring she stirred.

"Morning," she said in a voice full of softness and sleep.

The phone stopped ringing. "Morning yourself," I said. "You picked yourself a hard bed. Why didn't you bunk in here with me? There was plenty of room."

"I didn't want to be alone, but I didn't want to sleep with you, either, so I took the chair."

The phone began to ring again. Whoever had just called was compulsive enough to hang up and immediately redial just to be sure he had been right the first time.

Lisa stood up and stretched. "Duty calls," she said. She was gone about five minutes. When she returned she said, "That was Arcel Mayfield, Radio's manager. Radio has checked himself out of the hospital and is at his hotel with the sheriff. They want us to come over."

"Us? You mean F.T. and me, too?"

"Yes. Radio wants to meet you, and I guess the sheriff wants to clear up a few things."

"Do you have any idea where F.T. is?" I said.

"In the other bedroom," she said.

"Wake him up and tell him to get the car while I take a shower and see if I can get this knee of mine to work again."

She left but was back in a flash with a look of horror on her face.

"Snake, I think he's dead!" she said.

That brought me to my feet, nakedness, bad knee, and all. We hurried down the hall to the other bedroom. I looked in and breathed a sigh of relief.

"What are you talking about? He's not dead. He's just asleep," I said.

"But he's so green," she said.

38

"Oh, that," I said. "That's just the way he looks in the morning. Liquor doesn't agree with him." Lisa looked a trifle ashamed, so I went on. "But you're not the first to make that mistake. I remember we were staying in a hotel once, and the chambermaid came in and saw him like that. Thinking he'd had a heart attack, she jerked the cord out of a lamp, stripped the ends bare, and tried to jumpstart his chest. You should have seen him come off that bed when those hundred and ten volts hit him."

Her eyes got big as saucers. "Was he all right after she did that to him?"

"Yeah," I said as I turned and headed for the bathroom. "But the room smelled like burned hair for the rest of the day."

I closed the bathroom door and turned on the shower. As the steam started to fill the room, I checked out my knee. The ice packs and bed rest had done their job. There was pain when I moved it, but the swelling was almost gone.

Bracing myself against the sink, I stepped into the tub, being careful not to put too much weight on the knee.

The scalding water cascaded down me, cutting through the dirt and odor from yesterday. Its warmth seemed to loosen up the stiff inner parts of my knee, and a lot of the pain went down the drain.

I dried off and walked back to the bedroom like a normal man. While F.T. showered I wrapped the knee with the Ace bandages, being careful to leave them a little loose. That's the way you use an elastic bandage. You always wrap whatever's hurt looser than you would with a standard bandage, because the elastic bandage will tighten up all through the day until it can become a screaming torment if you start out with it too tight.

F.T. got the car, and Lisa directed us to the emergency road, and we made it to the hotel in no time.

As we entered the hotel, I felt like we were in a penny arcade full of Elvis clones made from old bus station cowboys. The lobby was filled with men all about six feet tall, with long sideburns, dark greasy hair, and wearing white jump suits covered in studs and sequins and open to the navel. Each had his own group of admiring women in their late thirties, sporting peroxide-blond beehive hairdos. The good life had broadened their beams so much they were in danger of busting through the bottoms of their mix-and-match polyester pantsuits.

The Elvis imitators preened and strutted under the attention, arching their eyebrows, checking their eye shadow, and giving out cheap colored scarves like a line of gay street hustlers. Which is not to say that, in the real world, they were either gay or street hustlers. No, in the real world they were frogs in a princedom of rotting lily pads and stagnant water. Day in and day out their contribution to the sum total of man's thinking was little more than a cacophony of belches, and the monuments erected by their hands amounted to a breeding ground for mosquitoes.

That is to say they were insurance salesmen, hair weave specialists, or merchants who sold umbrellas, incense, fake gold chains, and paintings on black velvet. They were the men who planted bugs in your basement during your free termite inspection. They were men who worked behind the two-way mirrors of supermarket meat departments, passing the day rewrapping brown leftover hamburger camouflaged with a dusting of new pink, and put out for purchase by concerned mothers who squeezed the Charmin and only bought the peanut butter endorsed by Annette Funicello.

Which is to say these men were men with no curves, only angles. Men looking for a shortcut to get a wad of fifties, and leave a wet spot on the sheets. In short they were the thumb on the scale of life.

But that was all behind them in this chunk of time and space encapsulated by a hotel lobby filled with rented plants, area rugs, and love seats covered in rough, stain-resistant Indian prints. Here they were no longer frogs. Now they were princes in the land of Fruit of the Loom, where a man could walk tall, and a sneer and a hip swivel would get you more than just a sneer. Foppish—yes. Plumage—yes. Erectile tissue—maybe, maybe not. That all depended on the broad-bottomed blond beehive and her soft little hand. But it was too early for one to contemplate where he would squirt his ecstasy. Why, breakfast had barely settled, and the sun wasn't over the yardarm yet. So look but don't touch, because there was work to be done.

There were autographs to be signed, and not with names like Joe Shit, the ragpicker's son, either. Good names like Sid-Elvis, Delvis Baron, or the Great Trellis. Names any self-respecting man would be proud to call his own. Scraps of paper or cocktail napkins to be filled in with phrases of undying communication like "To Flo, with love," or "Best wishes from—" or, for that special fan, "With heartfelt thanks." And if the old felt-tip was working, there were bras, panties, or even blue-veined, milk-white breasts deserving a more personal autograph.

Then there were the comparisons—god-awful, endless, boring, repetitious claptrap to illustrate how Greatness had chosen them to fill the vacant throne of Elvis. As we passed through the crowds, I heard snatches of conversation: "It came to me watching *Jailhouse Rock*. That's when I headed for Mexico to find a plastic surgeon . . ."; "I don't believe that stuff about Elvis and drugs. He believed in God . . ."; "Las Vegas called my agent last week. They want to give me the key to the city . . ."; "Anybody who is only in this thing for the money is fooling himself. Elvis is bigger than all of us . . ."; "Of course my sideburns are real . . ."

It was so ridiculous it was wonderful, vital, and exhilarating. It was a carnival full of rickety rides, bright lights, cotton candy, and teddy bears filled with poisonous flammable stuffing. I was in hog heaven, and I loved it. F.T. and Lisa had to take me by the arms and drag me to the elevator.

Radio Johnson had a corner suite on the fifth floor. When Lisa knocked, the door was opened by a deputy dressed in freshly pressed khaki. Except for him the room was empty.

"Everybody's in the bedroom. They're expecting you," he said without waiting to be asked.

It was nice of him to volunteer the information, but he didn't bother to indicate which of the living room's two closed doors led to the right bedroom, so we waited. Dealing with a closed bedroom door can be tricky, for until you open it you can never tell whether there is a lady, a tiger, or an unmade bed waiting on the other side.

Lisa took charge. "In there," she said, making a hitchhiking motion with her thumb toward one of the doors.

The deputy nodded.

This time she didn't bother to knock. Instead she opened the door, stuck her head inside, and said, "Knock, knock." It was an absurd thing for her to do. Call me a traditionalist if you will, but I don't like abstract representations of action. If the situation calls for a "Knock, knock," then double up your fist and let it fly. Don't stand there like a drooling imbecile making baby talk. Hit the damn thing. Rattle the hinges. Knock the pictures off the wall. Like the Good Book says (or should say, if it doesn't), "Make yourself known by your actions." Or, as in my case, by your overreaction.

The bedroom was furnished with a king-size bed, a desk and chest combo, a color television, and a circular table and chairs near sliding glass doors that led to the balcony.

The television was on with the sound turned low. I sneaked a peek. It was tuned to "Wall to Wall Street," a game show in which members of the studio audience lie side by side, on the stage, while contestants see how many of their necks they can step on as they cross the stage in a simulated corporate climb to success and a new Kelvinator. It was one of F.T.'s favorites.

Stretched out on the bed, drinking his morning coffee, was Radio Johnson. Once again I was stunned by his incredible resemblance to Elvis. He was wearing a royal blue bathrobe, and I thought he looked pretty good for a man who had been shot less than twenty-four hours ago. Then I looked again. His look of well-being came from the layer of makeup he was wearing, which gave his skin a healthy tone and concealed the dark circles under his eyes. But his eyes didn't go with the rest of it. They were dull, flat, and tired.

Four people were seated at the table: the sheriff, a balding man wearing glasses, and two women who bore a strong facial resemblance to one another—at least as far as bone structure went. One had a pretty face and short dark hair. The other had an elaborately frosted hairstyle that reminded me of gold cotton candy and '57 Chevies. Her face, while still pretty, had a beat-to-hell look about it. I knew at a glance I would not want the memories that gave her that look.

Before we could even get the introductions out of the way, the women, led by the pretty dark-haired one, were on their feet and embracing Lisa. The exact mechanics of it are unimportant. It is enough to know that tears flowed, and hugs were exchanged, with the dark-haired one offering the greater solace to Lisa. The gold-cotton-haired one was more tentative, touching Lisa's shoulders as you would a strange dog that you are not sure is friendly.

With these simple gestures, with the ability to convey concern through the unspoken subtlety of touch, these three—two women and a girl—formed the circle of grief, a circle stretching back even beyond the visit of the two Marys to the empty tomb of Christ. Back to the day the world first knew violence. The day Cain slew Abel, and Eve lost both sons in the process.

What we saw was not so much a ritual as a secret. A secret thousands of years old. A secret that only the bearers of life can know, for only through the pleasure of the sowing, the pain of the bearing, and the demand of the nurturing can the worth—and therefore the loss—of life be determined.

This time it was not a son or a savior. It was a hank of hair and a piece of gristle tough as a banker's heart, but above all it was a father. Like Abel, the first recorded man to die, Ace Feldman, too, was murdered. Only from the looks of things Ace died for the worst of all reasons: he was in the right place at the wrong time.

When things quieted down, the sheriff handled the introductions. Radio Johnson needed no introduction. The petite dark-haired woman was Pam, his wife. The one with the frosted hair was Joan, Pam's sister. The balding fellow with the glasses was Arcel Mayfeld, Radio's manager. When I got a closer look at Arcel, I realized he was younger than I had thought. The glasses and the baldness had thrown me off. Instead of being in his late thirties, he was no more than his late twenties.

After the introductions were completed Radio took charge. "Pam, honey, why don't you and Joan go out for a breath of air? I want to talk over some business with these gentlemen."

A look of hurt crossed her face. She started to protest, but Radio silenced her with a wave of his hand. Pam turned to Lisa and said, "We're going down to the pool. Come on down with us. Some sun will do you good."

Lisa shook her head. "Thanks, but you go ahead. This is the first chance I've had to hear what happened. I think I'd better stay."

Pam accepted this gracefully, but there was anger in Joan's eyes. Neither of them liked being excluded. They just had different ways of showing it.

F.T. and I took their seats at the circular table while Lisa sat down on the edge of the bed.

Radio reached out and patted her on the arm. "Feel like some coffee or some breakfast?" It was a simple question, but the way he said it made it more. The tone of his voice made it into a statement of concern and condolence that also seemed to say, "I know you're hurting. I understand that. Pass a little bit of it over to me, and I'll help you carry it."

Therein lies the essence of the entertainer: the ability to communicate the sense of emotion to others with the fewest possible words.

Lisa shook her head, but F.T. and I took it as our cue to pour ourselves a cup from the gold-flecked plastic carafe on the table. The sheriff waited until we had finished stirring and tasting before he turned to Radio and said, "I know we've already been through this a number of times, but would you go through it one more time for Snake and F.T.? There may be something they can add which will help us get to the bottom of things."

"Sure, but first I'd like to take a moment to thank you boys for what you did yesterday. You saved my life. I'm only sorry that we couldn't save Ace's.''

He was a charmer. What he said about saving his life wasn't exactly true. He was in no danger from his gunshot wound, but it still gave me a good warm feeling to hear him say it.

''Words aren't enough when a man saves another man's life. A bond is formed—''

''I don't mean to rush you,'' interrupted the sheriff, looking at his watch, ''but I've got to get over to the festival, so can you move along to the shooting?''

Radio shifted his glance from F.T. and me to the sheriff. A look of irritation crossed his face for a second but only a second. In that second I could see Radio was a man who did not like to be told what to do.

He smiled and said, ''There isn't much to tell.'' Shifting his gaze to Lisa, who was still sitting at his side on the bed, he continued. ''Yesterday I went to see your father to go over some last-minute details about the show. Minor stuff like what time our sound check was scheduled for. To make sure the auditorium was going to be barred to everyone else when we did it. What time to arrive at the dressing room. Who we followed in the show. Detail stuff, but stuff he was always lax about. You know how he was.''

Lisa nodded. ''He was never very good about details. Whenever he did anything, you had to follow along behind him straightening out everything—''

''That wasn't his function,'' interrupted Radio. ''He was a salesman, possibly the greatest salesman I've ever known. He could sell concert tickets to the deaf. I've seen him do it time and again. The man was a genius. He didn't need to be a detail man. He had you for that. You were always right there behind him, picking up the pieces and tying up the loose ends.''

Radio had maneuvered Lisa into a beautiful conversational pocket. She didn't know whether she was being chastised for speaking ill of the dead or praised for being important in her own right. So she did the only thing she could. She sat there quietly.

"He was at the desk doing paperwork when I arrived. I sat down in the chair and waited for him to finish up. After about ten minutes he got up and went to the bathroom.

"While he was gone, a woman came into the trailer from the tunnel to the auditorium. She was wearing one of those Elvis masks. I thought she was just another fan who had wandered in, but when she raised her hand, I saw the gun in the scarf. Then she fired, and that's all I remember."

The sheriff turned to us. "Is there anything you can add to that?"

"Not much," I said. "She was gone by the time we got into the trailer. You found the gun, the scarf, and the note in the trailer, and the mask near the auditorium exit. If we assume that the note gives us the motive and that the killer is a psycho, then unless we turn up more physical evidence, or she tries again, we'll never catch her."

There was silence in the room as everyone pondered the thought that someone could walk into a trailer parked in the middle of thousands of people, shoot two people, and walk away scot-free. It was a depressing thought but a particularly American one, since as a country, psychopathic assassination of public figures has become a way of life over the past twenty years.

F.T. was the first to break the silence. "How do you know the killer was a woman?"

"Several reasons," said Radio with a knowing smile. "She was short, about Pam's height and build, but I got a good enough look to know that those were real breasts bobbing around under that shirt."

"What color hair did she have?" asked Lisa.

"I don't know. She had a red and white bandanna tied around her head pirate style, like they wear down Louisiana way."

"Down there men wear bandannas tied like that, too," I said.

"I know, but this was not a man. This was a woman," said Radio.

46

"I was just thinking maybe it was a female impersonator," I said.

He shook his head. "How many female impersonators do you know that are the same height and build as my wife? She's too petite. God doesn't make men that small and feminine. No, it was a woman."

"Did she say anything?" said F.T.

"Not a word," said Radio. "She just walked up and shot me."

"How close was—" I started, but Lisa interrupted me.

"What about my daddy? Why did she shoot him?"

"I don't know. I didn't see her shoot him. He was still in the bathroom when she shot me. I guess he came running when he heard the shot, and that's when she shot him."

I tried again. "How close was—" Again I was interrupted by Lisa.

"But why would she want to shoot either of you? What had you ever done to her?"

"I don't know what her motive was. All I can figure is that she's a crazy fan who's pissed off at me, and when your father stumbled in on her, she shot him, too."

"What is it you keep trying to ask?" said Radio, turning to me.

"How close was she when she shot you?"

He thought for a minute. "Three or four feet," he said.

"How did you get her pissed off at you?" said Lisa.

Irritation started to show in Radio's voice. "How the hell do I know how I got her pissed off? If I knew the answer to that question, then I might remember something about her that would help us find her."

Lisa raised her voice, too, but not with irritation. "Try," she pleaded.

More irritation showed on Radio's face. He struggled for a moment to get it under control. When he did, it was replaced by fatigue. Getting ready for a show, then getting shot, questions from the sheriff, and now more questions from Lisa had just about drained his battery dry.

"I don't know. Lisa, you know how crazy Elvis fans can be. It might be simple, like when I kiss the girls in the audience while I sing 'Love Me Tender.' Maybe she tried to put her tongue in my mouth, and I wouldn't let her. Who knows?"

Both my research for the article and personal experience made me agree with him. Elvis fans were a breed apart where intensity was concerned. It was an intensity that sometimes crossed over into violence.

I was about ten years old, but I remember, clear as a bell, the day all hell broke out between Jim Henry and Roy over Elvis. It all started at Oscar Steele's filling station one sleepy summer afternoon back in the time when Ike decided the nation's fate with a putter instead of a sword, and William Bendix kept saying, "What a revolting development this is."

Jim Henry had been drinking, and so had Roy, but that wasn't unusual. They were always drinking. What was unusual was that Jim Henry had decided he didn't like Elvis.

All day long he kept saying, "If Elvis Presley were to stop here, I'd punch him right in the nose."

Whatever possessed Jim Henry to think that Elvis would ever come through Cannibal Springs, Tennessee, or if he did, why he would deign to stop at Oscar Steele's filling station, is beyond me. But in his alcohol-ravaged mind it made perfect sense so he kept it up all day. "If Elvis Presley were to stop here"—and he would point to the oil-spattered concrete by the gas pump—"I'd punch him right in the nose," he would say.

Roy, his brother, listened to that all afternoon. About sundown he began to lag behind a little in the drinking, letting Jim Henry do the lion's share. About suppertime—or what would be suppertime for regular folks—Jim Henry passed out. Roy looked at him for a few minutes, and then, calmly as you please, picked up the poker from the fireplace and proceeded to smash Jim Henry's face into an unrecognizable mass of blood and bone.

When the sheriff questioned Roy, all he said was, "I just got tired of hearing him talk like that about Elvis."

It was a good story, and I felt Radio could stand a little digression, so I told it. Everybody but Lisa enjoyed it. The knowledge that the story was true seemed to worry her all the more.

Radio countered with, "It's a good thing Elvis didn't stop at old Oscar Steele's gas station, or he'd have probably saved Roy the trouble of whipping Jim Henry's ass. All that karate stuff aside, Elvis always enjoyed a good street fight. Lord knows, when he was touring back in the fifties, he got plenty of opportunity to practice.

"I remember the time a gas station attendant fingered Elvis, or called him a name—I forget which. And Elvis got out of the car and whipped the guy's ass for him even though the other fellow had a knife."

According to my research that story was essentially true. In fact the gas station attendant later preferred charges and carved himself a niche in rock and roll history.

"Funny," I said. "I never knew Jim Henry made it as far west as Memphis."

Everyone laughed except Lisa, who looked more worried with each passing minute, but Radio seemed to take no notice of it. He was warming to what I was later to discover was his favorite conversational topic—Elvis's life.

"The papers and books have all made a big thing about Elvis's entourage and his love of guns, but they never say anything about the real reason behind them. He needed constant protection. The man must have received thousands of death threats during his life. I remember once he thought about canceling his show in Vegas because of a particularly serious one. The man carried guns and had bodyguards because he needed them," said Radio.

Lisa stared at Radio for a minute. "That's what you need—bodyguards," she said.

Radio laughed aloud, but it was a hollow, tinny laugh that didn't quite ring true. "Hell, I've got all the protection I need. I've got all five members of Fluid Drive plus Pam and Joan. Any crazy woman in her right mind would have to think twice before she tangled with that mob."

I noticed he didn't mention Arcel, but I put it down to an oversight.

"Mob is right," snorted Lisa. "I don't think two alcoholic musicians and a three-girl backup count for much protection."

"Aah, but you're forgetting about Joan. She's a pretty tough cookie," said Radio.

"Fuck Joan," said Lisa.

If silence can ever be said to be startled or astonished, the silence in that room certainly fit the bill. The quiet way Lisa said "Fuck Joan" made us all sit up and take notice. Her manly use of the dirtiest word in the English language stilled any thought in our minds that she might be proposing a quiet session of tweaking and diddling between Joan and another consenting adult.

She was talking about war. In her mind, Joan's place was at the foot of the table, making do with the crumbs tossed down from above, and if Joan ever got so cocky as to forget that, Lisa would be right there to remind her.

"What you need are bodyguards," she repeated. "How else are we going to protect you if that crazy woman tries again?"

Radio thought about it for a moment. "It wouldn't work. There's just no way I can afford it."

"Do you agree that it makes sense?" she asked. Radio replied that it did. She turned to the sheriff and repeated the question. He also agreed that it made sense.

"Good, then it's settled. The record company will pay for it," she said. "Now all we have to do is find some bodyguards."

"I think we've already found them. You remember the bond I was speaking about when one person saves another person's life . . . ?" he said, looking at us.

"Wait a minute. You don't mean us . . ." I said.

Radio just smiled.

"We're just magazine reporters," I sputtered.

This time Lisa smiled.

"We'll have to check with our publisher in New York," I said weakly as I looked at F.T.

He was smiling too.

Seven

I made the call to *Ultra Suave* from the phone in the living room. I explained to Al Saltzman what had happened. When I got to the part about Ace Feldman's death, he stopped me.

"I've heard enough. It's a good story. Go with it. See what you can turn up. Keep me posted if you find out anything."

The words were all in the right place, but Al's tone was wrong. Normally Al exuded enough enthusiasm and vitality to make a pickle grow into a watermelon, but this time his voice was flat and lifeless.

"Al, you don't sound right. Is everything okay?"

"It's Ace. I'm sorry to hear it. He and I go back a long way. I was still a free-lance writer doing pieces for the fan magazines when Ace started out. We did a lot of crazy things together. In fact I almost married his wife, but he beat me to it."

"You mean Lisa's mother?"

"That's right," he said.

51

For the rest of the call I tried to make it up to Al for the off-hand way I had broken the news of Ace's death to him, but my words had no effect one way or the other.

I could picture him sitting there in his corner office staring out the window at a mirror view of a like corner office in the building across the street. It was a rotten view, and when on those rare occasions, after a multiple-martini lunch, I would sit in that office with him, I would always say, "Al, with all your money, why don't you get a decent view? You can afford it. Get yourself an office that overlooks Central Park or the river. Or at least get yourself some decals like they put on van windows and give yourself some Alaskan sunsets or an eagle or two flying high and free. Something—*anything* but that rotten view across the street."

He would turn, look out the window, and say, "What do I want a view of Central Park for? All I could see is trees. Ever try to make friends with a tree? Or a river? If I wanted to be friends with rivers and trees, we'd be in Montana, not New York. No, this is the perfect view for me. Everywhere I look I see people. They live, breathe, eat, sleep, fart, and fuck. Sometimes they try, sometimes they don't. But they're always moving. They're my trees."

Yesterday someone had killed Ace Feldman. He wasn't a tree, but I suppose there is some sense in the metaphor. I also suppose there is some sense in the mirror view of the corner office across the street. Spending the day watching the fellow across the way watch you. At least it made more sense to me when I hung up.

I walked over to the glass doors leading to the balcony and looked out. All I could see was the other side of the U-shaped hotel. There wasn't a tree in sight.

I opened the door and walked out onto the balcony. Five floors below us was the pool ringed in a lime-green merkin of Astroturf. The lounge chairs were practically all occupied, mostly by women, already oiled up and 'acourting the sun.

As I looked down at them I realized what was eating at me about the job: Ace Feldman. Everywhere I turned I was getting a blast of grief. It was starting to get me down. What I really wanted was to drink, laugh, chase women, and be part of the rock and roll scene. Not to be the extra pair of hands on Ace Feldman's coffin rail. It was too much to ask when I didn't even know the man. Heading back to the bedroom I made a firm resolution to get back to the business of having fun. After all, there is more to life than dying.

"What's the good word?" said Radio as I sat back down at the table.

I spared them the details of Al's grief and simply said, "He liked the idea and said to go ahead."

For the next few minutes we went through business discussions. I won't bore you with the details of the paltry sum a man will sell his soul and services for, but within a few minutes we had agreed on the money, on rights to Radio's inside story, and to being made deputies by Sheriff McDuff.

When we were finished Radio said, "Now that's what I call TCBing."

"TCBing?" said F.T.

"Taking Care of Business. That was Elvis's motto." Turning to Lisa he said, "Hand me my makeup kit, will you?"

She got the lady's weekend bag for him, and he fumbled among medicine bottles and cosmetics until he found what he wanted.

"Give these to Snake and F.T.," he said to Lisa.

She gave us each a gold chain with a small medallion made up of the letters TCB with a lightning bolt through it. It was the same insignia Elvis had given the male members of his "Memphis Mafia" in the 1960s. Only this time the gold wasn't real.

"Wear these in good times and bad to symbolize our bond," he said, sounding like a passage out of a do-it-yourself California wedding kit. "Don't feel that this means you have to call me 'Boss' like Elvis's entourage did," he continued as I put my chain around my neck. F.T. just sat there looking at him.

"I think there's a couple of things we'd better clear up," I said. "While taking this job does make us part of your entourage, we're *not* going to call you 'Boss,' and we're not going to look after your every need like Elvis's entourage did. We're bodyguards and reporters—that's all.

"If you want a cheeseburger or pizza at midnight, send somebody else. If you want a fried peanut butter, bacon, and banana sandwich, get somebody else to make it. If you want somebody to light your cigar or get you a glass of water, look at somebody else. If you need toilet paper in your bathroom, don't call us, call room service. Do I make myself clear?"

Radio looked at me for a minute. Then he smiled and said, "You know a lot about Elvis, don't you? Where did you find out about the fried peanut butter, bacon, and banana sandwiches?"

I was still a little heated, so I said, "It's my business to know about him. That's what I'm here for. I'm a reporter."

He just laughed and then said to the sheriff, "I've done my part. Don't you think you ought to do yours and deputize them?"

The sheriff sighed and said, "Stand up."

We stood. Then we held up our right hands while he said some mumbo jumbo, made the sign of the cross, the crescent, the lion, and a few other galactical symbols with his hands, and pronounced us married to, or at least intimately involved with, the American law and order system, for better or worse, till death—God forbid—did part us. It was a nice ceremony, but at its conclusion I felt cheap and cheated. If I had known it was coming, I would have worn white.

Then he called his office and told whoever answered to rustle up a couple of badges, a couple of gun permits, and to call the gun shop and tell them we were coming.

Radio held up his hand. "Sheriff—" he interrupted.

"Wait a minute," said the sheriff. Turning to Radio he said, "What is it?"

"Make that three gun permits, will you?"

There was a moment of silence, then the sheriff told whoever was on the other end of the line to make it three gun permits.

Radio beamed.

When the sheriff finished his call, Radio took charge again.

54

"Now that that's done, let's move on to the next piece of business, where you boys are going to stay. I want you to go back to the trailer and get your things. While you're gone, Arcel will move Joan out of the extra bedroom so you can stay here in the suite with me. Got that, Arcel?"

Arcel had it, but he didn't like it. I could tell that by his face. "She's not going to like it," he said, shaking his head.

"I don't give a damn whether she likes it or not. She's moving out," said Radio.

"But the hotel is full . . ." countered Arcel weakly.

"Then she'll just have to stay with you, won't she?" said Radio.

Turning back to us he said, "When you get back here with your clothes, let me know, and we'll go to the gun shop together."

That signaled the end of the meeting. As F.T. and I got up to leave, the sheriff said, "I'm going to head back to the office. Why don't you follow me and pick up your badges and permits?"

In the elevator I said, "Just out of curiosity, would you answer one question for me?"

"What is it?" said the sheriff.

"Why did you hesitate when Radio asked for a gun permit?"

Again the sheriff hesitated. This time the elevator doors opened on the ground floor. As we stepped out into the lobby, which was still filled with Elvis imitators and admirers, he made a sweeping motion with his hand.

"You see this? He's part of this whole crazy scene. Notice I didn't say that I think *he's* crazy, not in the legal sense of the word, but he's not exactly chugging along on all eight cylinders, either. Otherwise a grown man like him would not be going around pretending he is Elvis Presley."

"What's wrong with pretending to be Elvis? I wouldn't mind doing it," I said.

"That's right, you wouldn't mind doing it, but the fact is you *aren't* doing it. You're busy enough being Snake Kirlin, and from what I can see, that's a full-time job. My point is, a grown man doesn't have to be somebody else to get attention. It doesn't matter whether it's Elvis Presley, Waylon Jennings, or Bugs Bunny, it's not normal, and I'm not supposed to go around issuing gun permits to somebody who isn't normal. It could be dangerous.

"On the other hand, somebody is gunning for him, and he deserves the right to protect himself, so I decided to give it to him."

As we walked through the lobby he continued, "I guess the reason I feel that way is that I met Elvis a few times, and I liked him. Now don't get me wrong—I still wouldn't have wanted my daughter to marry him, but I liked him.

"You know Elvis had trouble sleeping at night, and one of the things he liked to do was to ride around when it was real late. Well, one night a big long Caddy comes rolling by where I'm parked, and it's doing about ninety.

"I take off after it, and when I get it stopped, I walk up to the window all set to read the Riot Act to the driver—and who is inside but Elvis! He's all dressed in black from head to toe, and he's alone.

"I didn't give him a ticket. Hell, you couldn't give Elvis a ticket in these parts and expect to keep your job. We got to talking, and he wanted to ride around in the patrol car with me. It was a slow night so I said he could. We drank coffee and talked all night. He was the lonesomest man I ever met.

"We talked about his life, and I can't honestly say if he had had the chance to do it all over again, he would have done anything different, but I can say he would have thought long and hard about it.

"When he was a kid he wanted to be a highway patrolman, and I guess he never got over it. Can you imagine that? The biggest star in the world still wanting to be a highway patrolman?

"After that he would occasionally call up. If I was on the night shift, he would come down and ride around with me. One night he brought me a present, a Colt Python .357 magnum. It was a beauty. I was tickled pink, and he knew it, and it made him happy. The one thing, I think, that gave him

56

pleasure in life was seeing other people happy because of him. That night I gave him a deputy's badge, and you should have seen the look on his face. It was right around the time when he started collecting them, and it meant a lot to him. In a lot of ways he was just a big kid. It makes me feel bad to see all these assholes tap dancing on his grave.''

We followed the sheriff to his office, picked up our badges, and headed for the festival.

The deputy let us in the empty trailer. When we finished packing, we decided to stop for a beer.

As I stood there sipping, I looked around the living room and said, ''Now that we've heard what happened, let's act out the scene and see if it gives us any ideas.''

F.T. played the part of the late Ace Feldman. It wasn't a hard role. Ace didn't have many lines. I played all the other parts. It's a versatility that comes with years of practice.

F.T. sat behind the desk. I sat in the chair in which we had found Radio. F.T. pretended to talk for a couple of minutes, then got up and headed for the bathroom.

I assumed the role of the killer and came in from the tunnel. I stopped at the point indicated by Radio. Something was wrong. I called F.T. in from the bathroom.

''It doesn't work. If the killer was three to four feet from Radio when she shot him, she would have been directly in line with the hallway. Ace would have seen her, and she would have seen him. If that's the case, why would he walk down the hall to certain death?''

F.T. thought about it for a minute. ''I'll tell you why it doesn't work. He had the distance wrong. Remember that both of them had powder burns. That means that each was shot from a distance of less than two feet.''

He was right about the powder burns, which raised another point. How did Radio miss the distance so much?

It's easy for a person to misjudge the distance between three and four feet, but more difficult to miss between two and three feet, because that distance is near the invisible territorial border of self called ''our space.'' If another person comes inside that space and gets too close to us without invitation, alarm bells go off, and we feel uncomfortable, and move away to correct the distance, or take steps to repel the person.

"Let's try it at the shorter distance," said F.T.

This time he played Radio and sat in the chair. I walked over and pretended to shoot him. The distance worked out, and she was invisible from the hallway.

"Then she heard Ace coming, and moved over to the doorway to take him by surprise. As he reached the doorway, she shot him," I said.

"Then she walked back to Radio, dropped the scarf, gun, and note, and took off like Snyder's goose," said F.T.

We stared at the chair for a while before I said, "It all works out except for the distance."

F.T. shrugged. "He made a mistake."

I told him about my theory of space. He agreed that it was an interesting idea but one with little meaning.

"What it could mean," I said, "is that Radio knew the killer. That's why he let her get that close."

We went back to the hotel with our gear. Hearing voices from the bedroom, we stopped at the bar to avoid disturbing anyone. F.T. poured us a beer while we waited. From our vantage point, we could hear every ugly word spoken between Joan and Arcel.

"Who the hell does he think he is? Telling me to move out . . ." she was saying. She had a voice like sliding down a ninety-foot razor blade into a vat of alcohol.

"But honey, he's got to have someplace for the bodyguards to sleep. They suggested it—not him. He wanted you to stay here, but they said they couldn't look out for him if they weren't right here. You've got to admit it makes sense. There's no reason to have bodyguards if they aren't going to be around when you need them," he whined back in a beat-me, fuck-me, make-me-write-hot-checks voice.

"Bodyguards. Hah! He needs bodyguards like I need a six-hole bowling ball."

"Honey, you're forgetting somebody shot him—"

"Yeah," she interrupted. "And they didn't kill him, either, did they? They killed Ace, but they didn't kill him. Know why they didn't kill him? I'll tell you why. He wasn't worth the powder in another bullet, that's why. I don't know why my sister ever married that worthless piece of garbage. All his life he's been a failure. Do you know he couldn't even keep a job in a goddamned meat packing plant, that's how bad he was. He's had at least fifteen jobs since they've been married, and you know what? He's been fired from every one of them. Time and again I've told Pam to leave him, but she wouldn't. When he got this Elvis idea, it was the last straw. I thought she was going to leave him then, but no, she decided to stick it out for one more try. Then you come along, introduce him to Ace, and the two of you fill his head with a lot of crap about how he's the reincarnated Elvis. All of a sudden this worthless jug of frog piss becomes the King, and starts ordering people around like they were his slaves, and you just let him. You even let him throw me out of my own room."

"But baby, what could I do? There's only two bedrooms in the suite. Believe me, if I could, I would build an extra with these hands, but baby, I'm not a carpenter, and you're not a bodyguard."

"Oh, I'm not a bodyguard, am I?" she said. "Who the hell do you think looks out for Pam? Me, that's who. More than once she's needed a bodyguard, let me tell you."

"Honey, you're just exaggerating."

The door to the other bedroom opened and Pam stuck her head out. "There you are. Radio's been waiting for you. Come on in. You can put your stuff away later."

We did as we were told. Inside, I could see that Radio didn't like being kept waiting. "Where the hell have you been?"

"Outside," I said. "Waiting for Joan to finish moving so we could put our stuff in the bedroom."

"Let it wait," he said. "As slow as she is, it could take all day. We've got more important things to do."

"Like what?" said F.T.

"We've got to get you boys some guns," he said, rubbing his hands together with glee. His face was glowing with a boyish joy.

"Whatever you say," I said.

"Let's roll," he said. <u>Rolling</u> took more time than it should have. We were delayed while he checked his eye shadow, combed his hair one last time, and selected just the right pair of sunglasses. They were dark enough to look like a disguise and light enough for everybody to recognize him. When he had finally finished his elaborate primping, he turned up the collar of his jogging suit, and we were underway.

"Come on, Lisa. Are you ready?" he said.

"Sure," she said as she picked up her purse. She looked much better than when we had left her.

"What about me?" said Pam.

"Honey, you just stay here and rest. I've got plans for you later."

Again Pam looked disappointed, but Radio was already heading out the door, so he didn't see it.

At the elevator, F.T. took charge, stepping forward like Jack Palance playing a headwaiter. He held the doors open and ushered us in with a wave of his hand.

The lobby was still filled with Elvis imitators. The hissing was audible as they watched us walk through. The word was out. Radio was the champ, and they hated him for it.

Outside, he took a deep breath, clapped his chest with his hands, and said, "Aah, the summer's such a wonderful time. It brings out the green in the queens."

Lisa laughed and gave him a playful punch. "Be nice, now. You're a big star. You've got to be kind to the little man."

"And little do they know how little they are," he said like it was the natural ending to what Lisa had started.

"Behave," she said, giggling and pulling on his arm.

He turned to F.T. "Where is your car?"

"In the parking lot. Why?" he said.

"Don't you think you ought to get it?" said Radio.

F.T. doesn't like being ordered around, but he didn't say anything. Instead he went for the car. When he returned, the top was down.

I opened the door and pulled the front seat forward so Radio and Lisa could get in the back. When Radio saw the clutter of empty beer cans, old hamburger wrappers, tire irons, tennis shoes, paperback books, and dirty laundry, he shook his head and said, "Y'all are going to have to clean this car up before we do this again. I can't be seen riding around in the back of a garbage truck."

There was a long silence while F.T. did a slow burn. I stepped in to fill the void. "But at least it's a Caddy. You know how Elvis loved Cadillacs." Radio brightened at that remark.

"You're right. The man did love his Cadillacs." Then turning to Lisa and taking her by the hand, he said, "Allow me," as he helped her through the rubble.

"Why, thank you, kind sir," she said with a mock curtsy, turning her ankle on a beer can and sitting down with all the grace of an elephant plopping onto a whoopee cushion. She turned red from embarrassment, and we had a tense moment until Radio started to laugh.

It was not a snigger, or a giggle, or even a polite tee-hee or two. No, it was an honest-to-God, out-and-out fit of laughter. At first it seemed that she was even more embarrassed, but that passed, and she started to laugh too.

As I climbed into the front seat, I thought whoever said it was right: laughter *is* the best medicine. There's nothing that makes you feel quite as good as when you try to do something smooth, or cute, and it backfires; and you turn around to find not only was the world watching, but it's laughing as well.

At the gun shop, F.T. quickly took care of business, since as deputies we were able to dispense with the usual paperwork and waiting period to buy firearms. He selected a Colt .45 automatic, the kind we had used in the Marines, a belt holster that rode high enough to be covered by a shirt worn outside, and a box of ammo.

"I'd like to see that pearl-handled thirty-eight," I said, pointing to one of the cases. The proprietor obliged me. I hefted it, then twirled it around my finger a couple of times. It twirled all right, so I was sure it would do. Radio's eyes didn't leave the gun.

"I need a holster. I want a shoulder holster, left-handed," I said.

The owner hunted around until he found one and brought it to me. Before I could put it on, Radio took it out of my hands.

"Let me try this one," he said.

"Go ahead, it's your money," I said. He slipped the shoulder holster on, put the pearl-handled beauty in the holster, and checked out his image in the glass of one of the cases.

"This is real pretty," he said. "You know, Elvis had one just like it. I saw him wear it in a picture. It looked good, just like this one. I think I'll take it. You don't mind, do you?"

I did, but I didn't say anything. Something else in the case had already caught my eye. "No, you go ahead. It looks better on you."

"You really like it on me?" he said, still admiring his image.

"Yeah, it's definitely you. You look just like Elvis in the picture."

This time he turned. "You know which picture I mean . . . ?"

"Sure, you're talking about the 1970 Christmas picture taken of Elvis and his entourage after they had been deputized by the Shelby County sheriff. They were all holding their badges, and Elvis was sitting in a chair in the center of them. He was wearing a black shirt, white tie, and a shoulder holster with a pearl-handled revolver in it," I said.

"You're right. That's the picture," said Radio with amazement in his voice. "So you see why I want this gun—"

"I see and understand."

"Go ahead and get anything else you want," he said.

I took him at his word and turned back to the proprietor.

"Do you have another shoulder holster?"

"I'll see," he said. A few minutes later he returned with one. I tried it on, and it fit perfectly. Then I turned back to the case.

"I'll take that German Luger and a box of ammo."

The look on Radio's face told me that he knew he'd been one-upped. But he wasn't a man to give up easily. He bought four derringers, too. One for each of us, and one for Lisa.

The owner added up the bill and gave it to Radio. He passed it to Lisa and said, "Babe, take care of this, will you?"

Time slipped by us, and it was already midafternoon by the time we returned to the hotel. Pam, Joan, and Arcel, along with five people I didn't know, were in the living room of the suite.

The five people were the members of Fluid Drive, Radio's backup band.

On lead guitar was Marty Dokes, a friendly, good-looking guy with the sort of thick, wavy brown hair that looked like he had just stepped off a New York ad set for English Leather. He was wearing sneakers, chinos, and a faded golf shirt decorated with an alligator holding an Old Blue can over the left breast. When we shook hands, he offered his left, his chording hand, and his fingertips were rough enough to ruin the finish on a jeep. As I looked him over, he hit just the right tone, a tone of "studied casualness," the kind that takes hours of work to achieve.

On drums was a small, wiry fellow who drummed the table with his free hand while he played cards with the other. He sported a very natty beard, dark glasses, and a cowboy hat. His name was Tom Powers. When he stood up to shake hands I got the distinct impression that he had boxed earlier in life. He had that kind of body, like a tight spring, always aware of where he was, always friendly but always ready. He was too small to have much of a money punch, but I imagined that he had a left hand that could nickel and dime you all the way to the hospital.

I also got another impression. One that was darker. From his movements, from what I could see of his eyes through the dark glasses, and from the way he rattled on verbally, I got the idea Tom was a speed freak.

But the men weren't what drew and held my attention. What did, was the balance of Fluid Drive—a female set of identical triplets. All cut from the same dough with the same cookie cutter. All tall, lean, and lanky with dark shag haircuts, skintight jeans, concho belts, sunglasses, and blue work shirts open all the way down and tied at the waist. Over each girl's left pocket was a name embroidered in red. They were Sauté, Purée, and Flambé.

63

As we shook hands I said, "Those aren't your real names, are they?"

"No," said Sauté. "They're our stage names."

"How did you happen to pick those?"

"To let you know that when you're dealing with the Kellys, you're cooking with gas," said Flambé.

It made sense—I suppose. After all, who was I to argue with rock and roll?

The introductions completed, I looked around for our gear, which we had left in the living room. It was gone. Figuring it was better to steer clear of Joan and Arcel for the moment, I asked Pam if she had seen it.

"It's in your room. I unpacked it for you while you were gone," she said.

"Thanks, that was nice of you," I said.

"It was no bother. I wouldn't want you to be distracted from looking out for Radio by something as simple as unpacking."

Her gaze held mine. There was a slight smile on her lips. For some reason her tone of voice and facial expression did not quite match, but I didn't know her well enough yet to know why, though I had my suspicions.

Radio didn't hang around long, choosing instead to go into his bedroom alone, then closing the door.

F.T. and I drank beer and chatted with the assembled faithful for a while. The conversation centered around the evening's show. I tried to steer it toward the shooting, but nobody wanted to talk about it, and all I succeeded in doing was raising a verbal cloud of dust.

Later Pam went into the bedroom. She stayed a few minutes, and then came out and said something to Arcel. He went into the bedroom and closed the door. Pam came over to us and said, "Come on. He wants to go over security measures with y'all while he gets dressed."

We grabbed a fresh beer and followed her into the bedroom. Arcel was standing in the middle of the empty room.

"Where's Radio?" I said.

"In the bathroom. Make yourselves comfortable. He'll be out in a few minutes," said Pam.

We sat down at the table and waited. We were on our third beer when the bathroom door opened and Radio emerged, dressed in blue pajamas and carrying a book. I caught a glimpse of the title: *Mankind: One Foot On the Barrail to Cosmic Crossover*. Once again he had mimicked Elvis perfectly with the bathroom, the pajamas, and the pseudoreligious book. As the old bard himself, Uncle Willie Shakespeare, so aptly put it: All the world's a stage—even the toilet.

Taking her nose into her own hands, Pam went into the newly vacated bathroom, returning with a bowl of water into which she poured about half a salt shaker. Radio took it from her and sat down at the table with us. He placed the bowl on the table and lowered his face into it until his nose and mouth were underwater. Then he started to make loud swallowing noises. I looked at Pam.

"What's he doing?" I asked.

"Clearing out his nasal passages. It's an old yoga trick. When you swallow like that it pulls the water up into your nose and sinuses and cleans them out."

"Can't you drown that way?" said F.T.

"You could, but you only swallow until you can taste the salt in the back of your throat. Then you stop, blow it out, and do it over again."

While we watched Radio do this disgusting act for the next five or ten minutes, Pam busied herself heating a cup of water with one of those contraptions you plug in and hang over the lip of the cup.

"Where'd he get an idea like this?" I said, meaning the water business.

"From Elvis, where else?" she said in the tone of a sorely tried mother. "Before a concert he always cleaned out his sinuses this way. Then he'd drink a cup of tea with honey to loosen up his vocal cords and coat his throat. That's what I'm doing now, making the tea."

When the tea was made, Radio wiped his face, then started

to pace while he drank it. Addressing nobody in particular, except the world, he started to pump himself up for the show.

"Tonight is going to be a historic occasion. Tonight marks the return of Elvis to the stage. Through me," he said, stabbing his chest with his thumb. "He lives and breathes once again, and I will take up his work where he left off. I live for the greater glory. He believed in the hereafter, as I do. By his training, he knew that even when he left this world, he would be able to reach us again through chosen people. In his mind, there was never any doubt that somebody would carry on his work, and he would speak through them. Tonight the world will see—that someone is me."

He put down the tea and turned to face us, placing his hands in a cupping motion against his chest like a young girl offering her breasts. His eyes were fire-bright and shining like a gambler who has just drawn an inside straight. It was easy to see Tom wasn't the only member of the entourage who enjoyed a little speed now and then.

"I feel him in me. My spirit and his are one. Tonight, on that stage, it will be Elvis performing, not me. He has given me a message to bring to the world. It's his message of love, and nothing can stand in the way of that message being delivered."

What he was saying had truth in it. Elvis was a man who devoted a lot of energy to his beliefs about the "hereafter." Some feel it began as a boy, when his mother took him, week after week, to visit the grave of his twin brother Jesse. Possibly she gave the dead twin a living personality. Who knows? But one thing is certain: throughout his life, Elvis developed a stronger and stronger belief in his own "holiness," a holiness much like a minor god of Greek mythology, and in his own ability to communicate across the Valley of Death. Now, in this hotel room, in his absence was also his presence, making itself known through the body of Radio Johnson, a man of humble origins. It made cold chills run up and down my spine.

Arcel looked at his watch and gently said, "Radio, it's time to get dressed."

66

Radio stopped pacing, and for a time it was as if he hadn't heard. Then he looked at me. "Do you feel what I'm talking about?"

I nodded in the affirmative.

"It's for this reason there are those who would kill me and take my crown, the crown Elvis has chosen me to bear for him. That's why I need you—to keep the forces of evil and jealousy from taking that which was his and is now mine. Will you help me? I need your help. Elvis and I can't do it alone. I need you to protect me while I do his work. Will you do that? Will you lay down your life, if necessary, to keep his work going? Your rewards will be great. To the faithful will go riches, gold, and glory. Men will know you and speak of you as you pass. Women will desire you. All that you dream will be yours. Are you with me?"

I swallowed hard. The man across the room had grown until he threatened to bust the walls at the seams. The insignificance of Radio Johnson had been shed like a summer snakeskin. In its place was an energy, an electricity, an aura that crackled in the air.

"Are you with me?" he asked again. Again I nodded in the affirmative. My voice seemed to have left me, and I was having trouble breathing. The air conditioner was on, but the room seemed humid and cloudy, something I hadn't noticed before. As I struggled to breathe, I felt the sweat start to break out on my forehead.

Does the man have such power? I thought. *It's like being in a room with the devil himself.* Then I looked around and saw it. There was a vaporizer going full steam on the bedside table.

Arcel chimed in again, "Radio, it's time."

"You're right. Make ready," he said as he sat down.

Arcel unzipped a garment bag and brought out the Suit of Lights. He took a damp cloth and began to wipe away any scuff marks on Radio's white plastic boots, while Pam began to work on his makeup and hair. First, she got down on her knees and unbuttoned his pajama top. Radio's entire midsection was encased in bandages for his wound.

She took a bottle of Brut, poured a generous portion into

the palm of her hand, and began to rub it on his chest with lazy, sensual motions. The humid air of the room was soon thick with the smell of cologne—the same cologne Elvis had worn during his lifetime.

When she finished, she stood up and began to touch up his base layer of makeup. When his face looked smooth and rosy enough to stand even the harshest of stage lights, she started to work on his eye shadow. Radio had worn green during the day, but this time she gave him blue with a touch of silver, which gave his eyes a sense of silver sparkle that would work well for the audience near the stage. She added mascara to his lashes and touched up his eyebrows with a brown pencil.

He sat there like an eighteenth-century fop while she took a brush and added lipstick dark enough to go well with the lights, then she turned her attention to his hair.

First, she carefully combed and brushed it until it was perfectly shaped in the hairstyle known round the world, then she took a can of spray and proceeded to give it the full treatment. If she had been painting a car, she would have had a prize-winning fourteen-coat lacquer finish when she was done. As it was, she put enough on to make his head virtually bulletproof.

When she finished, Radio stood up, and Arcel removed his pajama top. Then he knelt and pulled down the bottoms. Radio stood there, in his underwear, impervious to all this handling. I looked at F.T. There was a nasty grimace on his face. I could see all this primping and preening didn't sit well with him.

Arcel brought a set of kneepads like basketball players wear. Radio looked down at them. "What are they for?"

"Your knees. We don't want to take any chances on stage."

"Forget them. I'm not wearing them."

Arcel dutifully forgot them, and returned with the white boots. He knelt and raised one of Radio's feet as one would that of a horse. He slipped the foot into the boot and zipped up the side zipper. He repeated the process with the other foot.

As Radio stood there waiting for him to fetch the Suit of Lights, I thought about one of the basic differences between

68

men and women. If you put a good-looking woman in front of you wearing nothing but her panties and boots, even other women have to admit she looks sexy. But if you do the same thing with a good-looking man, even the most devoted fan will want to laugh at how ridiculous he looks. Alas, the spirit of Don Quixote lives in the breast of all men.

Arcel helped him into the sleeves and zipped it to his navel. Last but not least, he reached around Radio's waist from the back and buckled the wide belt around his middle. As he did that, I could not help thinking of the scene from *Patton* where the orderly is helping Patton dress for battle, and George C. Scott is standing there with a crazy look in his eyes, talking about history and how this is personal between him and Rommel.

When Arcel finally finished, Radio walked over to the mirror to check out the finished product. Satisfied, he said, "Let's ride."

And ride we did.

Eight

The living room was empty. Lisa and Fluid Drive had already left for the festival. Armed to the teeth, we made our way through the silent corridors to the elevator.

Arcel pushed the button, but it wasn't his day. Three elevators in a row were full, something I found odd since the building only had six floors, and we were on the fifth. It made me wonder if the people on the sixth knew something we didn't.

Radio was nervous and pacing. It was stage jitters, but the drugs didn't help any. After the third elevator passed us by, he turned to Arcel and snapped, "Get on the next one, and when you come back, it had better be empty."

When the next one stopped, Arcel leaped aboard like a jackrabbit with positraction. Minutes passed. We read and reread the framed advertisement above the ashtray, in which the hotel proclaimed the food and ambiance of its Commodore Room to be such that it would delight even the most jaded, hungry, horny, travel-weary, and dyspeptic Bacchus to pass through its doors.

As the time ticked away, I began to worry about Arcel. What was taking him so long? Radio was snapping his fingers and muttering to himself. When the elevator finally stopped again, I saw my worries were for nothing. Arcel was the only passenger.

In the lobby, Radio was mobbed by a group of autograph seekers, all women in their sixties and seventies with gray hair done with a blue tint. They were like kids, begging and pleading for a kiss, an autograph, a lock of hair, a sequin—anything to show the folks back home they had been near their star, the brooding Adonis—the new Elvis . . . risen . . . risen . . . risen . . . too much man for even the grave to hold . . . boychild, man, savior, and genuine folk hero, all rolled into one.

Radio's face beamed with pleasure as he passed among them, hugging and kissing, and asking about their families. The ladies responded by gushing and swooning in such a sweet way I could not but think of that famous Wayne Newton song—"Red Roses for a Blue-Haired Old Lady."

F.T. leaned over and whispered, "Get him away from this, and I'll get the car. Bring him out the back way. We don't want to take any chances."

It took a few minutes to tear him away from the fans, but finally we worked our way to the hotel's rear entrance, where F.T. had the Caddy waiting. He had used the time to put up the top. The electrical tape repairs on the holes in the roof made it look less of a limousine than ever, but Radio didn't say anything.

Pam, Arcel, and Radio piled into the back seat while I rode shotgun in the front. Everything looked quiet in the parking lot, so I motioned for F.T. to proceed.

Once in traffic, Radio said, "Why did you put the top up tonight? It wasn't up today."

"If anybody is going to try to get you, it's more likely they'll try it at night," I said.

It was an explanation that seemed to make Radio uncomfortable.

The ride was as smooth as a presidential caravan. We took the back road to the emergency entrance, which Radio didn't like because it separated him from his fans, but it got us there in record time.

There was a guard at the entrance to the trailer who looked us over carefully before he let us enter. The trailer looked as if a cyclone had hit it. There was paper everywhere: paper cups, plates, towels, napkins, and every one of them had been used. There was stale beer in the cups. The plates were filled with chicken and rib bones covered in barbeque sauce. There was a lot of potato salad around, too. Everyone had used that as an ashtray, and the lumpy white mounds with the filters sticking out of them looked like little birthday cakes from the American Cancer Society.

We walked down the tunnel to the back entrance of the auditorium, where another guard gave us the once-over. I said the magic password, and he let us through.

Backstage was pure bedlam. Lisa was running around with a clipboard and acting very efficient. Her face showed her tiredness by the lines around her mouth, but her eyes were bright, and her jeans and blouse were crisp and unwrinkled.

"Thank God you're here! I was starting to worry. What took you so long?" she said.

"It takes Radio longer to get dressed than most," I said. F.T. smiled at that one.

"Never mind that now. Let's go down to the dressing room."

There was a guard at the head of the stairs leading to the basement dressing rooms. The basement was nothing special, just the usual concrete floors with drains in them, poor lighting, and cinder-block walls. Naturally, the air conditioning wasn't working, and the air was a bit close. I thought about Elvis's aversion to sweating. He hated sweating almost as much as he hated bathing. I looked at Radio, but he didn't seem to mind.

Lisa led us down the corridor to the second door. The dressing room was about ten by ten in size. One wall was filled by a dressing table made of cheap Formica in the center of which was a large mirror bordered by rows of lights on three sides. On the table was a small oscillating fan with pretty ribbons blowing in the breeze. There was a second fan, this one rectangular in shape, sitting on the floor. The two of them did a decent job of stirring the air. The room's only furniture was a coffee table whose finish had been tortured beyond belief with wet cocktail glasses and cigarette burns, a couple of folding chairs, and a couch that wheezed when Radio sat down on it.

By the time we all crowded into the room, the air was stifling. The smell of Brut and body odor was enough to make you want to throw up. Radio must have felt the same way because he waved us out of the room.

"Go find something to do till show time. I need to be alone."

Kinder words were never spoken.

Outside, Pam stopped Lisa. "Have you seen Joan tonight?"

Lisa checked her clipboard. "She's here someplace. I have her checked off as arriving. She's probably upstairs. Why don't you try there?"

The upstairs part sounded good, so we followed everyone back to the comfort of air conditioning. Pam started looking for Joan, and Arcel went off to take care of whatever business managers take care of. F.T. and I headed for the bar.

There was a lobby bar for the ticket holders, but to get served there meant we had to battle the crowds, never a good idea when you're wearing a loaded gun. Instead we headed for a washtub filled with ice and beer backstage.

Marty Dokes was there ahead of us. I ripped off the top from a can of Old Blue and poured about half the icy contents down my throat in a single swallow. The coldness was so intense that my face went numb, but I poured the rest down my gullet in a second swallow and reached for a refill, knowing all the while that that nice numbness, like all other good things in life, would end all too soon.

"Bodyguarding looks like thirsty work," said Marty. His

voice was already thick from drinking.

"About like being a musician," I said.

"Yeah, that's thirsty work too," said Marty.

"I imagine you're pretty excited about the contest," I said.

Marty took a swig and smacked his lips. "Yep, our ship has finally come in. What we've been waiting for all these years. Now it's ours, partners till the end."

"How do you mean you've 'been waiting for all these years'? I thought Radio had only been doing the Elvis thing for about a year."

"That's right, he's been doin' the Elvis thing for about a year," he slurred. "But we've been together a long time. Before the Elvis thing we used to call ourselves the Acetones. Pam thought it up while she and Radio was dating. She worked at a dry cleaners and thought it would be cute to name us after a cleaning fluid. Never liked the name myself."

"How did you come up with the name Fluid Drive?"

"That's not our name. We don't have a name now. Fluid Drive is the name the girls use."

"I'll bet when Radio got shot it gave you a scare," I said.

"Gave me a scare. Anything happens to Radio, there'd go the ship. Sunk. And it'd be back to the meat packing plant for us."

"I guess you hope we get that crazy fan before she tries again," I said.

"Crazy fan . . . crazy fan . . . it wasn't no crazy fan . . ."

"Marty, it's time to get your gear ready," said a hard, cold voice behind us. It was Tom Powers, the drummer.

"Yeah, you're right," mumbled Marty as he shuffled off.

Tom opened himself a beer. Through his glasses I could see his eyes were diamond-hard and speed-freak mean.

"Do you know what Marty meant when he said that the killer wasn't a crazy fan?" I asked.

"Yeah, he meant our fans don't go around killing people. They're just people out for a few laughs, and the worst thing that can happen with them is they'll hug you too hard, leave lipstick on your collar, or pinch you on the butt. They *don't*

74

go around killing people. Maybe Rolling Stones fans kill people. Maybe even some of Elvis's old fans, but not ours."

"If she's not a crazy fan, then who is she?"

Tom looked at me for a minute, then he said, "I've got to see about my gear," and he left.

Before I could discuss this interesting development with F.T., Arcel came running up to us.

"Have you seen Radio? It's almost show time, and he's not in his dressing room."

We dropped our beers and headed for the steps, passing the triplets of Fluid Drive as we were leaving. I asked one of them if they'd seen Radio. All I got in return was a giggle. The pupils of their eyes were so dilated you could see as far back as the dawn of time in them. Fluid Drive was stoned to the gills.

The guard at the steps said Radio had not come up.

We went through the dressing rooms one by one. All we found were clothes, makeup kits, and instruments. The place was deserted, and there was no sign of Radio.

The door next to Radio's dressing room led to a room that was dark and filled with stage props and other odds and ends associated with the building. The two bare light bulbs hanging from the ceiling weren't sufficient to pierce the gloom. They lighted a small patch around themselves, but if anything, they drove the rest of the area deeper into shadow.

"I don't like it," I said.

"Me neither," said F.T. as he drew his gun and pulled back the slide to seat a cartridge in the chamber. I did the same.

F.T. led the way, crouching low to make the best use of the gloom. I followed right on his heels. At times like this I had to rely on F.T. to be my eyes, since sunglasses in a dark room make me blind as justice on a cold morning. F.T. took his time, carefully checking everything before moving on, a lesson learned in his first thirteen-month course in the care and fertilization of rice paddies.

The storage room was close and humid, like being locked all night in Nero Wolfe's laundromatic orchid room. From somewhere ahead of us, I heard the sound of a motor. We slowly worked our way toward it. The source of the sound was a walk-in cooler with foot-thick walls and a door like a bank vault.

"I don't see him. Let's head back. He may be back in the dressing room," I said.

"Wait a minute. Let's check out the cooler," said F.T.

I followed him to it. Someone had shoved a screwdriver through the lock hole on the latch, making it impossible to open the door from the inside. F.T. removed the screwdriver and opened the door. Inside lay a crumpled figure dressed in white and sequins, looking for all the world like a Mr. Softee driver who'd been mugged by a gang of ice-cream-crazed eight-year-olds.

I stepped back and turned on the light at the outside switch. It was Radio. A claw hammer lay on the floor beside him. There was blood on the back of his head and the collar of his suit.

F.T. was beside him in a flash. He gave him the old professional once-over and said, "It's nothing serious. He's just been knocked out. Go get the sheriff while I see if I can bring him around."

I found the sheriff upstairs. He rounded up the doctor, and we headed back. When we got there, the doctor wasn't necessary. F.T. had revived him by placing cold cans of Old Blue in all the strategic places, and Radio was awake.

"What happened?" said the sheriff.

"I don't know. Somebody hit me on the head. That's the last thing I remember, till now."

"Were you in the dressing room when you got hit?" said the sheriff.

Radio hesitated for a moment before answering. "No, I was in here."

"What the hell were you doing in here? You didn't have any business in the supply room just before a show."

It took Radio a moment or two to think up an answer to that one. The blow on the head had slowed his reflexes considerably.

"It was hot in the dressing room. I came in to get a beer to cool me off," he said.

The sheriff gave him a look that fifth grade teachers reserve for bad students, then decided to let it pass.

"How do you feel?" I said.

"A little shaky, but all right," said Radio.

The sheriff picked up the claw hammer. There was blood on the claw part. "Did you get a look at who hit you?"

"No, I didn't see anything or hear anything. All I remember is the pain, and then waking up," he said, looking around. "What time is it?"

When I told him he said, "Holy shit, I've got to get moving. I'm due to go on."

As we helped Radio to his feet, the sheriff said, "Well, sports fans, there you have it—the show must go on."

Heading back to the dressing room, Radio was shaky, and a couple of times we had to take him by the elbows to keep him steady.

Once we were in the dressing room, he checked out his makeup and gingerly felt the back of his head where he drew his hand away with blood on it.

As he sat at the dressing table staring at the blood on his fingers, Lisa appeared in the doorway. "Where have you been? You're due to go on in a couple of minutes." Then she saw the blood on his fingers and said, "What happened?"

We told her the news. She came into the room, all motherly and anxious, touching him tenderly and examining the cut.

"Can you go on?" she said, her voice full of concern.

Radio looked at her reflection in the mirror and said, "Sure, just give me a minute to get myself together."

That was an exit line, but she didn't take it, choosing to stay and hover around him like the Goodyear blimp.

He called for his makeup case, which I handed him. He rummaged around in it till he found a medicine bottle filled with assorted pills. He poured several of them into his hand and chose three or four, which he washed down with a beer. Then he went through some theatrical motions to indicate he was getting himself together for the performance of his life, and then with a shrug of his shoulders reminiscent of James Brown or Gorgeous George, he stood up, and we were off.

F.T. and I flanked him while the sheriff led the way toward the steps and the stage above.

When we arrived topside, the band was set up and ready to go. At the high sign from Radio, Tom, Marty, and Fluid Drive, along with three guys I didn't know, took their places on stage.

I asked Lisa about the extra guys, and she said they were a studio horn section she had brought in to fill out the sound.

Pam and Joan were waiting in the wings with Arcel. Arcel placed a towel around Radio's neck and rubbed away the sweat. He noticed the blood and looked over at us, but he didn't say anything about it, which made me wonder what had happened to him after he had alerted us.

He massaged the muscles in Radio's neck as one would a fighter getting ready to go into the ring, talking all the while about him being the King, and how he was going to knock 'em dead.

The house lights dimmed, and the announcer's veterans-approved-broadcasting-school voice announced, "Ladies and gentlemen, for your entertainment pleasure—the one! . . . the only! . . . Radio Johnson!"

The band started on the theme from *2001: A Space Odyssey*, with Sauté pounding the bass keys of the piano, filling the air with an ominous, dangerous, rattlesnake sound. Then the trumpet started, its lonely sound announcing from far away that He is risen . . . He is coming . . . the King is coming. The sound growing as the rest of the horn section joined in and built it to a light swell, where Tom started to pound the drums like a jungle telegraph, repeating over and over—He is risen . . . He is coming . . . the King is coming. The horns came back, but louder and more insistent this time. The voices of Fluid Drive joined in harmony with Marty and Tom, like the voices of loyal subjects announcing and worshipping at the same time, each reaching higher and harder till their sheer power threatened to take my breath away.

I looked over at Radio where he stood stock-still, eyes glazed, drinking in the electricity from the amplifiers as the music surged, and the crowd hunkered tighter into their seats.

When the music finally reached the peak of its electric glissando, it paused, and Tom shifted into overdrive, kicking off the entrance number with drumming that seemed afire. The whole band jumped in, romping and stomping through a set of chords whose only meaning was to keep the tempo moving and get the star through the hardest part of performing: making his entrance without tripping over his feet.

They need not have worried. Radio took a deep breath and stepped out smartly, looking neither right nor left, waving to no one, and not smiling, but scowling.

When he reached the microphone, he just stood there with the band going hell-for-leather behind him. The thunder and roar seemed to pass through the plane that defines musical limits, and became more.

It became the sound of mechanized life, the sound of machinery in action, a sound as familiar to us as the whippoorwill to our forefathers. No longer music to our ears, it became music to our souls. It was the sound of the five o'clock whistle and the City of Big Shoulders. It was the sound of the bulldozer and crane dinosaurically leaving their mark on the face of the planet. It was the chug and rumble of the eighteen-wheeler and the whir of the Waring blender. It was the whine of the Snooz Alarm and the drone of the air conditioner. Therein lay its secret. Rock and roll aped the rhythm of our lives.

The driving music went on for at least two minutes while he stood there looking out at the darkness and the beast—the audience. Standing where we were, we could see what he saw, and it was easy to see, blinded by the lights, deafened by the sound, he was not performing for the crowd—the crowd mattered little—he was performing for the greater glory, marching in time to a master of time and space that only he knew, and through him, we could feel but not see.

As the music thudded and thundered, he seemed to grow taller, taking strength from it. His chest opened and ex-

panded, his stance growing more aggressive as he waited until
he felt the time was right. Then he stepped up to the mike and
strangled it like a male apache dancer in one of the Paris
waterfront dances of the fifties. Drawing it closer to him
against its will, he cuddled the mike close to his cheek, arrogantly sure of his power, cocked his hip, raised a rather limp
wrist in a gesture reminiscent of a Baptist choir director, and
the music stopped as surely and swiftly as if somebody had
pulled the plug.

After the roar, the silence was deafening. As he stood there
saying nothing and doing nothing, I found myself holding my
breath. By now I had figured he wasn't doing Elvis's "Aloha
from Hawaii" show, opening with "C.C. Rider" and following it with "Burning Love." No, what we were seeing was
something entirely different.

He stood staring into the lights until the audience began to
grow restless and jittery, like a person one stroke away from
orgasm with a partner who won't let him have the last stroke.

Finally, in a loud voice, he started, "Today I was sitting in
my room, and the spirit of Elvis came to me, and do you know
what he said to me?"

The audience wasn't quick enough to respond, so Radio
strangled the mike a little tighter and stalked to the end of the
stage. Pointing an intimidating finger at the audience, he
roared, "Children, I can't hear you! Do you know what he
said?"

This time the audience came back strong. "No!" they yelled
and screamed.

Radio returned to center stage and yelled again, "Do you
know what he said to me?"

And the answer came back this time stronger than the first.
He dragged the mike to stage right and screamed the same
thing, and when the response came back this time, I thought
the roof was going to come off the place.

Radio returned to center stage. "As I sat there and the Vision came to me, reaching out from across the Valley of
Death, wanting to be with us, and keeping his promise to
return, *HE* said—'Tonight is the night to boogie-woogie!' "

The whole place went berserk. The band hit it with a wall of sound like the driving wheels of Casey Jones's locomotive as it snarled, and thundered, and roared while the fireman poured on the coal, and Casey, with a smile on his lips and the devil in his eyes, pulled out the throttle all the way. We were underway, on the road bound for rock and roll madness, as grandmothers, mothers, and daughters alike threw roses, room keys, and even panties in an exuberant release of tension.

Radio romped and stomped, and did the old James Brown one-legged slide back and forth across the stage, dragging his reluctant partner—the microphone—back and forth with him. At center stage, he stopped and again raised the limp wrist high over his head, standing with one leg cocked, and caressing the mike against his cheek. As the hand went up, the band once again stopped on a dime. The audience took a little longer to pick up the cue, but Radio was in no hurry. He stood there patiently, waiting until they quieted down to nervous edginess before he started again.

"Ladies, when you're in your car all by yourself, or you're sitting home all alone, and you're feeling lonesome and blue. You're feeling like nobody loves you in the whole wide world, and you turn on your radio, and you hear Elvis sing, all of a sudden you feel the spirit and the power of the boogie-woogie, and you feel it touching you deep down in your heart. What you're feeling is not just music. You're feeling the spirit of Elvis. He's coming into your heart. He's coming into your life. He's going to make things right, and this is what he's saying to you. He's saying these words right here—That's all right, Mama."

The band was with him all the way in a driving, stutter-plucking variation of the locomotive beat as he moved in time to the music of Elvis's first record. The crowd was on its feet and moving toward the stage.

It alarmed me. "Things look like they may be getting out of hand. Don't you think we ought to move out a little so we can be closer to him if they get up on stage?" I yelled.

"Naw, he's got it under control," F.T. yelled back.

"Yeah, but you're forgetting there's a murderer out there."

Before F.T. could answer, Radio raised his hand again and the band stopped.

"Sometimes the spirit of the boogie-woogie is not enough for a woman," he said, cradling the mike to his cheek. "Sometimes she needs more. Sometimes she needs something else to make her feel special, something else to make her feel whole, something else to make her feel like all the trouble she goes to for everybody else is worthwhile. And if you ask her what that thing is that would make her happier than anything else in the world, happier than a big house, happier than a limousine, happier than a long vacation, she'll say these words—Love me tender."

The audience quieted down as he eased into the number, making the song personal and private to each woman, no matter how young or old. As he moved and sang, I forgot about the trivial things: Arcel dressing him, the salt water up the nose, the body odor, and his arrogant ways. On stage, he was magic.

It took F.T. a moment to shake free of the spell, too. Turning to me he said, "I told you there was nothing to worry about. If there's one thing he knows, it's how to whip an audience into shape."

He did little more than a verse of the song before he strolled to the edge of the stage and beckoned. The women came by the ones, the tens, maybe even the hundreds to be near him. Leaving the singing to Fluid Drive, he knelt and began to kiss them one by one. It wasn't an act of love or sex on the part of the women; it was an act of communion, performed with chastity, each careful to take only a little and leave some for the rest. When a woman did overstep the bounds of propriety and began to treat Radio as if he were made of chocolate, the others were quick to remind her of her place.

When he finished his rounds he returned to center stage, where he made a couple of flashy karate moves, and the band hit the finishing chords of the song.

He turned his back to the audience while Flambé plucked the bass strings—*tum-ta-tum, tum-ta-tum, tum-ta-tum*. Without turning, he began to complain in a low crooning way about how his woman didn't close her eyes when he came near her, how the good thing seemed to be cooling between them even though she was doing her best to keep it from him.

Flinging his arms like a petulant child having a temper tantrum, he spun around to face the audience and screamed in a voice filled with need, "Baby, I know you've lost that loving feeling." The band came in behind him on the old Righteous Brothers hit.

Radio begged and pleaded through a couple of verses to let everyone know he was serious about the old loving feeling, and if she would just forgive him and let things get back to normal, he would mend his low-down ways.

Then it happened. As he was musically working his way down through a series of "Whoa, whoas," he turned his head to his right and looked at me standing in the wings. A smile crept across his face. It was a he-cat smile that said it all.

To the imaginary woman, if she had seen it, it said, "I'll do or say anything necessary to get my way, then I'm going to keep right on doing whatever I want."

To me, it was a look of driving ambition. A look that said if a Judy Garland imitation was the way to the top, he would be on stage belting out "Somewhere Over the Rainbow" at the top of his falsies.

He turned his eyes back to the audience and started through the chorus again, complaining about how his baby had lost her loving feeling, but a subtle vocal shift had taken place. This time he was no longer accepting the blame for her loss of loving feeling. No, he was tossing the blame right into her lap. If there was any loss of loving feeling in this relationship, it was her fault, not his, but he was man enough to forgive and forget, if she would only quit acting so weird.

As the music swelled for the climax, he screamed, "Baby!" It was a he-cat scream that said, "I know what you need."

He pumped his hips hard a couple of times like good old dirty backdoor sex and screamed "Baby!" again. This time he might as well have yelled for the women in the audience to bend over the kitchen table, raise their skirts, and drop their panties because Radio was going to ride them hard and put them up wet tonight.

The music reached them on the old subliminal airways. The subject of sex had entered the discussion, and they responded in kind: yowling, wailing, screaming, and scratching till they sounded like ten thousand chain saws on high octane.

It wasn't a sexy sound. It was a frightening sound— frightening because of the intensity in some of those deep pools of still water. I disagreed with Tom the drummer; it *was* an intensity that could cause murder.

I turned to F.T. He looked a little white too.

"We'd better go down and check the dressing rooms again just to be sure there is no little surprise waiting for us when the show is over."

Nothing had changed since our last visit. The basement was still deserted. We drew our guns and went back into the storage room, this time for a more thorough search. Nothing we found yielded a clue to her identity. There was no carelessly dropped handkerchief or tube of lipstick. Nothing. This time she had been flawless in her execution except for one thing— Radio was still alive.

We took a beer and went into the dressing room. Nothing had changed there, either. As we sipped them, I noticed Radio's makeup case. It was so obviously an extension of him that it made me curious to see its contents, so I started to snoop.

It was filled with more goodies than Snoopy's doghouse. It was a veritable drugstore. There was makeup of every hue and color in the rainbow, and for every cosmetic purpose known to man. There was about eight pounds of junk jewelry: rings, bracelets, necklaces, and pins of assorted sizes and shapes, with a total retail value of about four dollars and thirty cents. There were about twenty bottles of pills, again of every hue and color in the rainbow. Some had prescriptions, some didn't. Having some knowledge of pills, I recognized several garden-variety uppers and downers. Others I didn't recognize.

There was also a pint of sloe gin and a note.

I unfolded the note. It simply said, "Radio, darling. Meet me in the storage room before you go on tonight. Love," and it was unsigned.

I showed the note to F.T. He looked at it and said, "How interesting."

"*Cherchez la femme*, as the French would say," I said.

"Those French have a word for everything," said F.T.

"Now we know what Radio was doing in the storage room. He was meeting someone—someone he is having an affair with."

"Who?" said F.T.

"I don't know," I said. I thought for a minute. "This note raises more questions than it clears up: Who is he having an affair with? Who else knows about the affair? Is the note from his lover or the killer? Or are they one and the same? If not, is the affair the reason behind the killing? But it does clear up one big point . . ."

"What's that?"

"Radio knows the killer, whether he realizes it or not. Right now he's so busy covering up his affair that he may also be covering up the killer's identity without knowing it. We have to get him alone and see if we can get some idea as to her identity."

"Whose? The killer or lover?" said F.T.

"Both," I said.

Radio was beginning his last number when we reached our former position in the wings. In the time we had been gone, something on stage had changed. The atmosphere had gone from the pure electrostatic tension that we had left to one which hung heavy with exhaustion. The band was still flying high from the excitement of the pretty lights and their own slip-and-slide, electroglide, rock and roll music, but Radio and the audience were a different story.

He stood there, at center stage, holding the microphone pole for support, his white jump suit almost transparent from the sweat that soaked it through. The sequins sparkled against the shiny white wetness, giving his body a luster and twinkle guaranteed to drive any self-respecting rubber freak mad with desire.

His hair, so carefully coiffed and sprayed before, now hung wet and limp, some parts sticking to his forehead and other parts sticking to the side of his face. Rivulets of sweat streamed down his face, cutting gullies of mud through his clay-brown makeup.

The spring was gone from his legs. The quadricep muscles above the knees had given out and would no longer hold his weight. Like a spent boxer, he stood there with knees locked and legs quivering. His posture was gone. His back was bowed, his shoulders slumped, and his head seemed almost too heavy for his neck to hold up. Standing there in the limelight, he looked for all the world like a man who had spent the last two hours doing the Virginia reel with a refrigerator for a partner.

The audience—that black, pulsating, fire-breathing mass of arms, legs, hair, and eyes that lay in wait, writhing in the darkness under the lights—had been fed, petted, and stroked to orgasm, and was now reduced to responding with a sigh instead of a roar.

Taking the mike from the pole but still using the pole for support, Radio began to speak. His voice was thick and slow with weariness.

"Today when Elvis appeared to me in my room, he gave me one more message to give to you. Normally he closed his show with 'Can't Help Falling in Love' from *Blue Hawaii*, but this is not a normal time. This is a special time, a time of love, and he wanted me to sing this song to let you know that love still lives even though he can't be here to deliver it to you."

Sauté tinkled the keys on the piano, and the band joined in quietly as Radio began to sing, "I'll Remember You."

There wasn't a dry eye in the house as each person sorted through personal memories of the King. From the handsome boy singer who, now in retrospect, looked so innocent and vulnerable, to the army days, to the god-awful movies, the Vegas days, the television specials, the drugs, the weight, the heartbreak, and finally the last Cadillac and the cemetery ride.

At the end of the first verse, Radio raised his hand and the band stopped. "I want to do this second verse for Elvis, to let him know that we'll remember him, too."

He started to sing, and one by one, people in the audience began to hold up lighted matches and cigarette lighters until the whole audience was aglow in silent tribute to the memory of the King.

When the song ended he said, "You've been a fantastic audience. God bless you."

The band and the applause started at the same time, climbing higher and higher until it was again a deafening roar.

Radio was shaky as he walked toward us in the wings. I wondered if his legs were going to hold him up. Arcel walked over to us and said, "Go out there and give him a hand getting off the stage."

As we took him on each side and helped him off, I was amazed at the heat on stage. The temperature must have been a hundred, maybe more. I guess that was to be expected. When you prop your feet on the dragon's teeth, you're bound to feel the heat.

Nine

 The applause finally died down enough for Lisa to walk out onto the stage. Nervously she fingered the microphone as she began to read from her notes.

"Ladies and gentlemen, my name is Lisa Feldman. I'm the president of Pyrite Records . . ."

A murmur ran through the audience at the sight of one so young in a position of such prestige and authority. Lisa waited for it to quiet down before she continued.

"Some years ago, my father and I began this company. Success didn't come easy. We had to work for it, but like everyone who believes in the American dream, and keeps on keeping on, it eventually came our way.

"What you've seen and enjoyed here this weekend, our tribute to the King of Rock and Roll—the late Elvis Presley—represents, in large part, our commitment to show our appreciation to you, the public, by using that success to make others successful too, just as Elvis, himself, would have wanted if he were still alive.

"This is a pleasure and duty which normally would have been my father's, but this weekend he was . . . he was . . ." She faltered. I held my breath for her. She swallowed hard and kept going.

"This weekend he was killed . . ."

Again a murmur ran through the audience.

"So I'm here to try and fill his mighty big shoes."

The audience burst into applause, and Lisa had to stop to wipe away the tears.

"Now," she continued, "the moment you've all been waiting for. It's time to crown the *new* King of Rock and Roll. Time to choose the man to carry on the great Elvis tradition.

"For the winner, this is a dream come true, for he will get to live the life of Elvis for one year. He'll receive a recording contract with Pyrite Records. One week from tonight he will once again appear here, this time in a solo concert to kick off his album and national 'Fifty-Fifty' tour, where he will appear in all fifty states of the United States in fifty days, traveling in his own private jet, and culminating in a one-week appearance at the famous Fiesta Hotel in Las Vegas.

"That's not all. When the tour is over, and he's tired, he'll have a place to come home to. What I'm talking about is his very own mansion—Dreamland."

She went on to announce, to nobody's great surprise, that Radio Johnson was the winner. Even if the contest hadn't been rigged, he would have won hands-down.

As he started to go on stage he stopped and said to me, "I wrote her a pretty good speech, don't you think?"

It was a good speech, but the sincerity with which the teenager had delivered it was more impressive.

Radio made a nice little speech and accepted a loving cup about the size of Rhode Island.

The band came out, and Radio dedicated his last number— "Heartbreak Hotel"—to the losers. Gracious winning was not a part of Radio's makeup.

He did one verse, waved good night to the audience, and trotted offstage.

Arcel gave him a fresh towel and said, "Great going, champ."

Pam gave him a kiss and said, "We finally did it, baby. We finally made it."

Radio looked more enthusiastic about the towel. Turning to us he said, "Let's get out of here."

Back at the hotel, I excused myself to take a shower and change clothes.

I turned the water on hot to let it scald the crud out of my pores. As I soaped and scrubbed, I used the time to think things over.

What did we know? We knew the killer was a woman, but we didn't know which woman. Given the fact that all killers are crazy, we now knew this one was no crazier than most. She was no psychopathic fan who killed from a perverted sense of cerebral outrage generated by a real or imagined slight, or from an arrested sexual delusion, or from a vitamin deficiency, or an overproduction of some obscure hormone whose name is thirteen letters long and made up largely of X's and Z's. No, this was a woman who wanted to kill Radio for a definite reason, at which judge and jury would nod their heads and accept as logical.

Tonight's second attempt on Radio's life had shown us several more interesting things. It had shown us, even with guards all around, she still had easy access to the backstage area, and even more important, to the dressing rooms below. That could only mean one thing: she was associated with the show.

Once downstairs, she did not hide in the storage room on the off chance that Radio would come in for a beer. No, she used the note we had found in his makeup case to lure him to the storage room. This meant she knew him and his habits well enough to write the note, and be certain he would follow its instructions. In other words, she was already close to him, possibly a member of his entourage. If so, one of the women—Pam, Joan, Lisa, Sauté, Flambé, or Purée—was a murderer. Which one was it?

It was safe to assume, that for the moment at least, she did not have a gun. Otherwise she would have used it in the storage room instead of botching the job with the claw hammer and locking him in the freezer. However, the gun situation was one we could not count on to remain static. Guns were too easy to come by.

As I thought about Radio lying there on the floor of the cooler, something didn't set right with me. Then it came to me. It was the wounds. When a person sets out to hit or shoot someone, he normally lines up directly in front of, or behind, the person he intends to assault. If that is the case, a wound from behind would be on the opposite side of a wound made from the front. That wasn't the case with Radio. Both wounds were on the same side, the right side.

I turned on the cold to rinse off, and all thoughts of our predicament vanished as I stood there shivering under the icy stream.

I used three towels to dry off. That left F.T. two washcloths, a hand towel, and the bathmat for all two hundred and fifty pounds of him. It was a drying job that would require ingenuity.

F.T. came into the bedroom while I was laying out my clothes. I told him about my questions concerning the wounds.

He thought for a minute before he said, "It's the approach angle. In the trailer, if you remember, she had to approach him from a diagonal on one side. In the storage room, it was the other side."

I thought about it while F.T. showered. What he said made sense. It was a matter of angles.

I changed into the bottom half of a royal blue sweat suit with white stripes, Nike running shoes, and a black T-shirt with a small taco embroidered over the left breast. The likeness was a good one. The taco was about the size of an Izod alligator, and in gold, red, and green, it was so detailed even the lettuce stood out.

Satisfied with my appearance, I wandered into the living room before F.T. had a chance to finish his shower and discover it was going to take Kleenex and toilet paper to finish his drying job.

The band was at the bar enjoying pizza and a round of cool

Art Bourgeau

ones. I decided to join them. As I popped the top on an Old Blue, Purée, the rhythm guitar player, said, "Radio's looking for you. He's in the bedroom."

"Thanks," I said. I knocked on the door, and Pam answered it.

"Oh, it's you. Come on in," she said.

Radio was standing beside the table, looking very regal from the neck up, while Arcel struggled to undress him from the neck down.

Without moving his head an inch, Radio cut his eyes toward me and said, "Where's your gun?"

"In the bedroom."

"Go get it. I don't want you going anywhere without it."

"Even here in the suite?" I said.

"That's right. Now go get it," he said.

When I got back to the bedroom, F.T. was drying off. I started to chuckle, but then I noticed what he was drying off with—my two-hundred-dollar silk cowboy shirt. The one decorated with the special hand-painted scene of the Alamo with John Wayne standing on the parapet, drinking an Old Blue in the midst of shot and shell.

"What the hell are you doing? That's my best shirt," I said with horror in my voice.

"Yeah, I know," said F.T.

"Well, stop it, for Christ's sake! You're going to ruin the painting on it," I said, grabbing it out of his hands.

I held it up to the light. The painting looked okay. I carefully hung it on a hanger.

"Why the hell did you decide to use that? There were plenty of towels in the bathroom."

"Yeah, if you like wet towels."

"What about the bathmat? You could have used that," I said.

"And get athlete's foot all over my body? You've got to be crazy."

"Don't be silly. I've dried with bathmats many times," I said.

"Yeah, and look at your skin. It looks like a fat woman

92

took a leak on you, wrapped you in swaddling clothes, and left you in a warm, dark place for three or four days."

That hurt.

"Zevich, that's what I don't like about you—you have no sense of humor," I said.

"Sure I do. That's why I used your shirt. I knew the look on your face would be funny as hell when you found out."

He had a point there, and I laughed. After all, I had started it. I should have at least left him another washcloth.

He laughed too.

I put on my shoulder holster while F.T. finished dressing. Looking at me in the mirror he said, "What's that for?"

I told him about Radio wanting us to wear them everywhere. He agreed that it made sense.

We picked up a couple of beers at the bar and went back to Radio's room where Arcel and he were seated at the table while Pam toweled his hair dry. Radio was now wearing a light blue terry cloth robe with a towel draped around his neck. He didn't look very good. The muscles in his face were sagging, and his eyes were dead flat. He had obviously shuffled a few downers to burn off the effects of the uppers, and the result was double tiredness: the extreme fatigue you naturally feel after being strung out on uppers, and the lethargic feeling of the downers.

"Arcel, I need a beer. Get me one," he said.

After he had gone, Radio said, "Sit down. I want to talk to you."

He didn't say a word until Arcel returned with the beer. Then he sent Pam and Arcel out of the room.

"I know you think I'm a little bit crazy to have y'all wear your guns around the suite, but you have to see my side of it. Somebody's trying to kill me. Your job is to keep that from happening. Tonight you didn't do that very well. She almost got me," he said in a flat, tired voice.

"Just to set the record straight, she *did* get you," I said. "The reason you're here now is we saved you before it was too late."

Radio dismissed this with a wave of a hand. "That's not

really important. What's important is—''

"What's important is this," I interrupted. "We *were* doing our jobs tonight. *You're* the one who sent us upstairs. While we were gone *you* got caught with your pants down and wound up in the cooler. We *were* doing our jobs when we went upstairs, and we were *still* doing them when we found you before you could freeze to death."

"You're right," he said in a placating tone. "I didn't mean you weren't doing your jobs. That's not it. What I guess I'm saying is somebody is trying to kill me, and I'm scared. You can understand that, can't you?"

F.T. and I knew the feeling only too well. Having somebody after you is very unpleasant.

"Do you have any idea who is behind it?" I asked.

"That's easy. It's somebody traveling with us. I don't know who it is, but I'm sure it's one of them."

"Why would anybody in the show want to kill you?" said F.T. "That's a little bit like killing the golden goose, isn't it?"

Radio's drug-deadened eyes brightened a bit. He smacked his fist into his palm in an emphatic gesture. "Exactly! That's my point entirely. It's not me they're after. Everybody in the show loves me. They'd do anything for me. No, what the killer is after is the *symbolic* me. If by killing me, she can keep us from taking our show to the people, she will have succeeded in her mission."

He was talking drug talk that made no sense at all. What was the "symbolic" him? And if everybody loved him, why would anyone want to kill him?

"How do you figure that?" said F.T.

Radio gave him a look normally reserved for the half-witted.

"Because if we go down, Pyrite Records goes down with us. Through the years Pyrite has been a small company that has held on by making rhythm and blues records for the black jukebox market. Ace made enough to live comfortably, but that's all until he came up with the idea for this festival. Everything Lisa owns is tied up in it. In fact *I've* even put money into it. If I go down, we all go down."

That part made more sense. Now we were talking about a

concrete motive. One we hadn't thought of.

"So you think somebody is out to ruin the record company by killing you," I said.

"That's right," he said.

"If that's the case, Ace Feldman's death wasn't a matter of being in the right place at the wrong time. It was premeditated."

"Right again. With both of us dead, there's no way Lisa could save the company. I owe Ace Feldman a lot. Without him, I'd be nothing. It's a debt I'm going to repay. I'm going to see to it this idea works, and nobody takes advantage of Lisa in the process. That's my job. Your job is to find the killer before she finds me."

I didn't go over any of my thoughts in the shower. Instead I just said one thing.

"Tell us about the note in your makeup case."

Radio stared at us blankly for a moment before he replied, "What note?"

I told him about searching his makeup case and finding the note, and of its contents.

"I don't know what you're talking about. Get the makeup case and show me."

I brought the case to the table and opened it. Inside was the same assortment of pills, cosmetics, junk jewelry and sloe gin as before, but that was all; there was no note.

"I don't understand. It was here before," I said.

Radio did me the courtesy of not asking why I was snooping in his makeup case. If the situation had been reversed, I wouldn't have been so generous, but people in the public eye soon learn to take it for granted that fans get a thrill out of going through their dirty laundry.

Instead he said, "What did it say?"

I felt kinda silly repeating the "Darling" and "Love" parts, but I did.

There was still no reaction from Radio.

"It doesn't mean a thing to me," he said.

I tried another tack. "How about this—are you having an affair with anyone?"

"What do you mean by an affair? If you mean am I sleeping with anyone, the answer is yes, but it's nothing that you could call an affair. I'm always sleeping with somebody, or several somebodies. That's the nature of the music business, and it suits me fine. You see, I'm the sort of man who'd fuck hog, dog, or frog—if I had the chance. One woman just isn't enough for me.''

"Who are you sleeping with now?"

He shook his head. "It doesn't matter. If I told you, it wouldn't narrow the list down much. Let's talk about this tomorrow. In the past two days I've had about all the excitement I can stand. Now I need some sleep."

The party in the living room was breaking up, and everybody was going to drive into Memphis to follow up on a rumor that Jerry Lee Lewis was going to stop by his favorite nightspot. It sounded like fun, and I could see F.T. wanted to go, so I volunteered to stay behind and guard Radio.

After they had gone, I got myself a cold beer and went into the bedroom where I undressed and hung my gun on the bedpost just like in the old Westerns. The room was quiet. I fluffed up the pillows and settled back to enjoy the latest bestseller, *Valium and Tears*. It was the story of three women who discover their hairdresser doesn't respect them as people, and the trauma resulting from this discovery. It tugged at your heartstrings all the way from the opening paragraph.

I doubt if I had read more than fifty pages before I heard a soft knock at the door. I told the knocker to come in. It was one of the triplets—Flambé, if the name on her shirt was to be believed.

"What brings you out in weather like this?" I asked.

"I thought I'd come down for a beer, but it looks like everybody has gone," she said.

"Everybody but me," I agreed.

"Where'd they go?"

I told her, and she allowed as how, since there was only the two of us left, we should have a drink together. I told her that I was nude under the sheet, so she would have to do the bartending chores. In a flash, I had an Uncle Jake's on the rocks and a fresh Old Blue to wash it down with. Flambé settled back in one of the chairs with an Old Blue and a joint, which I declined to share with her because I was afraid I would get too giddy to fulfill my bodyguarding chores.

"By way of proper introductions, tell me your real name," I said.

She shook her head. "Only if you'll tell me yours, Snake."

She had me there. "Kelly is your real last name, isn't it?"

"Right," she said.

"Tell me, how did the Kelly girls get to be Fluid Drive?"

"There's not much to tell. We're just three peas in a pod who came from a God-fearing family and happened to like to sing together, that's all."

It wasn't all. Her tone of voice told me that, so I pressed the issue.

Again she evaded with, "You wouldn't be interested."

I pressed again, and this time she gave in with a sigh.

"Nothing unusual about it. We grew up about a hundred miles from here, same hometown as Radio. We had a God-fearing daddy who feared God so much that we never got to do anything except go to church. No dates, no movies, no boyfriends, no parties—just church. That's where we got started singing. Ever since we were little we sang in the choir.

"When we were about sixteen, Daddy had a heart attack and had to stop working, which he regarded as a sign from God that his heavenly reward was at hand, and he was getting some advance notice to put his house in order. So he started to get tougher than ever. It was too much to bear, so we took off.

"We went to Memphis and worked at the usual jobs: receptionists, clerks, and so forth. Finally the three of us got jobs in a bar as waitresses, and wouldn't you know it, before long we fell in with bad company and started to sing."

I didn't believe a word of it. It sounded like something out of a movie magazine, or something you would hear when you ask, "What's a nice girl like you doing—" But I continued.

"How did you team up with Radio?"

"We were doing some studio work for Pyrite, and Lisa thought we would fill out his sound, so she put us together not knowing we already knew each other."

That part sounded fine.

"So you've known Radio a long time . . ."

"A good long time. We're younger, but you know how small towns are. Everybody knows everybody else's business."

"What kind of a guy is he?" I asked.

"In bed or out?" she replied.

The bluntness of her reply caught me by surprise. "I was thinking in general terms when I asked the question," I stammered.

She looked at me for a full thirty seconds before she said, "I'll show you."

She stood up and began to shed her clothes. As they dropped to the floor around her, I did not liken them to falling autumn leaves, nor did I liken her unveiling to flowers bursting open in spring.

She had nice breasts, but they did not remind me of pears, apples, cantaloupes, or the front end of a '57 Cadillac. Her nipples were a tad erect, but they weren't like erasers, gumdrops, cherries, or grapes.

When she walked over and stood beside the bed, I was on an eye-to-eye level with her mons veneris. Even that I didn't think of in any personal, endearing terms such as Temple of Venus, Lady Jane, or the Old Cabbage Patch.

No, instead the thought that kept running through my mind was, Why me?

Here I was in the middle of a murder investigation in which the killer was a woman, and a total stranger—albeit a good-looking stranger, but still a stranger—comes uninvited into my bedroom, and in less than fifteen minutes, starts to take her clothes off. It didn't make sense. I was nowhere near charming enough to generate that type of behavior from a woman.

So it was with as much curiosity as desire that I moved over and pulled back the sheet, extending the invitation for her to join me in bed.

I put my arms around her and tried to kiss her, but she twisted her head and pushed me away. Kissing was out.

In a flash her hands were at my crotch, kneading, stroking,

petting, jerking, pinching, and teasing. She had good hands, I'll admit that, but she was way ahead of me. I don't demand roses and candy in bed, but a little hugging, kissing, and general touching is nice.

She was having none of it. For her, it was all business below the beltline, and before long, her noodling had me harder than John Henry's punch.

She thumped it a couple of times like a person checking a watermelon for ripeness. After which I wouldn't exactly describe my state of arousal as turgid—a word I've always felt sounded more like a description of a Nazi U-boat than an erection—but she seemed satisfied enough to push me back on the bed and swing her leg over me with all the style of a fancy Dan cowboy mounting his horse in a forties two-reeler.

It wasn't but a matter of seconds before I was passing through customs at the entrance to her port o'call. As Elvis himself would have sung, that's when my heartaches began.

No sooner was I locked and loaded inside her, when she grabbed me by the throat and pinned me to the bed. With her other hand she reached out and pulled my pistol out of the shoulder holster. Keeping me pinned with one hand, she pointed the gun right between my eyes and said, "All right, mister, let's see you strut your stuff."

I didn't think she would shoot me over such a trivial thing— no sane person would. But it did leave two distinctly unpleasant possibilities. She could be the murderer. I had no reason to eliminate her. In fact she had now moved to the top of the list. If that were the case, she would most certainly kill me. Or she could shoot me by accident. There was a bullet in the chamber. All she had to do was accidentally pull the trigger, and I would be just a memory. In either case, the end result would be the same, so I chose to try to please her.

It took a while. The woman was a hundred and twenty pounds of bone, blood, skin, and hair built around a vaginal vacuum cleaner, and she was determined not to stop as long as there was breath in my body.

Throughout the event my body participated on its own while my mind ranged over a whole spectrum of confusing thoughts and emotions. First, there was shock that it was happening to me. Then relief that I wasn't dead, followed by a period of indifference in which I kept thinking of Masters and Johnson's definition of nymphomaniac: a woman who wants sex more often than a man. And finally—I'd be a liar if I didn't admit it—there was pleasure. But the overwhelming tone of the whole experience was impersonality. At no time was I ever a person; I was just a piece of tail. And her every action, including her own self-pleasure, was directed toward reminding me of that fact.

When it was over and I watched her dress, I can't exactly say I felt cheated or dirty from the experience. Nor can I say I felt empty. No, it was something different, a sensation that words cannot adequately handle, but it is to say that I felt divided, as if my sometimes willing, sometimes unwilling, participation in the act had divided my body and soul into two separate, distinct, disjointed parts. And neither part was willing to look the other in the eye.

She walked over to the edge of the bed and bent down and kissed me. She combed my hair with her fingers, straightening it like I was a little boy.

"Don't be mad," she said as she stood up to go. "You wanted to know what Radio is like. Now you know."

I wasn't mad. Anger is an emotion, and except for the fright, emotion had left the room and gently closed the door behind itself before Flambé and I ever started to couple. Instead, the coldly analytical fed on the impersonal, leaving my body sodden but the gears of my mind meshing and clanking as it picked up speed, fueled by the events of the last two days.

Earlier, Radio had said he felt the killer was trying to ruin the record company through him, but so far—other than the death of Ace, the man who happened to be in the right place at the wrong time—there was nothing to indicate he was right. Not one fact. Not one shred of evidence. I made a note to spend some time with Lisa. Maybe she could shed some light on it.

On the other hand, everywhere Radio's name was mentioned, sex was always mentioned in the same breath. On stage he exuded it. Offstage he continued the image. He admitted to numerous affairs, although he would give no names.

The first woman I asked about him said, In bed or out? An answer that indicated a certain duality of personality: there's what you see, and what you get.

This in itself was not unusual. Even the most well-adjusted people often have startlingly different sexual personalities than what the world sees in their outward lives.

This duality can be as harmless as the familiar example of the meek librarian who wears her hair in a bun and hides her eyes behind horn-rimmed glasses, but who, when given a chance, sheds those bland trappings and becomes a tiger in bed, much to everyone's delight. Or at the other end of the spectrum is the Jekyll and Hyde nightmare of the rapist.

What Flambé seemed to be saying was that Radio was a tease, much like a go-go dancer: all flash on stage, but there it stops. However, what she was also saying was that she had slept with Radio and it hadn't worked.

But what she *wasn't* saying was equally as important. She wasn't saying how she began to sleep with Radio. How long it lasted. Why it stopped. Who broke it off. Or how she felt about the breakup.

If *he* had ended it because of a new affair with someone else—the someone who supposedly sent the note now missing from his makeup case—then she might well have that famous fury of a woman scorned.

However, she wasn't the only woman scorned. There was also Pam, his wife, who was now twice-scorned in a group of only six women. Once by Flambé, and once by one whom Radio refused to name.

Of the two main motives for murder, sex and money, sex was looking better all the time.

Ten

Arcel woke everybody at the crack of dawn to get ready for the breakfast press conference. We had coffee and Danish in the living room while he went about his chores of girding the loins of the master.

This morning Radio outdid himself. He appeared wearing a gambler's rig if I ever saw one. It was a black suit with a long frock coat that reached almost to his knees. The collar was trimmed in velvet. With it he wore a white ruffled shirt, black string tie, a silk brocade vest with enough colors in it to make a rainbow look like rush-hour smog, and a belt with a dinner-plate buckle that proclaimed him to be the Nevada All-Around Champion Cowboy for 1928.

The press conference was a rousing success. Reporters came from far and wide. The contest and the million-dollar give-away were news. Ace's death and the two attempts on Radio's life were news. But the biggest news of all was Radio himself.

Once discovered, some people are natural newsmakers.

They don't have to do anything except just *be*, and the cameras and typewriters fall over backward in adulation. That was Radio.

He didn't bother with the humility pose. He just stood there arrogantly spouting on about being Elvis's link to the living world, and they loved him.

When it was over, the cavalcade for the drive to Dreamland formed. Hundreds of flashbulbs lived out their firefly, micro-second lives to preserve the event for future generations.

F.T. drove the Caddy. Joan and Arcel rode with him. I rode with Radio, Pam, and Lisa in one of the limousines. They took the back seat while I rode in the front with the driver.

As we got underway, I could feel Radio's sense of happiness. I was happy for him too. The caravan moved out slowly so as not to lose anybody. Those were Radio's instructions.

"Keep the fans in sight at all times," he told the driver. "I belong to them now. They've got a right to be able to get close to me."

Sheriff McDuff led the caravan, taking the local roads instead of the interstate. Red lights posed no problem to a group of our size. We made the thirty-minute trip in just under three hours.

Dreamland was just that, a big Southern mansion, pompous and pretentious enough to be a funeral home, set on twenty acres of farmland good enough to die for.

There was a large stone fence at least eight feet high all around the property. Entrance was through a set of iron gates to which musical notes and an iron guitar-wielding rascal had recently been added to make them like the gates at Graceland, Elvis's mansion. I could still see the fresh welds when we drove through the electrically operated gates.

By prior instruction, the deputies at the gate admitted only Radio and the entourage. Even the reporters were turned away.

The driveway was long and semicircular, curving in front of the house. We pulled up, and the driver opened the doors for us. Radio stood in the driveway, looking at the front of the house with its columned porch. Looking very proud, he put his arms around Lisa and Pam and said, "Ladies, we're home."

Pam didn't smile or look happy about the idea. In fact I could have sworn I saw a chill go through her as she crossed her arms across her breasts as if she were cold.

After everybody else arrived, we crossed the driveway and climbed the stairs to the front door. Before I could reach the knob, the door was opened by a black man dressed in a black suit, white shirt, and tie. He was of medium height, quite trim, and couldn't have been less than a hundred years old, but he bowed smoothly from the waist and said, "Welcome to Dreamland, Mr. Johnson. My name is Wilson. I'm your butler."

I said, "Thanks, but you've got the wrong man. My name is Snake Kirlin. Mr. Johnson is that dead ringer for Elvis Presley standing in the driveway."

He looked me over in a glance and did another slight bow.

"Thank you very much, sir."

I could see that he went with the house. His loyalty was to the land, not to the people. It was nothing new. Just something you don't see much of anymore.

We began the tour of the house. It was a huge monster, all done in flocked wallpaper, with loads of cheap Victorian-style furniture. It looked like the decorator had gone through a thrift shop with a blank check.

The basement held a bathroom, laundry room, and a large den with red and black plaid rug and lots of plastic furniture. There was a bar, a large console television, a good set of stereo components, and a huge slot car track so elaborate that it seemed as if you were looking at a miniature world.

The kitchen was also in the basement. It was large enough to feed an army. On one side was a dining table with a dozen chairs. The stove was freestanding and in the center of the room. Around the stove and accompanying sink was a bar and stools. There was a second sink among the cabinets running along one wall. The other wall was filled with three large matching refrigerators in copper. Ernestine, Wilson's equally aged wife, beamed as she showed us around.

The main floor had a formal living room that made you uncomfortable to be in. You'd have to be drunk or in a coffin to spend much time there.

Across the hall from the living room was the study. Its furnishings consisted of a pool table, couches, chairs, a desk, and bookcase-lined walls. I looked the books over. There were whole sets of the great books of the world in imitation morocco bindings. I picked up one and thumbed through it. Nobody had ever opened it.

Next to the living room was a formal dining room every bit as stuffy as the living room. Somehow I didn't see us eating many meals there.

Behind the study was the music room, and it was a honey. In it was a full-size grand piano bound in highly polished copper just like the ones at Pat O'Brien's in New Orleans. It was gaudy but beautiful. There were amplifiers all around the room and a full set of drums. Off to one side was a bar and refrigerator. One corner of the room was filled with a glass-walled closet that housed the control room. Today's music room was no longer for polite Sunday afternoon renditions of "Bicycle Built for Two." This was big business, and the music room at Dreamland had everything you needed to cut an album. I could see that we would be spending some time in this room.

The rest of the first floor was the servants' quarters. The second floor was taken up by bedrooms. None of them was remarkable. They were like hotel rooms. Two beds to a room and very functional furniture, adequate closet space, a television, and a bath for each.

Also upstairs was the master suite. This was where Radio and Pam would reside. It consisted of a living room with couches, tables, and chairs, a huge bedroom done in navy blue, and dark as Hitler's mind. The bed was king-size, and at the foot were three television sets.

There were two bathrooms attached to the suite. One was regular-size, and the other was about the size of a basketball court. Naturally, the big one was for the new Elvis. As I looked at it, it gave me uneasy feelings. It was the first time I had ever been in a bathroom large enough to have a couch and several chairs as well as a sunken tub and all the other items normally associated with a bathroom.

Behind the house was the swimming pool. Surrounding it was a large concrete patio filled with white iron tables with green Cinzano umbrellas. At one end was a bar with a thatched roof. One one side of the pool was a six-car garage, empty at present. On the other was the stable with three well-kept horses in it.

By the time the tour was finished, Wilson had unloaded the luggage, Marty was mixing drinks at the poolside bar, and the cook was starting to bring out food.

As we ate, I could not help but think of Pam's look of horror when we had arrived at the house. It was so completely out of character for her. She was a submissive woman who entrusted her fate to the winds, and her husband, in exchange for a bovine uninvolvement with her surroundings.

Not once had she expressed concern over her husband's danger. No emotion. No hysteria. Not even a question—not one.

She was a classic case. Pretty enough to turn a head or two, and smart enough to let the prettiness take up the slack in all the other departments that make a woman exciting. I could see why Radio had married her. She was perfect for him, her prettiness flattering his vanity and preoccupation with the superficial, while her lack of challenge in all the other areas we rate a person's worth, offered all the challenge he could physically or emotionally handle.

Now, as I watched her work her way through a hamburger and a plate of fries, daintily pulling back her lips to keep her lipstick intact as her little teeth tore away bites of meat and fixings, she looked at ease in her role as lady of the house. But when she had first seen the house, her look had been that of a woman who had just felt someone step on her grave.

Maybe when she had seen the house she had momentarily felt the weight of the age-old values question: "What price glory?" And for that moment temporarily abandoned her ostrich sisterhood with Mafia wives who insist their husbands are merely in the flower business. Realizing instead that rock and roll is a life and death business.

After lunch, Pam continued in her role as the happy hostess, while Radio retired to the house with Lisa to go over more details of the tour set to begin now in only six days.

I wanted to talk to Pam, but I didn't get a chance. For the rest of the afternoon she settled herself in the midst of Joan, Flambé, Purée, and Sauté for serious sunbathing and cigarette smoking.

F.T. and I also spent the afternoon in a time-honored way: sitting at the bar drinking beer.

Every so often Flambé would cast a glance my way and flash a warm smile. It was the sort of smile that said we shared a common secret. I smiled back with the knowledge that, in a world so jaded only the truly bizarre is memorable, hers was a memory that would be with me always.

Memorable because she had shown me the other side of the coin. A side normally seen only by women. A side in which sexual arousal was an itch, and the inadequacy of the partner's performance, the scratch that never came. Made all the more infuriating by the fact that the inadequate partner pulled away totally satisfied. Was it any wonder they call it the battle of the sexes?

Or to put it another way, in a quest for a more perfect harmony between man and his aloneness, philosophers from Plato to Bertrand Russell have searched the world over for the answer to three existential questions: Does a tree falling in the forest, with no one to hear it, make a sound? What is the sound of one hand clapping? Is there a man with a cock so small that he can't satisfy himself?

I could easily see Radio making love in that cold, hostile, demeaning way. Men to whom women are truly drawn are almost always disinterested misogynists. For those of us to whom the go-ahead nod comes all too infrequently, it seems odd, but that's the way it is. With the ease of access comes the contempt of familiarity.

Seeing that nothing more could come of the pool scene, I

left F.T. to his own devices and went inside to begin the rough draft of the story for *Ultra Suave*.

After a couple of hours of note making, I had the festival down nicely, but Radio lacked depth. I needed more, so I hunted up Tom and Marty.

I found Tom in the den watching a documentary on the life of Bud Collier, famous host of "Beat the Clock," a game show in which contestant after contestant revealed their own personal tales of horror when the buzzer sounded, and they went home with nothing more than a set of Samsonite luggage for their efforts.

I told him what I needed, and he agreed to help.

"You and Marty go back a long way with him . . ."

"We're his oldest friends," he said.

"When did you meet, high school?" I asked.

"No, long after that. Whatever gave you the idea we met in high school?"

"I guess I was confusing his life with Elvis's life. They seem like railroad tracks running side by side."

Tom gave me a look that made me feel like I had just crawled out from under an autograph book. "Radio is from Clarenceberg, about a hundred miles from here. Where we met was Cardoza, Mississippi, when we all worked at the same meat packing plant. Marty and I had a band with another guy. We were working roadhouses on the weekends, but the other guy had a girl friend who made him quit. Women are like that. When you're a musician they can't wait to get close to you, then once they do, they'll do anything to bust you up so they can keep you home."

"Is that why you don't have a girl?" I said.

"That's right," he said with a hard edge to his voice. "I'm in the middle of the good times—not past them. I've waited too long for my ship to come in. I'm not going to mess it up now."

"When the other guy dropped out of the band—is that when you teamed up with Radio?" I asked, leading him back to the subject.

"Yeah, you see, Radio didn't have any friends, men or

women. So when we rehearsed, he liked to come over and listen to us. Sometimes he'd sit in and sing with us, but he had no training, so sometimes he didn't sound too good."

"What about you and Marty? You had training?"

"Sure. I was the drummer for the high school band, and Marty's uncle taught him to play the guitar. Nobody taught Radio anything. He had to pick it up on his own. When the other guy quit, Marty and I talked it over and decided to give him a chance. As luck would have it, things worked out."

"Earlier you mentioned the problem with women. How did Pam take all this?"

"Radio didn't know Pam when we started. I told you, Radio didn't know anybody but us when we started. I don't think he had ever had a date before we went on the road."

"As good as he is with women? I find that hard to believe," I said with astonishment in my voice.

"Are you calling me a liar?" said the speed in Tom's system, taking my remark the wrong way.

"No, I'm just shocked. It wasn't what I expected to hear."

Tom leaned back and relaxed. A proud-poppa sound crept into his voice. "Before Marty and I showed him the ropes, he was green as a pup."

"How old was he when all this happened?"

"Twenty-four or -five I guess."

"Twenty-five?" I said with more astonishment in my voice. "I thought maybe eighteen or nineteen, not twenty-five. Where did Pam come in?" I asked in confusion.

"After Joan," he said. "We'd been playing together for a while, and Radio had gotten good enough that the women were starting to come on to him. When he realized what they were after, he started to make up for lost time. He took 'em all to bed. Old ones, young ones, ugly ones, good-looking ones, fat ones, thin ones—he took 'em all. He took 'em one at a time, two at a time, three at a time. He took 'em in the parking lot, in the back seat, in the bathroom, even in their houses with their husbands asleep in the next room. The things that boy could make a woman do would fill a book.

"About this time we started playing a joint where Joan was

Art Bourgeau

working as a waitress. She started up with Radio. He stayed with her a little longer than most because old Joan can do it all, let me tell you. If she ever offers to throw a leg over you, take her up on it because she's a real pleaser.

"Anyway, apparently she'd been talking about Radio to Pam, who incidentally is her half sister, not her whole sister. One night Pam stopped by, and that was all she wrote and smoked. When she got a look at him, she had to have him. Next thing you know, Joan is out of the picture, and Pam is *marrying* Radio."

"Love at first sight, was it?" I said.

"Not exactly," said Tom with scorn in his voice.

"Here Radio was, doing so well with the ladies, and then he drops it all to marry her. What else would you call it?"

"Her, not it," he said.

"What do you mean?" I asked.

"I'd call her a one-trick pony with a one-track mind. That's what I'd call her."

"What does that mean?"

"I think I've said enough," he said.

"Before, you mentioned women trying to break up a band to keep the men home. Did Pam try to do any of that after she started with Radio?"

"Let's just say Marty and I aren't her favorite people, but that's off the record."

"Off the record," I agreed, lying through my teeth. In the journalism business, nothing is ever off the record. If you want it off the record, then don't say it.

"She's always been jealous of us. She's always tried to break us up. When we were poor she tried to get him to stay home, but it didn't work. Now that we're doing well, she still wants to split us up, but it'll never happen."

The picture of Pam as a designing woman who would not hesitate to take away her sister's—pardon me, her half sister's—boyfriend was certainly a whole new slant to her character.

Even more interesting was the fact that Joan had known Radio first. Here was another woman scorned. I knew Joan harbored ill feelings from the conversation we had overheard

110

between her and Arcel at the hotel. Now I knew why she had those feelings, but I didn't know how deeply they ran.

It was time to talk to Radio.

After supper we retired to his suite where we made ourselves comfortable with a fifth of Uncle Jake's Sipping Whiskey and a stash of cold beer. Man talk was in the air. I assumed my best Barbara Walters intensely-interested, painfully-soul-searching, stare-'em-down-till-their-eyes-water look and plunged ahead.

"Tell me about what it was like to grow up in Clarence-berg," I said softly.

Radio positioned himself so that he could comfortably gaze at a corner of the room rather than me, then put it on automatic pilot, letting himself travel back in time.

"It was the fifties. Slow times in a slow town. People still drank malteds and thought hamburger joints were the greatest invention since the wheel. Kids spent hours trying to perfect their pinball game. Forty thousand points would make you a juke-joint hero for a week.

"We watched 'Leave it to Beaver,' 'Father Knows Best,' and 'Ozzie and Harriet.' Everybody wanted a pipe-smoking dad who spent all his free time either in the garage building things for the kids or standing another round at the malt shop. Everybody wanted a mother who always wandered around the house in high heels and spent the livelong day baking apple pies. Everybody wanted Christmas to come twice a year, and the worst thing you ever heard on Christmas Eve was Robert Young telling Bud his bicycle was going to be green instead of red.

"And when you grew up—that is, when you got to be sixteen and got a driver's license—you'd take your girl (who was Annette Funicello) and leave in *your own* car, never to be seen or heard from again until the two of you turned up on 'American Bandstand' in a spotlight dance, where Dick Clark recognized you and asked you to sing your latest hit single. And back home, every kid—I mean *every* kid—you ever knew just happened to be tuned in that day, and the sight of you filled them with envy and brought them to their knees, forcing

111

them to admit they loved, admired, and would give up their football jacket to be you for just one hour.

"It's the kind of dream every kid had in those days. The difference between me and the people of those days is that I still am the dream, they aren't. It's me the man was talking about in that song 'When You're Young at Heart.' I'm the dream maker and the dream taker. The center of light and motion. I'm the focus."

I started to clap. "Very nice," I said. "Where did you get that load of crap, outta some fucking fan rag you picked up in the toilet?"

He threw his head back and howled with laughter. "You're pretty goddamned sharp, I'll have to admit that. You're pretty sharp," he said, wiping his eyes with his hand. He walked over to his makeup case and returned with a magazine that he tossed on the table. "Here's where I got it," he said.

I looked down at the magazine. It was *Ultra Suave*. The article was called "Tube Dreams—A Retrospective" by Snake Kirlin. It was my latest article. What could I say?

After he stopped laughing he said, "Do you really want to know what it was like? It was a two-bit, pain-in-the-ass town, where you had to play football and take agriculture in high school or die. If you didn't, you didn't have any friends, and it goes without saying, you didn't have any girl friends, either. That's because girls learn early in life to go where the action is.

"It was a terrible town, with so many people fucking their first cousins that you expected everyone you met to have six toes on their left foot.

"I was the only child of a woman who owned a dress store. Can you imagine that in a town where you have to play football and take agriculture? Father dead and gone. It was hell."

"When did you leave?" I asked.

"Soon as I could."

"Where did you go?" I asked.

"Everywhere."

"Want to be more specific?" I said.

"No."

"Today I was talking to Tom about when you formed the band. Is there any reason why your original band now has no name?"

"We don't need one now. Things have changed. It's no longer *the band*. Now it's me, and they're the backups, that's all."

"What about Fluid Drive? They still have a name."

"I like it. It fits them," he said.

"He said you met in Mississippi, and you were pretty shy before you started singing."

"That's right," said Radio. "Another thing Elvis and I have in common. Shyness and a tremendous respect for womanhood."

"Just a few minutes ago you said that women learn early to go where the action is. That doesn't sound like respect. That sounds like a misogynist."

"What's a misogynist, a Japanese soup maker?"

"It's somebody who doesn't like women," I said.

"I didn't say I *liked* women. I said I *respected* them. I treat them as equals in a bad situation. That way we get along just fine. I keep on my toes, and they recognize this, so they spare me a lot of the usual crap."

"Most men don't have feelings about women as clearly defined as that. Sometimes they love them; sometimes they hate them; other times they're indifferent. It's largely situational. I suspect women feel the same about men. Why do you regard them as adversaries?"

"Because they like to hog the mirror," he said.

"Would you like to explain that?"

"No, I'd like to move on to another topic. Have you turned up anything new about the killer?"

"Not really," I said. "You see, for me to make any progress, you have to answer my questions, troublesome as they are."

Radio let out an exasperated sigh. "All right, go ahead. Let's get this thing over with."

"Who are you having an affair with?"

"We went through all this yesterday. If I remember right, you were running around with some crazy idea about a note which didn't exist."

"That's right, and you didn't answer the question."

"And I'm not going to answer it today, either."

I tried another tack. "There are six women in the entourage: Pam, Joan, Lisa, Flambé, Sauté, and Purée. One of them is the killer. So far I know that you have slept with Pam, Joan, and Flambé. Apparently you made a lasting impression on each. What I'd like to know is who else you've slept with."

He tried another gear. "Look, I've told you that I don't trust women; I also don't trust men. So the less said about who I'm sleeping with, the better. She's not the killer. Spreading her name around could only make things worse. We're a small group. It would get back to Pam, and there would be hell to pay. She's a possessive woman."

That certainly fit the impression Tom had given earlier.

"What makes you think her name isn't already spread around?"

"What do you mean?" he said.

"The note," I said.

"All right, there was a note. I went to the storage room to meet her. Only she wasn't there, the killer was. When we got back from the concert last night, the note was gone."

"Who could have taken it?"

"Any of them," he said.

"Tell me who you're having an affair with," I said.

Again he didn't answer.

Eleven

The next morning Lisa went into Memphis to take care of business. Pam and Joan organized an all-day shopping trip to Memphis for themselves and Fluid Drive.

Radio spent the morning in his pajamas, reading religious books, while Arcel answered the phone and took care of business for the upcoming tour.

Marty and Tom borrowed one of the limousines, returning about two hours later with three pretty teen-agers whose ages hovered close to statutory rape.

When Radio heard they had arrived, he changed into trunks and joined them at the pool.

"Where did you find these?" I asked Tom, with a sweep of my hand.

"They're just fans we met in town. I thought they'd be a nice treat. Something to pass the time with. It's one of the benefits of being a star. Why don't you wander over and try one of them for size? I'm sure they'd love it."

115

I shook my head. "I'd like to, but I don't think my heart would stand it."

"Aren't you man enough to ride a young filly like that?" he said, pointing to a young girl whose breasts stretched the front of her T-shirt until I couldn't tell if the shirt was advertising a beer joint, a health food store, or a transmission rebuilding service.

I shook my head again. "Christ," I said. "I must be getting old, but they don't attract me. I like women of my own age. It doesn't matter if they don't look like teen-agers. I don't either. The idea of physical perfection isn't as necessary as it once was. A woman who has been around excites me, not a teen-ager."

"Suit yourself," he said as he turned away, the victor seeking the spoils. Raping and pillaging never seem to go out of style.

Radio was not of my mind. He was in heaven, organizing a water polo game. The girls coyly mentioned they didn't have suits. Radio dismissed this with a grand wave of his hand, as if, in his presence, clothes were the least essential thing in the world. The more they pretended shyness, the more aggressive he became in his moves, and it wasn't long before he had them pulling up their T-shirts to show him their charms. Next, he had them stand beside each other while the boys judged who had the prettiest breasts. It was a scene straight out of a cattle auction, but the teen-agers beamed with pride in their glory, and from there to bare-assed naked in the pool was a short step.

"I think I'm going inside. I need to work on the article," I said.

Nobody paid any attention, but F.T. joined me for the walk to the house. Once inside, he headed for the pool table.

I went to our room, which adjoined the master suite, and started to organize the material into two categories. One category was for information I was happy with. The other was for things that needed clarification. I didn't notice the connecting door was ajar until I heard Pam burst into their bedroom, closely followed by Radio.

She was mad and loud. I would have had to have been deaf to have missed a word of a tirade that would have blistered the paint on an oven door. But hearing is one thing, seeing is another, so I quietly maneuvered myself to where I could see through the crack in the door without being seen.

"You bastard," she hissed. "What the hell do you mean by bringing a bunch of teen-agers up here and setting up some sort of poolside orgy?"

"Baby," stammered Radio. "It wasn't what you think. They're just fans. It's nothing serious."

"Nothing serious? I come home and find my husband in the company of three naked girls, each young enough to be his daughter. If that isn't serious, I'd like to know what is!"

The first punch usually wins the fight, and Pam had scored strongly with a verbal left hook to the chin. Radio was already reeling.

"You just don't understand. These things happen when you're a star. Don't make a mountain out of a molehill."

She put her hands on her hips and cocked her head. There was fire in her eyes. "Star, bullshit. You're some fucking star."

The gloves were off, and the Marquess of Queensberry cowered in a corner, covering his crotch with a volume of his rules. Somewhere high in the heavens, in a gym that doesn't smell of cigar smoke, sweat, fear, armpits, or feet, the ghosts of John L. Sullivan and Gentleman Jim Corbett sadly shook their heads.

But those were ghosts. Everybody knows ghosts have no fight in them. The same could not be said for Radio. He had plenty of fight in him as he spoke to her as if she were an ignorant child.

"Baby, we've talked about the big picture before. I thought you understood there are things you have to put up with. I don't belong to you any more. It's bigger than that, and we agreed that it's what we wanted. I belong to the world. I have an obligation to my fans. I'm the one destined to carry the Elvis glory forward. Don't spoil it now that we're finally there. I'm a star."

Pam shrugged off this undiplomatic statement of position as easily as water off a plastic raincoat, and aimed a verbal karate chop right to the gonads.

"Some star," she snorted. "You aren't even the star of your own house. It'd be nice if you'd put in the occasional guest shot in your own bedroom instead of lying there night after night, fantasizing about what you're going to say on 'The Tonight Show.'

"When we got into this thing, you stopped being a husband. You haven't paid any attention to me since the baby. Every time you look at me, I feel like you blame me. But it wasn't my fault.

"As if it wasn't bad enough when there was only the three of us—you, me, and Elvis Presley's fucking ghost—now we have a house full of ass-kissers hanging around, trying to get rich by turning you into something you're not. I was happy when we were struggling, but not anymore. We did the wrong thing. When you quit struggling, it cut off your balls. Now you're a fat old woman waiting to be waited on hand and foot. You've turned into a sexless, no-dick bastard. And you can't hide it any longer, so you have to turn to kids. That's all you're capable of anymore. They won't know how bad you really are. What a cripple you are between the legs. No fire, no gas, no go, just a scrawny limp dick and a hang look, that's all you are, Mr. Star."

With that, she thrust out her chin like she was daring Radio to do something. He took the dare. As he hit her, the slap rang out like a pistol shot. She reeled from the blow, and he hit her again on the other side. Her hair swirled with each blow as he hit her, first on the one side, and then on the other.

"You bitch, I'll show you who's a no-dick bastard," he said through clenched teeth as he slapped her again and again.

"I'll show you. You want hard cock? I'll give you hard cock! I'll give it to you till you choke on it!"

He reached out and pushed her down on the bed and knelt forward, putting his knee right on her crotch, pinning her in place.

"I'll show you some sex. You want cock? You're going to

118

get cock,'' he said as he grabbed the front of her dress, ripping and tearing it with all his might.

She tried to push him away. "You're hurting me! Stop it! Stop it!"

Here the action took a decided turn. What before had been fast and furious, filled with passion, now became slow and deliberate. Radio's voice kept its hard tone, but a subtle change crept into it. No longer did he sound like an irate husband. Instead, he now sounded like a stern, reprimanding father. Pam's voice also changed. It became lower and more sexy in tone as she begged and pleaded for him to stop.

He wasn't having any. He slapped her again and again as she lay there. She ceased to resist, except to whimper and plead verbally. He grabbed the top of her bra and ripped it open.

As he pinched and twisted her nipples, she thrashed her head back and forth, saying, "You're not going to make me let Snake and F.T. do this to me, are you? You're not going to make me let them take my clothes off and touch me where they want, are you? You're not going to make me do *things* to them, are you?"

I must admit, my heart picked up a beat at the sound of my name used in such a physical context. Apparently it had the same effect on Radio, who intensified matters by turning his cruel attentions to her panties, jerking them high into the tenderness of her womanhood, and twisting them, and sawing back and forth like he was cutting firewood. The panties finally gave way under the torture and ripped to shreds. He didn't bother to pull them off. Instead he pushed them up, holding her down by the throat while he pushed down his trunks until his butt and genitals were exposed. He was erect as he climbed on, ramming into her like a battering ram. As his pelvis slammed into her pelvis, she arched her back, and started to thrash her head back and forth, the blood from her nosebleed spraying her face and his. He rammed, plunged, snorted, and heaved like a stallion, holding her hands to keep her in place. Her body fought back, moving with him, arching, bucking, and challenging.

"Don't make me do this! Don't make me lie here while you shoot all that white stuff in me! Don't, please . . . Don't . . ."

That did it. Radio went over the edge with a snarl and a growl that reached all the way back to a time before the invention of the adjective. A time when men spoke only in nouns and verbs of one syllable. Back to a time when finger painting on stone walls was considered an art form instead of graffiti. Back to the days before the mastodon and the saber-toothed tiger were endangered species. Back to the dawn of man. Back to the days before television.

When he was done he collapsed on top of her, lying there sounding for all the world like a set of leaky bagpipes as he gasped and wheezed. She put her arms around him and rocked him like a baby.

That just goes to show how you can misinterpret what you see. What I had originally thought to be a normal quarrel between a married couple was in reality a statement of need and very subtle, sophisticated foreplay between two people who understood the signals perfectly.

Shakily Radio got to his feet and pulled up his trunks.

"I think I'll go back to the pool for a bit," he said.

She nodded but didn't say anything. They might have begun with a fire fueled by her jealousy, but none remained when he left. As he closed the door, she smiled a confident smile and curled up in a catlike position, her face still smeared with blood, and went to sleep.

Now I knew what Tom had meant when he had called her a one-trick pony.

Once she was asleep I quietly eased out of our room and went to find F.T. He was still pushing balls around the pool table. When I finished describing the S&M scene I had just witnessed between Radio and Pam, I asked what he thought.

He laid down his cue and looked at me.

"I think if she ever gave me even the hint of a nod for anything like that, I'd be on her fast enough to make Sea Biscuit look like a one-lung rickshaw driver."

Sometimes F.T. is not very sensitive. Except for me, people mean little to him. He gets along fine with animals. Even though he loves guns, he will not hunt, out of respect for them. He likes cold beer, hot sex, and old movies. His dislikes are few. He dislikes ever being totally sober, and he hates to go to sleep. Both of those come courtesy of Vietnam, where he learned what hell war really is. All those wonderful traits notwithstanding, F.T. is still not sensitive. He does not get sympathy cramps when that time of the month rolls around. He cannot discuss the theory of open education for more than ten minutes without becoming furious. And never have I ever seen him cry over the sight of a wine list.

So when I said, "I think something happened there that was more interesting than the sex," he just picked up his cue and went back to the game.

"What?" he said in only a faintly interested tone.

"The part about the baby," I said.

F.T. didn't see how that had anything to do with it. To be truthful, neither did I, but it didn't fit in the little routine of pet phrases they had gone through.

I left him at the pool table and went off in search of more information. The subject of babies is best discussed with women, so that's where I headed—to find a woman. Lisa was in Memphis, so that was out. I couldn't discuss it with Pam. Joan wouldn't give me the time of day. That only left the triplets, and of the three, Flambé was the only one I had had any contact with.

The girls were boycotting the teen-age orgy at the pool, and I found them in the den. I got Flambé aside and asked her about the baby.

She made a face and said, "Shucks, I thought you were going to ask me for a date tonight."

"Well," I stammered. "I didn't know we were going to do anything special tonight."

"We're going to play 'Elvis at the movies.'"

"I haven't heard anything about that," I said.

"That's because Radio is just now figuring it out. We girls planted the idea in his mind. He's very suggestible, you know. I imagine right now Arcel is phoning around to rent a theater."

"It sounds like fun, but tell me about the baby," I said.

"What baby?" she said.

"Pam's baby," I repeated.

"I don't know what you're talking about. Pam hasn't had a baby, or even been pregnant since I've known her."

That left me scratching my head. I knew there was more to it than that. I wandered out to the pool and sat at the bar, trying to figure it out. Radio saw me and waved me over to where he was talking with the butler.

"Tonight I'll be leaving the limousines for the boys. I'll be traveling in my staff car, the white Caddy, with my bodyguards. I'd like you to clean out those beer cans in the back seat. They've been in there so long that I'm afraid if I cut myself on one, I'll come down with lockjaw, and we'll all be out of work."

The butler didn't look too happy about his assignment. I couldn't blame him. Our back seat was no-man's-land. Radio turned to me. "Snake, show him where the Caddy's parked, will you?"

"Sure," I said.

We walked together. "You don't have to bother," I said. "I'll do it."

He didn't look at me. There was a lot of nastiness when he spoke. "No, sir, I'll do it. Mr. Johnson has made it clear that my job is to do what he says when he says it."

I understood that in his mind, he and the house were a unit. They were here before us, and they would be here after us. All we were to him was the nuisance that paid the bills.

"And you don't like it," I said, verbally finishing my train of thought.

"I'll do my job like I've always done my job, but I want one thing understood—"

"What's that?"

"I'm a Christian man. I go to church every Sunday," he said.

I looked at him in surprise. "What's that got to do with it?"

"You people have just got here and already you have a lot of drinking, naked women, and who knows what else. I just want you to know that I'm not going to be a part of it."

I jumped when I heard Radio's voice. I hadn't heard him come up behind us.

"Don't worry your pretty little head about it, Sunshine. Ain't nobody going to ask you to take off your old butler suit and join in, so you just keep that old nose of yours stuck up in the air where it belongs and out of my business. Otherwise you're going to find yourself looking at your beloved mansion from outside the fence, if you get my meaning. Now get Snake's keys and get over there, and get that car cleaned out. While you're at it, I want it washed and waxed for tonight."

"Yes, sir," he said with all the bruised dignity he could muster.

As he turned to go, Radio stopped him again.

"Long as I'm here, there's one thing you'd better remember: shit flows downhill, and as far as I'm concerned, you're the one living in the valley."

Close to midnight we all gathered in the living room. On the stroke of twelve from the old electric grandfather clock in the hall, Radio made his appearance. He was dressed in a snow-white jogging suit with a gold stripe down the sleeves and legs. Contrasting with the simple gold and white ensemble was his black shoulder holster filled with the pearl-handled .38. The man knew how to dress. He looked like the centerfold for *Guns and Ammo*.

Taking the room in at a glance, he said, "Everybody here." It was a statement, not a question. "Good, let's ride," he said.

As we headed out the door, he took Pam by the arm. "Honey, why don't you ride with Joan in one of the limos? I want to go over some things with Snake and F.T. on the way."

"Fine," she said in her usual placid tone. Apparently the afternoon had cooled her out.

Our Caddy was so clean I thought we had the wrong car. The dirty laundry was gone. The old food wrappers were gone. The beer cans were gone. Even the newspapers, magazines, and books were gone. With so much more free space, the inside looked like a basketball court.

I opened the door and pushed down the front seat to make it

easier for Radio to get in. The ripped seats had not been repaired. They were past that, but the old butler had put a piece of carpet over the tears. We were riding in style.

Radio made himself comfortable, and the caravan got underway. As we pulled out of the driveway, he opened the cooler and passed us each a beer.

"Snake, I'm sorry you had to see that little scene between Pam and me today."

That caught me by surprise. I didn't know he had known I was in the adjoining room.

"Lately, things haven't been going too well between Pam and me. Pam's an insecure person who likes to control things. It's a side of her personality that I don't think she's even aware of.

"Like most women, she was brought up all her life believing that her pussy was the greatest thing in the world, and men were sex-starved animals whose every thought was directed toward one thing—getting into her pants. Well, that ain't exactly the case. After you've done it a few times, and the new starts to wear off, you settle into a routine, like eating and sleeping. I know this ain't romantic, but it's facts. A secure woman understands this. But for an insecure woman like Pam, it's a hell of a blow to discover the one thing in her life that she *knew* was important, ain't as important as she thought it was. Don't get me wrong, it's important, but it's nothing to die for.

"After this Elvis thing started, her insecurities got worse and worse until I finally decided to leave her. I just couldn't stand it anymore. The fun was all gone. She was like a stone around my neck, pulling me down, dragging me back—needing, needing, needing, all the goddamned time. Never a minute's peace."

"How come you're still together?" I asked.

"When I told her I was leaving, the first thing she did was get pregnant. That stopped me. I couldn't leave her like that. Fortunately, she had a miscarriage."

"You're still here. Have you changed your mind?"

"Not a fucking chance," he said. "Only this time I'm the

one who'll be doing the calling of the shots."

It made sense. Not in the way Radio intended, but in the picture I had begun to piece together. For sex to be fulfilling to Radio, it had to hurt the woman. He didn't make love; he made hate. By keeping Pam around, he got double duty. First, there was the excitement of the hidden affair that held everybody's interest until he conveniently let Pam find out about it. Then there was her inevitable rise to the bait, and the surge of excitement he felt as he physically abused her and made her grovel in humiliation.

But one thing made me curious, so I asked, "You said Pam likes to control things. What did you mean by that?"

"You saw it this afternoon. When you play the hard game, the one who controls things is the one who gets hurt. Not the one who does the hurting. They set it up and lead you on, like they were playing a violin.

"Last night you asked me about Joan. She knew more than any woman I had ever met, always ready for a party or a good time. And I was happy with her—until I met Pam.

"Pam knew everything there was to know about how to make sex dirty. The first night, when I left her, my nerves were flayed to the bone from all the things she made me do. Things, even in my dirtiest thoughts, I had never imagined. It was a whole other world she showed me. I never knew women liked to do things that dirty and exciting."

I had been right in my thoughts about what Tom had meant by a "one-trick pony."

"So why did you decide to leave her, if she was so exciting?" I said.

"Even other worlds get boring after a while," he said as he turned to look out into the night.

The sidewalk in front of the theater was pure bedlam. It looked like a world premiere. Even though it was midnight in a small town, there were about two hundred people milling around. Some carried signs that read WE LOVE YOU BOTH, ELVIS AND RADIO. The colors were pink and black, Elvis's favorite combination during his early days. The crowd was mostly women. When they saw the caravan they began to scream and yell. If I hadn't seen the signs proclaiming undying love, I would have assumed them to be a lynch mob.

The sight of the crowd perked Radio up. "Circle the block and give the others time to get there before we stop. It'll make the fans worry when they don't see me."

He was right. The crowd was crazy by the time F.T. pulled up in front and said, "Get him in the movie theater while I go park the car. We don't want this thing turned into souveniers while we're gone."

I got out and pulled the seat forward so Radio could get out. When the crowd saw him, the noise got louder. It was like a big strong jolt of electricity for him.

He was gracious, kissing the ladies and giving autographs to whoever thrust whatever under his nose. I kept a weather eye out for trouble, but there was none. We made it inside the theater easily.

Our crew, with the exception of F.T., was already inside waiting for us. The concession stand was open, and everybody was arming themselves with popcorn, sodas, and enough sugar-saturated junk to rot the teeth out of a shark.

Keeping in mind what Radio had just said about control, I looked Pam over carefully. Her cheeks were a little puffy from the slapping, but there was not a mark on her. Except for the bloody nose, much of it had been more illusion than reality.

Women like Pam create confusion, and the continuation of many misconceptions about wife beating. Having had no experience in the world of S&M, other than the occasional midnight fantasy, the sight of two people with such highly developed sexual pain instincts was disconcerting. While the idea of "Daddy's naughty little girl" or the "French maid" scam are exciting, the idea of actually hitting a woman in anger is repulsive. But that was apparently not the way Pam felt about it. I suppose, at the heart of it, are basic questions of identity and perception of the world, as well as values trade-offs (a more sophisticated version of the old "would you for a cookie" routine). But intellectually discussing the identity question and values trade-off of the battered wife is one thing;

emotionally understanding it is another. And emotionally, I didn't have the ghost of a clue about it.

F.T. arrived with the cooler.

"That's a hell of a crowd out there. Did you check the theater out yet?"

"Not yet," I said.

"We'd better do it, just to be on the safe side."

We had Arcel and the manager keep everybody out and turn up the house lights. We went over the place from the projection booth to the stage. All we found were empty popcorn boxes, candy wrappers, and a used condom.

It was what I expected. We had the killer with us, and I was beginning to get strong feelings about her identity.

Satisfied there was nothing lurking in the theater, waiting for its chance to strike, we took Radio to his seat. Being nearsighted but too vain to wear glasses, he needed a seat near the front. Once he was seated alone in the middle of the row, Arcel scurried up with popcorn and soda. Radio placed these on the seat to his left and proceeded to light up a small, sweet-smelling cigar with a wooden tip.

Arcel moved into the row behind Radio and took a seat nearby, to be on hand if anything else was needed.

During the opening of *The Pink Panther*, I went for popcorn. While I waited, I looked outside. The fans were still there. Somehow it struck me funny that there was all that love outside, from people outside who wanted inside, and inside were only people sitting alone in the dark—a selfish, shit-assed lot if I'd ever seen one. Which is to say that they were filled with the sawdust that inflates politicians and beggars alike.

Marty came out and joined me.

"What are you looking at?" he said.

"The people outside," I said.

"Why's that?"

"I don't know," I said. "I guess I was just looking out there and thinking how confusing all this must have been for the real Elvis. Just imagine what it's like to have been the first superstar. Oh, there was Caruso, Jolson, and Sinatra before him, but none of them came close to Elvis. The world had never seen anything like it. He was the most photographed man in history.

"Just imagine what it was like to be a shy boy from Memphis who had to spend twenty years in a goldfish bowl, living the life of a recluse, doing what we're doing, going to the movies at midnight. Say what you will about the way he lived and died, but he did a hell of a lot better with it than I could have. He was the man for the job."

"True enough, but now there's another man for the job," said Marty.

"Yeah, I guess," I said absently.

"It was the smartest thing Tom and I ever did when we took him on. Look at us now. We got a three-way split of a million dollars, right down the line, a third each."

"When I was talking with Tom, he mentioned some problems with Pam. Something about her being a little jealous," I said.

"A little! Pam hasn't liked us from the start, but Radio has kept her in line. She's his problem."

"From where I stand, it looks like one woman isn't enough for Radio. He's getting a little on the side, isn't he? Tell me, who is it?" I asked.

"I don't know," said Marty as he turned to look back at the crowd outside.

But from his tone of voice, I could tell he was lying.

Twelve

It was shortly after noon when I woke. My dreams had been muddled affairs of finding Radio and Ace in the trailer. As I bent over to examine their wounds, an insane Inspector Clouseau kept leaning over me, looking at the back of my neck with a magnifying glass. When I'd ask what the hell he was doing, he would giggle and say, "I'm looking for clues."

It must have been the chili dogs with raw onions on top of the popcorn and the beer that did it.

F.T. was still sleeping. I dressed in a pair of shorts, T-shirt, and shoulder holster. I picked up an old Len Deighton spy novel from the bedside table and headed downstairs. The house was quiet. Everybody else was still asleep too.

Ernestine, the cook, was not around, so I put on the coffee and poured myself a large glass of cranberry juice to sip while I made breakfast. As the bacon cooked, I chopped up a small tomato, onion, and a handful of mushrooms. When the bacon was done, I put it on a paper towel to drain, and cooked the

tomato, onion, and mushrooms in the hot bacon grease.
When they were done, I spooned them out of the grease and
poured in the beaten eggs. As the omelet began to take shape,
I put in the toast.

About halfway through breakfast, Lisa wandered in.

"Mind if I have a cup of coffee with you?" she said.

"No, go ahead. There's plenty in the pot."

I watched as she poured, then added a lot of milk and sugar.
It looked like she didn't care much for coffee. She sat down
and fumbled in her purse for her cigarettes.

"Want some breakfast?" I said.

"No, thanks," she said as she lit her cigarette. "A cup of
coffee and a smoke will do fine."

"Don't you think you're a little young to be starting the day
off with a cup of coffee and a smoke? I mean, you've still got
things growing," I said with a leer.

She ignored my leer and addressed me with the proper tone
of a schoolmarm.

"I had breakfast when I got up. That was about four hours
ago."

"I stand corrected," I said.

"Which brings up the next question," she said. "What are
you doing staggering down here for breakfast at almost one
o'clock while the rest of the house is still asleep?"

"We had a hard night," I said.

"What happened?" she said.

"Not much. Arcel rented a movie theater and we watched
Patton and *The Pink Panther* from midnight until dawn."

"Just like Elvis. How cute."

"You might think so," I said.

Her smile changed to a look of concern. "Didn't you have a
good time?"

I shook my head. "Not really. Even Peter Sellers starts to
wear thin after a while."

"Poor baby," she said in her best tough-girl voice. She took
a drag on her cigarette and blew the smoke out in that attractive way women have of taking a routine movement and giving
it a bit of grace.

"Where have you been the last couple of days?" I said, changing the subject.

"My father's funeral. Have you forgotten?"

"No, not really. But for some reason that day seems long ago," I said.

"Maybe for you," she said. We sat in silence for a couple of minutes before she continued. "I know that you and F.T. aren't real detectives. You're magazine reporters. But have you come up with anything that might help catch her?"

"Not a thing."

"Do you think we'll *ever* find her?"

"Not unless she tries again," I said.

"Try again?" she said as if the idea had not occurred to her.

"Yes, she's here in the house with us now, just waiting for the right moment. This time she's going to finish the job. No mistakes. And there's probably nothing we can do about it unless we can figure out who she is."

"You're sure she's one of us?"

I went back over the details of the shooting in the trailer, and the attack in the storage room, but I omitted the details of the note and the mistress situation, choosing instead to concentrate on Radio's theory.

"Radio seems to think she doesn't hate him, she hates the record company, and by killing him and your father, it would ruin the company. Do you know any reason why someone in this house would hate Pyrite Records that much?"

She replied immediately. "No, that's crazy. Why would anyone want to ruin the company? It's the company that's making everyone here rich." Then she hesitated for a moment before continuing. "Also, it's not exactly true about their deaths ruining the company. My father's death hurt the company. No doubt about that. There was no insurance. We have debts at the bank. They're uneasy now that he's gone, but our accountant thinks we're in good enough shape to make it. I know I can count on her to take care of the bank and Radio to take care of the singing, so I'm not too worried.

"If Radio was killed, we'd *make* money. He's insured for a million and a half. The company gets a million, and Pam gets a half, so we'd be ahead of the game."

When we finished breakfast, I wandered out to the pool. The water was blue and inviting. I stripped off my shoulder holster, T-shirt, and glasses, and dived in, breaking the water cleanly with my famous, modified belly-buster. The hot August sun had warmed the water to just the right temperature. I swam a few lazy laps and got out.

I was still contemplating my conversation with Lisa when Arcel joined me.

"Radio's up, and he wants to see you," he said, pointing to the house with his thumb in a hitchhiking motion.

Radio and Pam were in their suite, having coffee and juice. Pam was dressed and cheerful. Radio was another story. He was still in his dark blue bathrobe and looked like a warmed-over bad dream. He was pale with dark circles under his eyes. His hand shook slightly as he sipped his coffee, and his eyes were lackluster. Judging by Pam's cheerfulness and Radio's drained appearance, they had enjoyed a further resolution of yesterday's difficulties by more intense activity in the marriage bed.

"Want to see me?" I said.

"Yeah. Sit down and pour yourself some coffee," he said. Even his voice sounded weak.

While I went through the usual business with the cream and sugar, and the stirring, and the tasting, Pam kissed him good-bye and headed downstairs. After she had gone, Radio took out a bottle of pills and washed down a couple with his orange juice.

"Pam and the girls were talking at the movie last night," he said. "They remembered that Elvis used to divide his entourage into two teams. Each team had its own uniform. And what they would do was compete against each other in their activities. Sometimes it was slot car racing. Sometimes it was bumper cars at the carnival. Sometimes it was roller skating. You know, stuff like that. Anyway, the girls thought it would be a good idea if we did the same thing. Only this time it would be the girls against the boys. How does that strike you?"

"Depends on the game, I guess."

"They've decided that. We're going to have a duel with Roman candles," he said.

It was the stupidest thing anyone had ever dreamed up since Hitler invaded Russia. I jumped on the nearest soapbox, and put wings on my tongue and sunglasses on my eyeteeth as I spewed forth pearl after pearl in a vain attempt to talk him out of such foolishness. It was no go. His pride was at stake, and God knows, having pride is like having an erection; it only takes a moment for either to get you into a lifetime's trouble. So talk as I would, nothing I said made an impression. After all, it was old Elvis's favorite game.

He told me to get the crew together to go shopping, and the meeting was over.

F.T. and I assembled the crew as directed. When Radio came downstairs he looked better, but not much. The paleness and dark circles were still there, but his eyes had some life in them. A nervous life derived from the recuperative powers of a glass of orange juice and a couple of mother's little helpers.

I was hoping he would ride with us, so we could further discuss his stupidity, but he was having none of it, choosing instead to ride in one of the limos with Pam and Lisa.

We had the top down on the Caddy, so Fluid Drive decided to ride with us. No sane woman can resist a ride in a convertible.

Radio knew where he was going. Choosing the back roads, we gradually worked our way through the black section of town. There was little economic distinction within the neighborhood itself. Neat, sparkling, white clapboard houses with well-kept lawns coexisted peacefully next to run-down shacks overgrown with junk-filled weed patches for lawns. There were no sidewalks anywhere, but that didn't surprise me, because there were no sidewalks in the white neighborhoods either.

Children played in some of the yards, but with little energy. The day was still too hot for that. Old people sat on the front porches of some of the houses, fanning and rocking, the movements of their chairs ticking off the seconds as they sat patiently, watching the world drift by.

133

Our passage brought the occasional nod or wave from the old rockers. One old duffer, sporting a very natty set of bright red suspenders, gave us a big grin full of where his teeth used to be and blessed us by making the sign of the cross with a flyswatter.

Finally we pulled into the parking lot of a small shopping center anchored at one end by Rowena's Country Kitchen and at the other by E-Z Al's Loan Emporium. Rowena's looked and smelled like a soul food restaurant, with the air full of the heavy smell of fatback slow-cooking and bubbling away as it gently softened garden-fresh green beans until they would melt in your mouth.

E-Z Al's also looked its part. With a window full of battered musical instruments, junk jewelry, and multicolored guitars, it looked like what it was—the savings and loan of last resort, a pawnshop.

We parked and got out. The parking lot was so full of Cadillacs, Buick Electras, and Olds 88s that our small fleet was virtually unnoticeable.

After we'd gathered around him, Radio made a sweeping gesture with his hand and proudly said, "Here it is."

I looked around to see if I had missed anything special but couldn't see that I had. There was a long silence while everybody else did the same and apparently came to the same conclusion.

F.T. was the first to speak. "The place ain't much to look at, but I'll bet it's got a lot of soul."

Radio beamed. "Right, and that ain't the half of it. Just wait till you see Levitsky and Son."

Truer words were never spoken. Levitsky and Son may sound like a high-class funeral parlor, but it's not. In reality, it's the finest low-end clothing store I've ever seen. Located in the center of the shopping center, Levitsky and Son had the large plate glass frontage of what had probably been a K-Mart in whiter times. But franchise America's loss was our gain, because Levitsky and Son was nothing short of pure unadulterated joy. In short, it was a Sears gone soul.

We went through the turnstiles and into the store itself. It had that special smell of a Woolworth's, with the smell of popcorn and roasting peanuts and cashews mingling with the smell of new dry goods and the rubber soles of thousands of pairs of Taiwan sneakers as yet unworn.

While the crew looked around, F.T. and I made our way to the food section in search of popcorn. Before we found it, we stopped at the lunch counter.

"Forget the popcorn—this place is the real thing. Look at that menu," said F.T. "They've got chicken feetsies. Christ, I haven't had them since Asia. Let's have some."

"What are chicken feetsies?" I asked.

"Chicken feet, what else?" said F.T.

"How do you eat them? There's not much meat on a claw," I said.

"You don't really eat them. You suck the marrow out of the bone. They're a real delicacy in the Far East."

We sat down at the counter. Before we could order, F.T. nudged me. "Look at that," he said.

"Look at what?"

"They've got Champale on draft. What a place!"

That was it. The idea of eating chicken feet and drinking Champale was too much for me, so I left F.T. to take care of my share and went to look for the others.

As I wandered the aisles, I found clothing wonders. Nationwide, jogging suits were all the rage, but Levitsky and Son had done them one better. They had jogging suits with ruffles, with sequins, with hand-painted sunsets, sunrises, and zodiac signs.

They had T-shirts so art deco they looked like fudge ripple and pistachio orgasms. They had every jogging shoe ever made, from high-top Converse sneakers to Adidas and Nikes in every color of the rainbow. They even had patent leather jogging shoes with Cuban heels.

It was easy to find Radio. I just went to where the crowd had gathered. In addition to our crew, there was a group of well-wishers and autograph seekers. Radio was making like a politician and kissing a woman's baby. After I got him through the crowd, I said, "Cute kid."

He looked at me with disgust. "All babies are cute," he said. "There's no such thing as an ugly baby. Hell, I'll bet when the Cyclops was born, everybody stood around and said, 'What a cute kid. Look at the beautiful eye he's got.' "

He had a point there.

We finally worked our way around to the jump suit section where F.T. was sipping on a Champale while he waited. Radio tried a sip, liked it, and sent Joan and Arcel to bring back a round for everybody.

Thus suitably fortified, we finally began to shop. Before some enterprising Seventh Avenue garment maker discovered it, the jump suit was known as coveralls, and was high fashion only for the jet-setter who was fortunate enough to work in a gas station in the dead of winter. But that was all changed. Now they came in all colors and fabrics.

There was much discussion back and forth before each team decided on the proper one. The men took dark blue in a light-weight cotton, which Radio liked so well he got a couple of extras. The girls chose fire-engine red suits made of a shiny fabric that hugged their curves so closely that it looked like they'd been dipped in nail polish.

Everybody happy, we paid up and headed back to Dream-land, where we spent the rest of the afternoon around the pool doing irreparable damage to our livers. But as a famous man once said, I'd rather be a liver than have one.

Around sundown, Radio sent Arcel for the fireworks. He followed his instructions perfectly and brought back enough firepower for a Chinese New Year.

After supper we all went to change into our new outfits, and then to team meetings. The girls were having their meeting in the den. The men were meeting in Radio's suite.

When we arrived, Radio had just finished one of his infre-quent showers and was still in his robe with a towel draped around his neck. But he wasn't the only one who wasn't dressed. Tom was still wearing jeans.

This took Radio back a bit. "Tom, where's your suit?" he

said in a voice filled with a combination of curiosity and irritation.

Tom was a bit flustered. "When I put it on, I found the whole ass was out of it."

"What do you mean 'the whole ass was out of it'?" said Radio.

"The seam had split all the way up the ass, that's what I mean."

Radio smiled. "Is that all? I thought for a minute you meant the material was gone. If it's a seam, that's easy enough to fix. That's the trouble with this kind of shit. It never holds together. Probably made in Taiwan or some such godforsaken place." Radio went into his bedroom and returned with his suit, which he tossed to Tom. "Here, take this one. I'll wear one of the others."

As Tom changed into it, he grumbled about the size and complained, "The thing smells kinda funny. What is it?"

"Spot remover, I guess. Pam spilled something on it this afternoon and had to clean it off. Guess it's not quite dry yet," he said.

Radio looked at his watch. "Arcel, it's time."

The rest of our team meeting was spent with all of us sitting there, watching while Arcel helped Radio into his jump suit. With that accomplished, we headed downstairs to do battle, like old Robin Hood and his merry men.

There were no lights on near the patio or the pool, but the light from the moon bathed everything in a pale glow, the furniture standing out like debris from a lunar fire sale. The girls were already waiting for us. They were all standing and had positioned themselves in the moonlight, for maximum visual effect, with the studied carelessness of a department store window. The effect was eerie and breathtaking. The moonlight played off the skintight, shiny fabric giving it the look of armor, their bodies no longer kindling bedroom thoughts. Now they were the warrior cat: sleek, hard, and capable. But what was even more eerie was the fact that none of them had any hair. They were bald as a half-dozen cue balls. I did a double take before I realized they were wearing white rubber bathing caps, complete with chin straps.

Radio laughed nervously. "Looks like y'all are ready to go."

The girls said nothing.

"Arcel, divide up the fireworks," said Radio.

As usual, Arcel, the man with a heart so small you could put it in a thimble and still have room for a carburator, did as he was told. When he finished, we each had a half-dozen Roman candles in front of us and a cigar to light the fuses.

The girls still had not said anything, nor had they moved from their positions.

"Arcel, light us up," said Radio.

Arcel advanced to light Radio's cigar first, but Joan's whip-crack voice stopped him. "Arcel, ladies first."

Arcel looked at Radio, who nodded approval. He went down the line with his Bic disposable until all the ladies had cigars with the tips glowing red-hot in the summer night.

That was where the civilities ended. Before Arcel could get our cigars lit, the girls grabbed Roman candles and lit the fuses. It was a rout as the men took cover. Radio scurried around behind overturned furniture giving us each a light, and by the end of the ladies' first salvo, we were frantically puffing away on our cigars as wave after wave of fireballs burst over our heads.

Radio took a count of the troops. Nobody had been hit, but in the general confusion we had lost our Roman candles and were unable to return fire.

F.T. and I were hidden behind a table where, if the girls didn't rush the position, we were safe from harm.

At the end of the first salvo, the girls decided to play the waiting game, knowing they had ammunition and we didn't.

Radio made his way over to us. "Boys, it looks like we're in big trouble. What do you think we ought to do?"

"Why don't we crawl back to the house and watch the late show? If we're quiet, they'll think we're still here and stay out here all night," I said.

Radio didn't think much of the idea. That made us even. I

hadn't thought much of this game from the beginning.

He turned to F.T. "What do you think?"

"We've got to distract them long enough to draw their fire. It'll take a couple of seconds for the candles to get going, and in that time, one of us ought to be able to get out there and get our candles. Then we can make a fight of this thing."

"That sounds good. Can you handle the distraction while Snake runs out and gets them?" said Radio.

"Sure," said F.T.

"Wait a minute. Why don't you send Arcel?" I said.

"He's too slow. They'd mow him down in a second. No, it's got to be somebody with experience in this line of work. That's why I picked you."

That was certainly a case of being damned with faint praise, but I reluctantly agreed to it.

"All right, I'll go around to the other side with Radio. Wait till I draw their fire, and then go for it," said F.T.

They went while I waited nervously. There was enough acid in my stomach to go up like an exploding car battery if one of those fireballs landed on me.

The wait didn't seem like hours. If anything, it was all too short as I lay behind the table. When I heard the first noise, I pulled my feet under me and got ready to go. There was more noise. It was enough to strain the girls' nerves to the breaking point, and they started the second round.

I waited while the first wave of fireballs flew through the night toward F.T.'s position, then the second, then the third. Finally, feeling that this salvo was about finished and I should be able to make it before they could get another going, I made my move.

It was a short move, no more than three or four steps before I tripped on an overturned table and fell facedown toward the concrete, managing to take most of the skin off my knees in the process. As I struggled to my feet, I heard one of the girls say, "There he is! Second line, let him have it!"

The girls were smarter than I had figured. They knew the limitations of a Roman candle, and had staggered their firing line like the Revolutionary War Minutemen. Somewhere in the midst of all those nice breasts beat the heart of a general, cigar and all.

As the fireballs came my way, I scurried on in a crouch, bobbing and weaving as best I could to avoid being hit. Our candles were scattered everywhere, so I had to scoop up a few, then run a couple of steps, scoop up a few more, and so forth. Fortunately, Roman candles aren't the most accurate weapons in the world, so I kept my wits about me and took care of business as my companions from the barricades cheered me on.

But unfortunately, with the last batch of candles I overstayed my welcome, and the girls got the range. As the round with my name on it came toward me, I stood there, frozen like a jacklighted deer. It seemed to take forever as the little sunburst came at me like a freight train in slow motion. In that split second, I braced and waited for the horrible feeling of bursting into flame. The impact was like being hit with a wad of cotton candy. It was nothing. At first I couldn't believe it, but I had plenty more opportunities to find out as ball after ball hit me. Then I understood why Elvis had liked this game. It gave you a sense of invincibility. It was fun.

I straightened up, took the cigar out of my mouth, beat on my chest, and let go with my best imitation of a Tarzan yell. Tossing the candles to my comrades, I lit one and aimed it at the girls. It was like being a kid with a water pistol.

The rest of the team stood up and started to advance on the girls, and the air became thick with fireballs flying from both directions. Everybody was laughing and moving around in general confusion.

Radio was chasing Lisa, who shrieked with delight. Pam was chasing F.T., who also shrieked with delight. Joan was chasing Arcel, who shrieked with fear, and the rest of the group moved around at random—except for me.

I had Flambé firmly in my sights and was bouncing marshmallow fireballs of red, orange, and gold off the shiny red fabric covering her shapely derrière.

She scrambled about, trying to hide behind furniture, but it was no use. Being around Radio had shown me that a bit more passion and daring between men and women was always appreciated. Nobody likes a laid-back lover.

When I caught her, I was going to throw her over my shoulder caveman style and run back to the house with her, where I was going to peel that red jump suit off like a Rudolph Valentino grape.

Then the scream started. It started high and hard on the register, a scream full of the knowledge of awful pain, and from there it climbed and wailed until it was unbearable.

We all stopped and turned toward it, our burning candles forgotten in our hands. Tom was on fire. His jump suit had ignited across the chest and was spreading down his arms as he turned and started to run.

"Stay!" yelled F.T. as he ran after him. I followed, but there was no way we were going to catch a man fueled by pain so great only the dead can swap stories about it.

Tom ran toward the stables, the horses inside whinnying in terror from the smell of the burning meat. His legs were now afire, and still he ran on, arms outstretched like a hideous Ku Klux Klan cross, lighting the night.

He died before he could reach the stable.

The party was over. The candles forgotten. A sight of pain burned into our brains that each would carry the rest of his days.

There was no hysteria or Miss America tears. No, there was just numbness, and the thousand-yard stare known to soldiers and merchants at Christmas everywhere. It was a sensory overload resulting in shock.

No one wanted to be near the place where F.T. and I stood. No one wanted to look at Tom's body. Instead they turned and with stumbling, shuffling gaits headed back to the house to await the sheriff.

Thirteen

 "She killed him," I said as the sheriff knelt by the grisly remains. "Sure as hell, she killed him."

The sheriff stood up and dusted off his hands. In the moonlight he looked as big, hard, and old as the trees around us.

"What makes you think that?" he asked.

I explained the game to him.

"While we were playing, I got hit at least a dozen times and nothing happened. Everybody else got hit, too. Nothing happened to them. So why did it happen to Tom? It was because he was wearing Radio's suit.

"Tom's suit was torn, so Radio loaned him his. While he was putting it on, he complained that it smelled funny. Radio said it must be the spot remover Pam had used after she spilled something on it. Spot remover is flammable. Soon as he got hit, he caught fire. Only he wasn't the one who was supposed to catch fire, Radio was."

"Are you saying his wife is the killer?" asked the sheriff.

142

I hesitated for a moment. It is a tough thing to pronounce a death sentence on someone.

"Yes," I said. "We know she put the spot remover on the suit, and we know Radio was supposed to wear the suit. She's the one."

"Not necessarily. Normally you don't have to look much further than the immediate family in a murder case, but here we have close friends and acquaintances who could have a motive too. The fact that she used spot remover on his suit doesn't make her a murderer. You've got to have more than that to arrest somebody."

"How about this," I said. "Originally he was Joan's boyfriend, and Pam took him away from her by playing little spanking games, letting him do sexual things to her that a normal woman wouldn't. Even so, he still got bored and decided to leave her. She got pregnant to hold him, but it didn't work. She had a miscarriage. He still intends to leave her, and she knows it. There's another woman. She can't stand losing out to another woman, so she decided to kill him."

"That could explain it. It could even be what the whole thing is about, but it doesn't prove it. There is nothing to link her to the shooting. There's nothing to prove she hit him on the head and locked him in the freezer. And no jury in the world would convict a woman for murder because she put spot remover on her husband's clothes. You need more, you need some physical proof that will convince a jury. You need somebody who saw her leaving the trailer after the shooting, or somebody who saw her coming out of the storage room after Radio was locked in the cooler. And you can forget the spot remover, because you'll never convince a jury that it wasn't an accident. No, the only thing we can do is question Pam and see if she lets anything slip, and to tell Radio what your suspicions are—off the record, of course."

I sighed. "I guess you're right," I said.

We headed back to the house, where everyone was gathered in the den. Fortunately, the girls had the presence of mind to remove their bathing caps, so there was at least some semblance of normalcy to the gathering.

The sheriff told Radio that we would like to speak to him alone. We went to the music room and closed the door.

"Now, about this evening—" the sheriff began.

"I know," interrupted Radio. "It was a goddamned silly-ass game, and I should never have let myself get talked into it. Now one of my two best friends is dead because of it."

"Whose idea was the game?" said the sheriff.

"I don't know. It might have been mine, it might have been Pam's. You see, we were talking about things Elvis used to do when he was alive. Dividing the entourage up into two teams and having competitions was one of those things. She thought it sounded like fun, and so did I."

"What kind of competitions did Elvis have?"

"The usual kind: bumper car battles at the carnival, slot car races, basketball games, stuff like that."

"Who picked this game?" asked the sheriff.

"Pam, I guess."

"You guess?"

"I don't remember clearly. We were talking about it, and I agreed to it."

"Snake reports that you loaned Tom the suit he was wearing. Is that right?"

Radio looked at me. "That's right. There was a hole in the butt of his, and he couldn't wear it. You know how cheap clothes are—the seams never stay together."

"He also says that your wife spilled something on the suit this afternoon and that she used spot remover to clean it up. Would you tell us about that?"

"Sure. She was having a drink, and we got to wrestling around, and she spilled it on me, that's all."

"What do you mean, you were wrestling around?"

Radio actually looked embarrassed. "Sheriff, my wife likes to play little games—little dress-up games—if you get my meaning. This afternoon, when we got back, she wanted me to put on my jump suit and pretend I was a garage mechanic, and she was the mayor's wife who happened to stop in with a car problem. And . . . And . . . I was attracted to her, but she was too nice for anything like that, so I had to force my attentions on her. That's when she spilled the drink on me. I'm sure you understand."

We *all* understood.

"Anyway, when we finished, she put some spot remover on it to clean it up. That's all."

"Fine. There's a couple of other points I'd like to clear up," said the sheriff. "I understand you and your wife haven't been on very good terms lately."

Radio looked at me again. "That's right. A few months ago I was going to leave her, but she got pregnant. So I stayed. Then she had a miscarriage."

"Why didn't you leave then?"

"The timing wasn't right. I was in the middle of the Elvis thing, and I didn't have time to make any more big changes then, but it's over and she knows it. As soon as things settle down, we're parting company."

"How does she feel about that?"

"She's not too happy about it."

"Made life hell for you, has she?" said the sheriff.

"No, not at all. Just the opposite. She's done everything I wanted up and down the line. She knew it was her only chance. When a woman's not sure of a man, she'll do anything to make him happy. It's when she *is* sure of him that she'll make his life hell. No, for the past few months, life for me has been one big bucket of Kentucky Fried Pussy—red-hot and finger-licking good."

"What about the other woman?" said the sheriff.

"What other woman?"

"The other woman in the group you're having an affair with."

Radio sighed. "All right, I'll tell you—it's all of them."

"All of them?" said the sheriff, F.T., and I in unison, our minds boggled by the thought of such conspicuous sexual consumption.

"Yes, all of them. What do you think I keep them around for? They're not good for anything else. The triplets barely pass as musicians. Pam can't cook, she's too damn high and mighty to clean, and too fucking dumb to understand anything you tell her. And to top it off, she's got a memory like a concrete block, so you have to keep going over the same territory again and again. As for Joan, she's so goddamned lazy she wouldn't pick up a stick to kill a snake. No, sir, if they didn't have pussies, they wouldn't have a friend in the world."

I'd never seen the character of a bunch of normal women dissected under such a harsh light. Women were a sore point with Radio, and back along the way, there was a reason for it, and along with the reason was the woman who caused it.

I say "woman" instead of "women" because bitterness that deep would not have been caused by a number of trivial misunderstandings with several women. Those adventures do not cut that deeply. They are just part of the give and take of life. Also, in any such series, there will be a heartwarming success or two to tide you over. No, his problem sprang directly from a systematic mind-fucking by one woman who had dearly wanted to trim his balls with a set of pinking shears.

I knew it wasn't Pam. She didn't have the grit for the job. No, it was somebody before Pam.

The sheriff finished up with Radio for the moment, and sent for Pam.

"Sit down, please," he told her. She sat down on the piano stool, but I can't say that in her red jump suit she conjured up any images of Victorian Sunday afternoon chamber music sessions.

He skipped the amenities and got right down to business.

"Are you aware that the probable cause of death was the cleaning fluid you put on Tom's suit this afternoon?"

"I didn't put any cleaning fluid on Tom's suit. I put it on Radio's," she said with confusion in her voice.

There, she had admitted it. The sheriff was certainly a sly old fox.

"You did put cleaning fluid on Radio's suit," he repeated to confirm her statement.

"That's right. He made me spill my drink on it, so I had to clean it up."

"You say he *made* you spill your drink. How did that happen?"

She blushed and looked down at the keyboard. "This afternoon we got to playing around a little, and he made me spill my drink. What's that got to do with Tom?"

"His suit was torn. He was wearing Radio's when he caught fire."

"Oh, no!" she said. She said it as if she were horrified, but it didn't ring true.

There were a couple of possibilities for the false note. One was that she was the murderer, so none of this came as a surprise. The other was that she hated Tom, so it was hard to be sad when he had died instead of Radio.

The sheriff questioned her at length about the type and amount of cleaning fluid she had used. She stuck to her story that she had used only enough to clean the spot, and that wouldn't be enough to catch fire.

As she talked, I remembered Marty talking about how the band's old name had been the Acetones. A name Pam had conjured up while working in a dry cleaners. If anybody in the group had a knowledge of cleaning fluids, it was her.

The sheriff sent F.T. to the master suite to get the cleaning fluid. Pam sat there nervously while he was gone. The sheriff asked no questions, choosing instead to let her ponder things.

F.T. returned empty-handed.

"It wasn't there," he said.

"But it must be—" said Pam.

"Why don't we go have a look?" said the sheriff.

We trooped up the stairs to the master suite. Pam led us into her bathroom, but there was no cleaning fluid. We had discovered what looked to be a serious loose end.

The sheriff called for deputies who began a search of the premises, concentrating on obvious places like garbage cans. It didn't take long to find the empty bottle in the kitchen garbage.

While it wasn't evidence to take to a jury, the empty bottle strengthened the case against Pam. If the killer had been someone else, she would have left the bottle there, but in Pam's case, the bottle had to be moved to avoid guilt by association. Only this time it backfired.

The sheriff held up the bottle. "How do you explain this?"

Pam stammered and yammered like anyone unused to answering questions from a policeman.

"I don't know—" was the jist of it.

The sheriff came back stronger, demanding explanations she didn't have. But in the end she stuck to her guns, and with no new evidence, the sheriff stopped short of accusing her and let her go.

After she had gone I said, "What do you think?"

The sheriff skirted the issue. "I don't get paid to think. I get paid to gather evidence. The thinking part is done by the jury."

"In other words," said F.T., "you don't know."

"That's right. Let's talk to her husband again."

We went back downstairs and summoned Radio to the music room again.

After he was comfortable, the sheriff began. "Based on the two previous attempts on your life and this," he said, handing Radio the empty bottle, "we feel there is a good possibility that this boy's death was another attempt on your life that went astray. Unfortunately, the evidence we have is all circumstantial, so we can't make an arrest, but I do feel that it is my duty to warn you that much of the evidence points to your wife."

"As the killer?" said Radio.

"It's a possibility. You've told us you are going to leave her. She knows about it. And even went so far as to get pregnant to stop you. We know she put cleaning fluid on your suit. We just don't know how much. We also know that she had access to both locations where the previous attempts took place. What we don't have is physical evidence that we can take to court. So all I can do is warn you."

Radio had a faraway look in his eyes. "The insurance policy," he said.

"What insurance policy?" said the sheriff.

"Ace was starting to run low on money, so I put some money into the festival. When we wrapped up the deal, the record company took out a policy on my life for a million and a half. The company gets the million, Pam gets the half."

"Whose idea was that?"

"Pam's," he said.

"Was this after she knew you were leaving her?" I said.

"Yes."

"Then why did you do it if you knew you were leaving?"

"Because I was calling the shots, and it didn't matter. I didn't know anybody was going to try to kill me."

"Now we have a double motive, but there's still no evidence," said the sheriff.

"No evidence? What about the insurance policy?" said Radio with more life in his eyes.

"It's important, but it's still not evidence that will get you a conviction. You know, under our system, you only get one chance in court, so you have to be sure you're right."

"That means you can't arrest her," said Radio.

"That's right."

"What about me? You tell me you suspect my wife is the killer. Then you tell me you can't arrest her—"

"We have no evidence. Now, if you can identify her as the one who shot you—"

"But I can't. I'd be lying if I did. All I can tell you is that it was a woman about Pam's height and build, but she was wearing a mask and bandanna, so I couldn't even tell you what color her hair was."

"Then there's nothing we can do except get a court order barring her from the premises," said the sheriff.

"Forget that," snorted Radio. "Can you imagine what the newspapers would do to me if they found that out?"

"Then our hands are tied," said the sheriff.

"Well, mine aren't," said Radio. Turning to me he said, "We've only got a couple of days to go till the tour starts. Stick close to me till then, and when the tour starts, we'll leave her behind."

"What about till then? Don't you think we ought to move her out of the suite?" I said.

"I don't think she'll try anything in the suite. Everything would point to her," he said. "It'll be all right to leave her there till we go. I'll just smooth things over a little, and she'll never even know she's being left behind till she sees our smoke."

It was a poor solution. In fact it was no solution at all. All the elements of the problem remained the same, but by issuing such vague instructions as "stick close to me," Radio thought he had handled things.

It was late when the sheriff finally decided to call it quits, and it was not a minute too soon for me. My nervous system had taken all the abuse it could stand for one day. My glands had squirted their last and given up the ghost, leaving behind a stumble-footed, slump-shouldered exhaustion almost crippling in its intensity.

I skipped a shower but managed to brush my teeth without mishap. F.T. poured us each a stiff shot of Uncle Jake's Sipping Whiskey. This was not a night for sipping. I knocked mine back in a gulp, followed it up with another, then another, and finally hopped into bed. I was asleep before I got comfortable.

It was the sleep of the little death: a great engulfing blackness so intense that it was impossible to tell whether its origin came from within or without. A time when the body turns into a flaccid, paralyzed, boneless mass while the soul, octopuslike in the darkness, contemplates breaking out of the rib-cage bars of its jail to once again be free with the wind.

Then through the blackness came a faraway tapping.

"Go away," I said, but it wouldn't. It kept coming back again and again until it cracked the eggshell of blackness, and the business of keeping body and soul together through another night was resolved.

I swung my legs to the floor and sat on the side of the bed. The tapping came again. This time I recognized it as a knock at the door. Not bothering to dress, I answered the door nude. Joan was outside. As I stood there, rubbing the sleep out of my eyes, she gave me the once-over.

"See something you like?" I said through a yawn. I was starting to sound like Radio.

"Not exactly, just different," she said.

"Different?"

"Yeah, without the sunglasses and gun you look different, almost human," she said.

"Thanks. What's up?"

"Radio wants us all downstairs in a half hour. We're going over to the funeral home to say goody-bye to Tom. Arcel is over there now, making arrangements to have his body taken home for burial."

"We'll be ready," I said.

As I dressed I thought about Tom's body. Logically he was too badly burned to bury. He should be cremated, but fortunately this wasn't going to be the case. Southerners have a revulsion to cremation. Maybe it's from our strong Protestant upbringing, with its deeply implanted fears of hellfire and eternal damnation; or maybe it's our strong tie to the land, and things green and growing. Who knows? In Tom's case it would take a cold-hearted bastard to consign that broken body to the fire again. His place was in the earth, where its coolness could draw out the heat and hurt until once again it could rejoin those things green and growing.

It was a somber crew that gathered downstairs. As usual, Radio kept us waiting, but it was worth it to see his funeral outfit.

His long black hair was combed straight back and sprayed stiff. He was wearing dark glasses with wide ear pieces so filled with holes that they looked like they were made from the fender of an old Buick.

His outfit was black velvet. The jacket was short and Mexican style with a high Napoleonic collar, velvet covered buttons, and flared cuffs.

His shirt was black silk and secured at the neck with a wide white tie. At the waist of the velvet bell-bottoms he wore a belt at least ten inches wide. Under the short jacket I could see the outline of his shoulder holster. I imagined the pearl handles of his revolver contrasting nicely with the black outfit. The effect was the Cisco Kid gone Mafia.

In his hand he carried a large five-cell flashlight like those carried by policemen and night watchmen. I wondered why he was carrying it.

We loaded into waiting cars and headed out. Radio had Marty in the limo with him. This was as it should be, old friends sharing old memories. Arcel was already at the funeral home. The women took the other limo, leaving F.T. and me alone for the ride.

Funeral homes all look alike. They are always substantial but ordinary buildings with an air of gloom about them that permeates everything: the bricks, the boards, the sidewalks, even the grass in the yard. Inside, the furnishings are sparse: lots of folding chairs and a Coke machine.

The worst part is the smell. It's the smell of cleanliness and dead flowers. There's no smell of anything living: no dust, no food smells, no cigar or cigarette smoke, no dog smell—only dead flowers.

Everybody waited in the parlor while Radio and Marty went in to pay their last respects.

In a few minutes the door opened, and the funeral director asked us to come in.

Radio was standing in front of the coffin. Marty was standing off to one side. Everybody else formed a semicircle around the coffin, and Radio began to speak in a quiet voice.

"We're here today to say good-bye to Tom, our friend. He meant different things to each of us, but to me he was special. More than anybody else, he was an example of willpower and won't power. I'd be tired, depressed, and ready to quit, and he would say to me, 'Radio, we *will* make it. We *won't* quit.'

"Words aren't enough to express my sorrow. The only consolation I have is that he's up there with Elvis now, and when Elvis finds this out, I'm sure Tom will be the drummer in Elvis's heavenly band."

He motioned for the funeral director to come over.

"Open the coffin," he said.

"Are you sure? He was badly burned," soothed the funeral director.

"I'm sure. I want to see him," said Radio.

The funeral director opened the top half of the coffin. Radio turned and looked down at the body. Nobody moved to join him. I didn't blame them. I'd seen the body.

In a soft, haunting voice he started to sing "Danny Boy." As he sang, he reached into the coffin and touched the body, holding one of the clasped hands. When he finished the song, he took the five-cell flashlight and gently placed it in the coffin.

"When Vikings died, their friends always placed their belongings with them, so they would go with safety to the next world. I'm putting this flashlight in here so that you can find your way back to us through the darkness. We'll be waiting, and we won't be forgetting."

He bent over and gently kissed that poor burned forehead, and without another word walked out of the room, tears streaming down his cheeks.

When we got back to the house, Radio took Pam and retired to the suite. The rest of us walked around on eggshells for the afternoon as her screams and protests filtered all the way to the first floor. It was nerve-jangling, but nobody, not even Joan, went up to see if she needed help.

Finally, late in the afternoon, he came down to the study where F.T. and I were playing pool.

"We need a group activity tonight. It'll get everybody back together. What can we do?" He thought for a minute, then snapped his fingers and said, "I've got it. We'll do what Elvis used to do. We'll have slot car races in the den. We'll get Winslow or Watson—or whatever that fucking butler's name is—to pop some popcorn. We'll drink some beer, maybe do a little speed, stay up all night, and have a fine old time. That'll loosen everybody up nicely. I've never done it before, but I'll bet you can race slot cars drunk or sober."

It wasn't the sort of activity I would have thought of, but that was one of the reasons he was the boss.

After supper everybody straggled into the den. Finally, around nine, we had a quorum present, and Radio made his appearance dressed in his white jogging suit, sneakers, and shoulder holster. Behind his glasses I could see his eyes had

that feverish glow that indicated he had been into the phar-
maceuticals again.

Looking the crowd over, he began at once to treat us like an
audience. He passed out beer, squeezed hands, shoulders,
butts, and breasts. He tweaked cheeks and, in general, took
physical liberties with everyone. I wondered how he got away
with it. If I tried it, I'd wind up wearing store-bought teeth
before I'd even warmed up. But when he did it, nobody took
offense no matter how intimately he touched them. Everybody
in the room was under the Radio Johnson spell—even Pam,
who for all her screams, looked none the worse for the afternoon's wear.

Sure enough, his good humor, physical assaults, and
general prodding brought the crowd back to life.

Before long some people were playing cards, others were
watching television, and still others were racing slot cars.

The butler was bringing in popcorn by the bucketful, and
we were eating it, or throwing it, as fast as he could make it.

Radio put out a box of cigars, and before long everybody,
men and women alike, were puffing away. In a few minutes
the air was so thick it reminded me of the day the tire warehouse caught fire. My first impulse was to throw myself on my
knees and try to crawl to a window, but F.T. stopped me.

I decided to try my hand at slot cars. The track was on four
large sheets of plywood on sawhorses. Being similar to a
model train track, it ran over a terrain of hills and valleys
made of papier-mâché. It crossed rivers of blue airplane dope,
and wound through towns of plastic houses, past fields filled
with plastic cows and plastic cow shit, and on toward its
destiny, which was to start over and cover the same ground
again and again. Life in the rut. When I looked at it, I felt I
was looking at one of life's messages, but since it wasn't
painted on any of the little plastic billboards, I said to hell with
it—and chose a Porsche.

On my second or third lap, I forget which, Sauté joined me.

"Want to race?" she said.

"Sure," I said.

She looked the cars over and chose a Corvette. I smiled inside. A Corvette is a good car, but it isn't up to the likes of a Porsche on the old slot car track. She spun its wheels, kicked its tires, or did whatever you do to determine a good slot car, and said she was ready.

I checked the position of my Porsche and said I was ready, too.

Before we could drop the flag she said, "This is a friendly race, right?"

"Right," I echoed.

"Then don't you think we ought to make a friendly little wager before we start?"

"What did you have in mind?" I asked.

"Since it is a friendly wager, how about the loser has to do whatever the winner wants for one hour, immediately following the end of the race?" she purred.

My pulse picked up a beat on that. It was my kind of game. Two people on the same wavelength, both winners.

However, not wanting to show too much early enthusiasm, I merely said, "Like old Harry Truman said, If you can't stand the heat, don't wear a fur coat when you go to work in the laundry."

She looked up from her car. Her face had a questioning look on it, but she didn't say anything. I gave her my warm, fatherly look. It was the least I could do. The poor child was so beautiful, but she was also so ignorant in the ways and sayings of men who have trod the paths of greatness. A problem I intended to rectify when we found ourselves with a free hour.

She reached over to set the timer for the opening bell, but I stopped her.

"With so much at stake we need something better than a bell to kick things off."

"What do you suggest?"

"My cigar," I said.

"What?"

I held up my cigar so she could see it. "Like in the Westerns. I'll put it on the edge of the table, and when the ash drops off, that'll be our signal."

"Fine," she said.

I positioned it on the edge of the table. Fortunately it was a cheap cigar, so we didn't have long to wait.

As the ash finally began to dip earthward from its own weight, Sauté leaned over and whispered, "Nudge it a little."

A bare touch was all that was necessary to send the gray column tumbling downward, but at that moment I was distracted, and Sauté pulled out to a commanding lead.

I hit the power for my own car only to find that it wouldn't run. I repositioned it on the track, and we were off to the races.

She was far in the lead. Too big a lead for me to expect to overtake by sheer engine force. This required subtlety. I had to go at a fast enough speed to cause her to make a mistake. If she went off the track or stalled out, I was the winner.

I took the papier-mâché hills and valleys at not quite breakneck speed, saving my extra burst for the straightaways after the blue airplane dope rivers. I roared through the little plastic towns at full tilt hoping that no little plastic people or dogs got in my way.

By the time we reached the back part of the course, I was close enough that I didn't have to keep looking back and forth to keep us both in view.

I took a second to steal a glance at my opponent. She was leaning out over the track, her nostrils flaring from the excitement. It was a shame. A fine woman like that didn't deserve to lose. But that's life. I inched the controls up another notch as we neared the last turn.

It was a sharper turn than I had expected, and I went into it too fast. I found myself leaning, too, as the laws of gravity, inertia, and centrifugal force took over the destiny of my little Porshe. But the little Porsche was not about to be counted out. You could almost hear its little tires scream as it tenaciously hung into the turn, fighting its way through and onto the final straightaway like a stone from a slingshot.

I put the pedal to the metal and let her roar as we came down the stretch, the little armature motor rising in pitch until it reached a whine. I was closing the distance, and closing it fast. Her Corvette was no match for the Porsche. She was running flat out, but it wasn't good enough as I relentlessly closed the distance.

The finish line was up ahead. I had her if I could just get a little more out of the Porsche. Letting up on the control for a second, I let inertia keep the speed up, and then at the crucial second, slammed it open again. My little car flashed by the finish line, but it was too little too late. She had beaten me, crossing the finish line a scant few inches ahead of me.

I turned to her and extended my hand. "Best two out of three?" I said.

"No, thanks. I like to quit while I'm ahead. Now, come along," she said.

As we marched upstairs, I was smiling on the inside. When we stopped at her door, I was grinning on the inside like a Cheshire cat.

Once inside I reached to kiss her, but she pushed me away, saying, "Oh, no, this is my hour, remember?"

I relented. "What do you want me to do?" I said with my best leer.

"Come in here with me," she said as she led me to the bathroom. This offered a number of dramatic possibilities. A total vista breakthrough. It was kinky. I liked it.

Inside, I cast a quick glance to discover our most likely route. Was it going to be something like a bubble bath by candlelight, or were we going sexual left wing with enema bags and water sports? There was nothing that gave me a clue.

"Now close your eyes and put your hands in the sink," she said.

I did as she said, and in a moment I felt her drop a pair of soft, silky panties on my outstretched hands.

Damn, I thought. *That little minx can certainly undress fast.* Then I felt a second pair, and then a third. I opened my eyes to find that she was holding an armload of bras and panties, and was dropping them into the sink one by one.

"What gives?" I asked.

"Our bet, remember? You lost," she said.

"So?" I said.

"So, you're going to be my maid for the next hour. First

you're going to suds out my undies, then we'll see what else we can find for you."

"But I thought . . ." I sputtered.

She tweaked my cheek and said, "A bet is a bet."

I was right. It was dirty. But I was wrong. I wasn't going to enjoy it.

"Get the soap," I said with resignation in my voice.

"Spoken like a true sport," she said. She fished around and came up with a container of mild detergent and some Woolite.

"You use Woolite for your underwear?" I said.

"It keeps them nice and soft. You wouldn't want me to go around with hard, rough panties, would you?"

The sexy way she said "panties" sent a shiver up my spine. When said properly, the word "panties" is one of the naughtiest words in the English language.

I began my sudsing in earnest. Still in the same seductive voice she said, "Be sure to get the crotches nice and clean."

That broke the mood. Crotch is not a sexy word. It's a dirty word. Not a sexy dirty word, just a dirty word. It's something that smells bad and needs washing. I decided to give her a little return fire.

I held the soapy material in my hands and rubbed it vigorously in the time-honored hand-laundry method. Then I stopped and looked at my efforts.

Frowning, I said, "Christ, don't you ever wipe? These rabbit tracks must have been in here for three months."

No woman I know would be comfortable without straightening up before the maid arrived. And this was even worse. Truly dirty underwear would either be wrapped in newspaper and shoved in the garbage can where prying eyes would never see it, or it would be sudsed out in the middle of the night in a dark bathroom with the door locked and the curtains drawn. Something to laugh at? Most certainly not. It's a matter of pride and form, and something to be applauded.

Sauté was beside me in a flash, looking over my shoulder, but I was back, vigorously sudsing away, so there was nothing to see. She was bouncing on tiptoe, poking me.

"Let me see. Let me see," she said.

Without breaking the rhythm of my washing, I looked over my shoulder and said, "Really want to? It's not pretty."

"Yes," she pleaded.

"All right," I said and slowly fanned out the panties like a poker player opening his hand one card at a time.

When she could finally see that I had been teasing, she gave me a light slap on the shoulder and said, "Bastard," but she said it with warmth and style.

She sat down on the windowsill and looked at her cigar with disgust.

"I can't take any more of this thing. You want to finish it? I'm going to have a cigarette."

"Sure," I said. She came over and put it between my teeth. I took a puff. This was the first time I had ever smoked a cigar with lipstick marks on the business end of it. It wasn't bad.

She returned from the bedroom with a pack of Newports and a bottle of Uncle Jake's Sipping Whiskey. Something she saw stopped her in her tracks, and she threw back her head and started to laugh.

"What's so funny?" I said, still sudsing away.

"You are. You're the funniest sight, standing there hunched over the sink, wearing a shoulder holster, and sudsing out underwear with a cigar clenched in your teeth."

I raised my eye level to check this vision out in the mirror. She'd forgotten one thing—the red face I was sporting from embarrassment.

"What you need is a drink," she said.

"Amen to that," I said.

She took the toothbrushes out of the glass and poured a stiff one. She kept the bottle for herself. This girl was nobody's fool.

I stopped long enough for a sip. The glass was cruddy inside, the way toothbrush glasses get when you don't wash them. I tilted it back, tasting her toothpaste on the rim of the glass. As the warm strong whiskey hit my lips it was like drinking a mint julep with Fluoristan.

She went back to sit on the windowsill. After lighting her cigarette she said, "I don't mean to put a damper on things,

159

but I can't get the sight of Tom burning out of my mind. What a terrible accident.''

I looked up from my wash. "It wasn't an accident. It was murder.''

"Are you sure?"

"Sure as can be," I said.

"Do you have any idea who it is?"

"We know who it is, but we don't have enough evidence to make an arrest.''

"That's scary," She said, hugging herself as if she were cold.

"You're from Radio's hometown. Tell me about him as a kid.''

"I didn't know him as a kid. We're younger than he is. By the time we got old enough to know him, he was already gone.''

"I was talking with him the other night. There's a gap of several years between the time he left home, and when he hooked up with Tom and Marty. Do you have any idea what he was doing during that period?''

She shook her head. "No, I don't. As you've probably noticed, he doesn't talk about himself much. Really, all I know about him dates from when we got together.''

I had the feeling she was being evasive. She knew more than she was saying, but she knew Radio didn't want it said, so she was keeping quiet. I tried another tack.

"He didn't have much good to say about Clarenceberg. Is it as bad as he let on?''

She thought for a minute. "No, it's not that bad. It's dull, that's all. We all had problems with parents. I think that affects the way you remember a place you spent your childhood in.''

"You said 'we'—meaning Radio too?" I said.

She hesitated, then smiled and said, "Like I said, I didn't know him before we teamed up.''

I was beginning to get a feeling that the past held a secret I needed to know. A secret that, except for Radio and Fluid Drive, had remained in Clarenceberg.

"Flambé was telling me that *your* lives were kinda tough. That your father was pretty tough. I guess that's what you mean."

"Yes, that's what I mean," she said, relaxing visibly.

"What about when Radio was working the bust-out joints? Did you know him then?"

She fluttered her eyelids hard enough to hover and laid a lazy hand against her breast, apeing the Blanche DuBois prototype.

"Why, sir, how you abuse me. No woman of breeding would ever set foot in such a place."

"I stand corrected. You know how it is with us hired help. No manners," I said as I held up a lace-trimmed, gossamer, crotchless job by Frederick's of Hollywood.

"Seriously, we were already in the music business, working steady at studio work, while he was still banging his guitar in the men's room at the bus station, but he moved up quick once the Elvis thing got rolling. He saw his chance and took it."

"How do you mean?"

"He took out a little insurance by putting up some money when Ace started to run low, and he even covered that by starting up with little Lisa."

The way she said "little Lisa," she might as well have been saying "I've got shit on my shoe."

I didn't know whether to pursue her dislike or her statement first. I chose the statement.

"You mean he's having an affair with Lisa?" I said.

"Since it's just us girls here doing our undies, I guess I could tell you. After all, you know how girls gossip. They've been having an affair since the thing started. How do you think Radio won that contest?"

"I know the contest was rigged, but it was rigged because he's good. He's packing the gear. He's the one who can do the job."

"True enough, he's good. And he *might* have won the thing on his own, but that's not how I heard it. I heard it took money and little Lisa to bring home the bacon."

"But she's so young—"

"As you men always say, Old enough to bleed, old enough to butcher. Isn't that what you always say?"

"But how? Here I thought she was the young innocent. The way she talked about Ace, and how strict he was, and how her whole life was the control room—"

"Most of that's true. She *is* good in the control room. She's got an ear that hears it better than it really sounds, and she can work a control board until she makes the tape sound like she heard it. That's a gift."

"What about Ace?" I said.

"Ace was a tyrant and a shit who always had a coke spoon stuck up his nose and two fingers inside your panties, just to make sure your motor was running. If you weren't wet when Ace decided to check you out, you didn't work for him. I can honestly say K-Y Jelly kept our jobs.

"But when it came to Lisa, it was hands off. Nobody could come near her. If they did, he would have killed them. That's why Radio kept it so quiet."

"Tell me, what is there about Radio that makes him so attractive?"

"I don't know if I can," she said. "Some men were born to make fools or slaves out of women. Elvis was one. Radio *is* one. When you get near them, they make you afraid and attracted at the same time. They make you ache in places I'd rather not mention. It's magic. You know he's bad, but you'd lie to your husband, risk your marriage, or humiliate yourself in a thousand ways just to spend the night with him. And he's not even that good in bed—men like that never are—but you always feel like it was your fault he wasn't, not his. As to how he does it, I can't tell you, but I'll give you an example. If I had won the bet with him tonight, and we'd come up here, and I'd handed him my laundry, he would have dragged me all the way down the stairs by my hair, and in front of everybody, made me tongue-wash *his* nasty old underwear while he was still wearing it."

"And you'd have done it—"

"I think our hour is about up. We'd better get back downstairs," she said.

162

The party was in full swing when we rejoined them. F.T. was talking to Purée. Lisa and Flambé were watching television. Pam was bartending, and Joan was helping out by making sure her barstool was occupied. Marty and Arcel were racing slot cars while Radio watched.

Their race wasn't much fun to watch. Poor Arcel was even all thumbs at slot car racing. The man was so unphysical.

As Marty's car streaked across the finish line half the course ahead of Arcel's, Radio challenged the winner.

I wandered over to the bar.

"What'll it be, stranger?" said Pam in her best Western voice.

"A shot of redeye, ma'am," I said.

"Redeye, redeye," she said, pretending to look among the bottles. "Don't seem to have it here."

"Since you haven't got any redeye, how about a beer?"

She opened one and slid it across the bar to me. "Glass?" she said.

"No, thanks."

Radio, Marty, and Arcel came to the bar. "Honey, how about fixing us each one of those drinks that Marty likes. Whaddaya call them—haymakers?" said Radio.

"Right," said Marty.

"What's in a haymaker?" I said.

"Not much. Couple of ounces of Irish whiskey and the rest is Guinness stout. Just an Irish boilermaker."

She took their glasses and refilled them. The glasses had a design on them, which made them part of a set, but I couldn't see the design clearly, so I picked up Radio's. It had a picture of Elvis on it.

"Neat glass," I said.

"Yeah, it's part of a set—Dead Rock Stars. We got 'em off television. There's Elvis, Janis Joplin, Jimi Hendrix, Jim Morrison, Buddy Holly, and Otis Redding. I always use the Elvis glass," said Radio.

Somehow that figured.

"Snake, come here. I want you to see my new car," said Radio.

I followed him over to the track where he showed me a sleek miniature Ferrari. "Watch how she runs," he said. And run she did, just like a scalded dog. One lap was enough to show me that my little Porsche was going to be no match for him, so I headed back to the bar.

Marty and Arcel carried the drinks over to the tracks, and I resumed my seat.

"Where'd you learn to bartend?" I asked Pam.

"It was just one of the jobs I had when Radio and I first married."

"Let's see, you worked in a dry cleaners and as a bartender. What else have you done?"

"Oh, I worked in a restaurant, a drugstore, a clothing factory. Lots of places like that."

"What was your favorite?"

"The drugstore."

"Why's that?"

"It was clean, air conditioned, smelled good, and you got your cosmetics at a discount."

"She's lying," said Joan. "The real reason she liked working there was every payday the guys would all come in there to buy their rubbers, and they'd get embarrassed when she'd wait on them."

"Joan, that's not true," said Pam. But from the beet-red color of Pam's face, I could tell that Joan had violated a confidence.

"I remember when no decent boy would go anywhere without one in his wallet. 'Course you could see the outline right through the leather. Snake, did you ever carry one in your wallet?" said Joan.

"Uh, no. I never had much opportunity to use one."

"Can we talk about something else, please?" said Pam.

"Sure. What would you like to talk about?"

"Have you made any progress today? Toward finding the killer, I mean."

"Not much. She's clever, and she hasn't left a whole lot to work with."

"Do you think you're going to catch her?"

"If she stopped now, we wouldn't catch her. Our only chance is if she tries again."

"Think she will?" said Joan.

"I hope not. I'd rather let sleeping dogs lie."

"Quiet, everybody!" yelled Flambé. "They're talking about us on the news."

We all turned toward the set. The newscaster was one of those drip-dry male models who has gotten too good to do the Sears catalogue anymore. Now those guys are journalists, complete with pancake. He did the lead-in and then cut to a remote unit that happened to be stationed in front of Dreamland's gates. The newscaster with the remote unit was wearing his regulation Walter Winchell trench coat, even though it was ninety degrees out.

"Today, tragedy once again struck—"

He got no further, for the television exploded right before our eyes. The sudden explosion caused me to jump about two feet off the barstool. I looked around. I wasn't the only one. F.T. had drawn his gun. I quickly scanned the room.

Standing by the slot car track was Radio. He had a grim look on his face, and his gun was in his hand.

"I always wanted to shoot out one of those bastards, but I never had the excuse before."

Fourteen

It was just after breakfast when Joan found Marty's body.

Having had a temperate night, I was already up and shaving around the edges of my beard when I heard the pounding on our door. I went to answer it with shaving cream still on my neck.

Outside was a very distraught Joan. "It's Marty, and I think he's dead!"

F.T. and I grabbed our guns. Joan led us down the hall to his room.

Sure enough, Marty was stretched out on the bed, and he was cold as clay. While F.T. checked for vital signs, I searched the bathroom and closets. Nothing looked unusual.

F.T. stood up and said, "He's dead, all right. Joan, you'd better go tell Radio while we call the sheriff."

While F.T. did the calling, I looked the room over. It was messy. Clothes—some dirty, some clean—were spread everywhere. Tom's things appeared to be gone from the closet, but with the general untidiness of the room, I couldn't be sure.

F.T. hung up the phone. "The sheriff is on his way," he said.

"How do you think he died?" I said, looking down at the waxy gray look on Marty's face.

"It wasn't violent. No loss of blood. That only leaves three possibilities: heart attack, hemorrhage, or poison."

"Guess we agree on which—poison, right?"

On the bedside table was a glass with about half an inch of liquid in it. The glass looked like a peanut butter jar with a picture of Elvis on it, and the liquid was the color of motor oil.

I swirled it around in the glass and took a whiff. It had the unmistakable odor of Guinness stout.

"I guess a nation of Irishmen can't be wrong, but I'll never understand how they can make a steady diet of this stuff."

"Me neither," said F.T.

I held it up to the light. "Just look at it. You can't even see through it."

Radio came rushing in. He had the wild-eyed, disoriented look of a man who forced himself to go to sleep with a system still in high gear from speed. I've heard it said that you can't go to sleep when you're like that, but it's not true. You can sleep, only it's a light, restless sleep full of weird dreams, and any sudden noise can wake you with a heart-pounding, nerve-shredding effect.

"What's the matter here? Joan said something is wrong with Marty."

"Marty's dead," I said.

Radio walked over to the bed. "What happened?"

"We don't know. Joan found him and came for us."

"How'd he die?"

"We don't know that, either. The doctor will have to tell us. There doesn't seem to be any sign of violence, so it has to be heart attack, hemorrhage, or poison."

Turning his back on the body, Radio said. "With two people murdered in the past week, I'd say poison looks good."

"That was our thought, too."

Joan took Radio by the arm. "Why don't you go back to your room until the sheriff gets here? You need the rest."

Radio looked at her for a moment. "All right. Call me as soon as he gets here."

When the doctor finished examining the body, we joined Radio in his room. The doctor confirmed our suspicions.

"It looks like death from a drug overdose. Somebody spiked his drink with belladonna. The strong odor and taste of whatever he was drinking covered up the distinctive smell, but it's still there if you know what to look for. I'll have the contents analyzed, but it's just a formality. Belladonna is what killed him."

"Wait a minute. I thought belladonna was a medicine you took for a bad stomach," I said.

"That's right, it is. In small quantities it's a powerful muscle relaxant, but it's poison in larger doses."

I noticed Radio staring at the glass. "You say that's the glass he was poisoned with—"

"That's right," said the doctor.

"He wasn't drinking out of that glass. I was. It's one of a set. You were looking at them—the Dead Rock Stars set," said Radio, looking at me. "I *always* use the one with Elvis on it."

Then I remembered. "That's right," I said. "When y'all were racing slot cars just before the news you must have gotten your glasses mixed up, and he must have taken it to his room with him."

"Do you know anybody in the house that has a stomach problem and uses belladonna?" asked the sheriff.

"No," said Radio.

"Did you make this drink?" asked the sheriff.

"No . . . Pam did," said Radio.

A look of sadness crossed the sheriff's face. He rubbed a hand the size of a catcher's mitt across it as if he were trying to erase it, but when he was done, the look stayed.

"I guess that about clinches it. Let's go talk to her," he said.

"Wait a minute. Does that mean you intend to arrest Pam?" said Radio.

"That's right," said the sheriff.

"Then you're going to search the premises—"

"That's right too," said the sheriff.

"Do you have a search warrant?"

"No," said the sheriff.

"Then you're going to have to get one. If you're going to arrest my wife, it has to be done right. I could have lied and identified her the last time we talked, but I didn't because it wouldn't have been right. Elvis believed too much in the American way for us to start taking short cuts, no matter what it costs."

It took less than an hour for the warrant to arrive. The sheriff presented it to Radio, and we began our search. Tom's room revealed no more than it had when I had checked it out earlier, but the master suite was another story.

We watched as the sheriff examined Radio's makeup case. All the makeup was still there. The junk jewelry was still there. Even the sloe gin was still there. But the drugs were gone.

That was the reason Radio had insisted on the warrant—to give him enough time to get rid of his nonprescription stash of uppers and downers. He was taking no chances on getting busted for possession.

Pam wasn't so lucky. The empty belladonna bottle was in her purse. It was the physical evidence we had needed since Tom's death.

The sheriff sent me to bring Pam to the den, but she was not in the house. I found her at the barn, returning from her morning ride.

"Here for your ride? If I'd known, I'd have waited, and we could have ridden together," she said.

"No, I was looking for you," I said.

She dismounted. "How nice. What can I do for you?" she said with just a hint of flirtation in her voice. Her glowing skin and flirtatious tone made me think maybe there was something to the old business about riding being a turn-on for girls.

"Well, actually it's the sheriff who wants to talk to you. He has a few more questions he'd like to ask," I said.

Her face darkened at that. "Whatever he wants will have to wait until I finish taking care of my horse," she said.

"No problem there. Can I help with anything?" I said.

"No, I like to do it."

I watched while she unsaddled him. She had been using a heavy Western saddle, but she handled the weight with ease, throwing it over a sawhorse in the tack room.

She led the horse into a stall and unbridled him. Then she took the combs and brushed him down, making long sensuous strokes along his back and over his rump. Her hands were hypnotic as they stroked and stroked. Each one brought a little chill up my spine, as if she were rubbing me.

When she finally finished and turned to look at me, a knowing look crossed her face, and she smiled. I swallowed hard and took a deep breath. It was a raspy breath. When I tried to speak, it came out like a croak.

"I guess we'd better be going," I croaked.

"Yes, I guess so," she said, her eyes never leaving mine. She took my arm as I turned to go. As she came up against my side, I could smell her. She smelled of sweat, and soap, and starch, and horse. It was a smell that cast a spell, and all I could think of, for the moment, were lusty things I wanted to do with her right there in the barn.

She let me think these things for a moment. Then she tugged my arm and said, "I thought we had to go."

"Uh, right," I said.

F.T. and the sheriff were waiting for us in the den. Radio was not with them. Pam stopped and looked at our faces, going from one to the other. She found little sympathy or compassion there to warm her, but she showed no surprise at that, just a slight wariness in her eyes that she kept under tight rein.

"Sit down, please. There's a few things we need to go over," said the sheriff.

Pam sat down in the middle of the couch, but she did not relax. She sat forward with her elbows on her knees, like *The*

Thinker. Even though she was wearing jeans, she kept her knees together and angled away from us, as if she were wearing a short skirt and did not want us taking liberties with our eyes.

"This may take a little while. Would you like some coffee or something to drink?" he said.

The sheriff's tone was all kid gloves, but his face was cloudy with anger. He had the look of a rigid, punishing father who has just discovered his son playing with dolls. It was an anger that stemmed as much from the supposed violation of sexual roles as from the act itself. It was a change of roles that he—or the world, for that matter—did not understand. Men murder; women are murdered. It has been that way since man first lifted his hand in anger.

But if Pam was aware of this line of thinking, she did not show it.

"No, thanks, I'll just have a cigarette," she said as she picked up a pack of Marlboros lying on the table. F.T. gave her a light. She took a drag or two on the cigarette, and it seemed to relax her. Smoking gave her something to do with her hands, something else to think about, other than what was about to happen.

She settled back, straightening her blouse slightly and touching her dark hair to be sure everything was in place. Like Radio, she was forever the vain sexual animal. When all else fails, show them your crotch before you bare your jugular.

The sheriff began. "We found Marty's body this morning. It appears he was poisoned."

Her eyes opened wide with shock. "Poisoned? It can't be. How . . ." It clearly wasn't what she expected to hear.

"He drank a drink that was meant for your husband. The glasses got mixed up," said the sheriff.

"Oh, no!" she exclaimed. As in Tom's case, her exclamation had a hollow ring to it.

"Before you say any more, I must warn you," said the sheriff, and he went through her rights. By the time he was finished, all the color had drained from her face. Her worst fears were confirmed. The blade had fallen.

"Are you arresting me?" she said in a shaky voice.

The sheriff ignored her question.

"Last night you were bartending at a party here. Is that correct?"

She nodded in the affirmative, eager to do anything to please.

"During that party you made drinks for your husband and Marty. What were they drinking?"

"Haymakers. That's a mixture of Irish whiskey and Guinness stout," she said.

"You made these drinks in glasses from a set with rock and roll stars on them."

"That's right. They're Radio's favorite."

"And your husband usually drank from the glass with Elvis on it—"

"*Always* . . . he *always* drank from that glass." She stressed the word "always" as if she were giving away a long-held family secret. She looked at us again, from one to the other, as if she were waiting to hear that this trivial admission was what we were looking for.

"The drink in that glass was poisoned with belladonna from a bottle which we found in your purse. Can you explain how this bottle happened to be in your purse?"

She couldn't. She tried, but she couldn't. She hemmed and hawed and stammered, but in the end it was all gibberish, and she didn't say anything worth two cents. That struck me as odd. In each previous case she had been careful enough to be sure no evidence could be found near her, and now this fatal slip.

She took a nervous puff on her cigarette.

"Why would you suspect me?" she said, seeking positive reassurance to the contrary, but instead, this was when the sheriff knocked the props out from under her.

"Because you have a very strong motive. We know that your husband is leaving you and that you know this, too. Women do not like that sort of thing to happen. Of the almost one dozen women on death row in Southern prisons, all but two committed crimes directly related to either holding a straying husband or boyfriend, or punishing one who'd already gone."

Pam tried to look confused, but he had hurt her. When he had read her rights to her, the whole thing had been a bad dream. Now it was a nightmare. He was serious about arresting her for murder, but what was even worse was that he was calling her a bad wife to her face. A wife who could not satisfy her husband. He was slashing away to the core of her identity, and she knew he was going to do it again and again, each time in public. She *had* to defend her position. She got up from the couch and began to pace.

"Leaving me? He's not leaving me . . . I don't know who told you that, but it's a lie. He's not leaving me. He loves me. He needs me. Nobody does the things for him that I do. No, no, he loves me. He's not leaving me," she said, her voice rising like a thermometer on a hot day. Looking at me, she said, "You watched us make love the other afternoon. You know he loves me. Tell them. Tell them he loves me!"

She startled me, and I jumped. I was embarrassed at being put on the spot for my little touch of voyeurism, and because of it, I too was angry. The sheriff looked at me, waiting for my answer. I struck back.

"It's true, I did watch you the other day, but I can't say that I saw you make love. Tom described you as a 'one-trick pony with a one-track mind.' What I saw was a prime example of that, not love. Radio told me that you'll do anything to have control. At first I thought he was wrong, but then, when I thought about it, I realized he was right. You found his hot spot, and you used it to keep him in line. I don't think that's what folks commonly call making love."

To allow myself to get angry was a mistake in self-control, I realized, but sometimes mistakes are like dominoes in a line. When you make a mistake and topple the first, all the others follow suit. That's what happened here. My anger brought a rise out of her. Her eyes flashed, and her voice was filled with anger and scorn when she spoke.

"What do you know about love?" she asked me scornfully. "Nothing, that's what. You're just like every other man. Love for you is a woman cooking, and cleaning, and staying home, barefoot and pregnant. You want a maid who fucks, that's all. You don't know the first thing about sophisticated love. About what it's like to be married to a man with needs as strong as Radio's. About what it takes to express those needs to a woman—that's love. And the love it takes for a woman to service those needs. What you saw us *do* wasn't love. Love was me *tolerating* what you saw us do. Don't fool yourself into thinking I liked it. It's a woman's duty to service her husband, and because I love him, I fulfill my duty.''

It was a good speech, but it didn't explain the satisfied look I had seen on her face as she curled up to go to sleep afterward.

"That doesn't change the fact that he's the one who told us he was leaving," said the sheriff.

Pam stubbed out her cigarette and lit another, buying a little time.

"All right," she admitted. "At one time he *was* going to leave me, but all that changed when I got pregnant. He decided to stay."

"Tell us about your pregnancy," said the sheriff.

"Radio was thrilled when he heard about it. He forgot all about leaving, and we were happy again, planning for the baby. We wanted a girl." She looked down at the table, avoiding our eyes as if she were ashamed. "But I lost the baby. I had a miscarriage."

"In other words, you knew he was leaving, so you got pregnant to keep him, but it didn't work," said the sheriff.

"No . . . No . . . you've got it all wrong. We *wanted* a baby. That's why I got pregnant, because I love him," she said, her voice rising again with emotion.

"Had you been trying to have a baby before?"

"No, we had decided to wait until we could afford—" Looking from one to the other, she said, "I know what you're thinking. It's not true. He does love me. We *did* want the baby."

None of us said a word. None of us believed a word she had said. It was that "control" thing again. When all else fails, get pregnant. That way it is two against one. Not all children are conceived that way. Not even a sizable minority. But the number of men and women who involve themselves in the child-bearing process for reasons other than love and mutual desire is certainly high enough to validate our thoughts.

She kept looking from one to the other. Having a highly developed sense of the social currents that flow between men and women, she realized we didn't believe her, so she decided to move to a more easily defensible subject. This did not mean that she was conceding one inch on either the subject of her marriage or her pregnancy. No, in her mind, she was putting them aside, adequately defended; in our minds, they had no defense.

"Besides, why would I want to kill him if he was leaving? With all the money he's got now, I'd get a good settlement," she said, choosing what she thought to be logical, solid ground.

The sheriff played a hole card. "The insurance policy." It was all he said.

"What insurance policy?" she said.

"The half million you get from the record company if he dies."

She denied knowing anything about it. The sheriff turned to me.

"Radio told us about it. You might as well admit it. We know it was your idea."

She stubbed out her cigarette and crossed her arms like a child in a pout. Where she had supposed solid ground, she had found quicksand.

"He's right," said the sheriff as he began to tick off the evidence on his fingers. "First, we know that you made the drink that killed Marty. You've admitted that. It was a drink made for your husband, and Marty got it by mistake. Second, we know you once worked in a drugstore where you could've picked up the knowledge of which drug to use. Third, we found the empty bottle in your purse.

"Fourth, we know you put spot remover on the suit Tom was wearing when he caught fire. This was also your husband's suit. Again, you worked in a dry cleaners, so you would know about cleaning fluids.''

Here I interrupted. "We know that you suggested the Roman candle fight."

"But I didn't," she said. "It was Radio's idea." There was panic in her voice.

The sheriff continued. "You had access to the dressing room and storage room in the basement."

I interrupted again. "You faked the note from Lisa. That's how you got him to the storage room."

"What note?" she said, lighting another cigarette. "You don't mean he's having an affair with Lisa?" Here she made a major concession. Knowing she was getting deeper and deeper into trouble, she returned to the subject of marriage and gave ground.

"I know he sees other women from time to time, but not Lisa."

It didn't work. True enough, Radio had been very good about covering up his affair with Lisa, but covering it up from a stranger like me was one thing. Covering it up from a wife as aware as Pam was another matter entirely.

The sheriff went for the wrap-up.

"You knew he was going to the trailer that afternoon. You followed him, found him alone, and shot him. Then, when you saw Ace, you shot him, too. I'm afraid it's all over. The best thing you can do is to confess."

We waited in silence while Pam finished her cigarette and lit another. In that time I sensed he had gone for the wrap-up too early. He had not built a sufficient imprint in her mind of our airtight case and her impending sentence of death.

He had not made her see the electric chair in her mind, or feel the matron shave her head, or hear the priest give her the last rites, so she wasn't ready to swap a confession in return for a promise of life in prison.

She weighed the odds and knew it was going to cost dearly; it was going to cost everything, but she had no choice. It was that, or her life. She was ready to trade. And we had blown it.

"All right, this is what happened. I didn't kill Ace. Radio

did. You see, Ace wanted me. He always had. Every time I was around him he was always touching me. Touching my breasts. Putting his hand between my legs. I had to let him for Radio's sake, but I kept him off by never being alone with him. Finally, just before the contest, he told Radio that if I didn't sleep with him, he'd have somebody else win the contest. Radio said no. It wasn't worth it even for a million dollars. They quarreled and Radio shot him.''

There it was—the trade-off. Her appearance in court would cause a nick or two to her self-esteem, and she would lose the money. But she would go free, and Radio would be punished for his infidelities. From what Sauté had said, her statement accurately summed up the kind of man Ace was, but it didn't sum up Radio. He'd have given her to Ace with his blessing, and it didn't address the facts of the shooting.

"Who shot Radio, then?" I said.

"Why . . . he shot himself," she said.

It was neat, but it didn't explain the mask in the hallway, the scarf, or the note.

"If he did this, then why did he tell you?" said the sheriff.

"Because he needed somebody to talk to, and I am his wife," she said, drawing back her shoulders proudly.

"Wasn't he afraid you'd tell?"

"Of course not. Everyone knows a wife can't testify against her husband."

The sheriff had regained some ground. While we didn't have a murder confession, he had tricked her into confessing to conspiracy.

"If that's the case," I said, "he intended to kill Tom and Marty all along. Why? They're his oldest friends."

"That's the reason. When they took him into the band, they signed a contract—a lifetime contract—splitting all the money three ways, a third each, and they wouldn't let him out of it," she said.

That was an excellent point. I knew they did have such a contract, but I didn't know anything about Radio wanting to break it.

"Tell us about the cooler," said the sheriff. "How did he

hit himself on the head and lock himself in the cooler? Especially when it has to be locked from the outside.''

This time she didn't have an answer. The game was over. She didn't confess, but the sheriff still arrested her, even though, without a confession, the case was substantially weakened.

While he handcuffed her, we went to tell Radio about it.

He was in the bedroom of the suite. When I told him what had happened, he seemed sad and relieved at the same time. I could understand both emotions.

All he said was, "Go along and make sure she's treated right. I'll have Arcel get her a lawyer.''

As we were leaving, I turned to look at him. He was staring off into space with a blank look on his face. No doubt he was trying to reach Elvis for guidance and commiseration.

Fifteen

Nobody accompanied her to the jail. Nobody stood up on her behalf and protested her innocence. Nobody even came out to say good-bye and wave as we drove away. In short, the Queen to the new King of Rock and Roll, in the twinkling of an eye, had become just one less plate at the dinner table.

At the jail the sheriff continued to play it hard, hoping to get a confession, but it was useless. Pam was now too scared to confess. She used her one phone call to call Radio, but he wouldn't talk to her.

F.T. and I watched while the deputies went through the admission procedure of fingerprinting and photographing and the body search. They did it all according to Hoyle, even to the point of bringing in a woman to do the body search. Nobody violated Pam's rights in any way. But the kid-glove treatment did not change the look of fear and loneliness in her eyes as they took her to her cell.

Neither of us had anything to say as we tried to sort out our thoughts during the ride back to Dreamland.

We parked the car and went in through the front, where we found Lisa supervising the butler as he struggled down the stairs with a load of luggage too heavy for a man of his years to handle.

"Somebody going on a trip?" I said.

She ignored the question and flashed us a chipper smile.

"Snake and F.T., just the men I want to see. Got a minute?" she said.

"Sure," I said.

"Good. Why don't we go down to the den where we can talk?" she said.

As we followed her down the hall, I noticed the door to the music room was open. Inside, two men I had never seen before were unpacking cases.

"Who are they?" I said as we passed.

"The new musicians for the band. I guess you've forgotten; we have Radio's free concert. Then the tour starts. We have to rehearse today."

I know show business is tough. "Break a leg" and "the show must go on" and all that other stuff, but this was ridiculous. Tom had been dead less than forty-eight hours. Marty's body had only been removed a couple of hours ago. And already their replacements were here and tuning up. Dreamland was starting to take on Shakespearean overtones as Radio went through people like I go through shirts.

In the den she motioned for us to take a seat at the bar, while she went behind it and stood in the same spot Pam had stood only last night.

"Drink?" she said.

"Beer for me," I said.

"Me, too," said F.T.

She opened two Old Blues and set them in front of us. Then she opened one for herself and held it up in a toast.

"What are we drinking to?" I asked.

"To success, what else?" she said.

It was a strange toast, and I asked what she meant.

"You did what you set out to do. You caught the woman

who killed my father and tried to kill Radio. That's success."

She was right, it was success, but I had an uneasy feeling that it had an even larger meaning in her mind. A darker, more personal meaning.

We drank, and she never mentioned Pam. She never showed the slightest curiosity about her motives or methods, which was unusual. I assumed Radio had told her what had happened, but there should still be a question or two. Only there wasn't.

Instead she reached into the pocket of her jeans and pulled out a wad of hundred-dollar bills. She peeled off a number of them and pushed them across the bar to me.

"Radio asked me to give you this, along with his thanks for all you've done." In a softer voice, she added, "You saved his life, you know."

Business first, I pocketed the money before I asked, "What does this mean?"

She took a deep breath and said, "It means the job is over, and thanks. Radio and I will never forget you."

We'd been fired.

"When do you want us out?" said F.T.

"There's no hurry," she said. "Arcel is taking care of your packing, and he won't be done for at least a half hour. Why don't you relax and have a few more beers before you go?"

She had tried to keep her voice steady, but triumph kept edging its way into it.

I finished my beer and stood up. "Well, I guess I'll use my half hour to go upstairs and say good-bye to Radio."

She opened another beer and put it on the bar in front of where I had been sitting.

"Radio asked me to say good-bye for him. The day has just been too much for him already—new musicians, getting ready for the tour, and everything."

I looked at her and nodded in graceful defeat. It is difficult to know what to say when the phrase "and everything" neatly sums up three murders and the arrest of a man's wife. Although it's easy to see how they could be shunted to the back burner in the excitement caused by a new drummer and a new guitar player. Now, *that's* news.

I sat back down and reached for my beer, only to find that ours was not the only status that had not remained quo. A whipcrack voice rang out behind me, saying, "Just what the hell to you think you're doing, having all my things packed and put in the hall?"

We all looked toward the door where Joan stood, looking hard-eyed and mean.

I looked back at Lisa. There was a look of shock in her eyes, but it wasn't there long before it was replaced by fire.

"Why, Joan, how nice of you to drop by. Radio and I were just talking about you this morning. He was saying how nice he thought it would be if you took a little trip back to Mississippi. By bus, of course. That's how you usually travel, isn't it?" she said in a voice filled with the sweet sound of acid etching glass.

Joan put her hands on her hips and stuck her chin out.

"Where's Radio? I'll fix your little ass real quick."

"Joan, dear," she purred. "He doesn't want to see you. Not now, not ever. It's too late. The only thing left to do is to scoop up the elephant shit as a memento, because for you, honey, the parade has done gone and passed you by."

For Joan—who, at the best of times, had a disposition only a tad mellower than Attila the Hun—this was too much.

She marched across the room and slapped Lisa with all her might. The blow rang out like the first shot on Fort Sumter. Lisa came back in a flash. She grabbed Joan by the hair and began hitting her, yelling, "You fucking bitch, I'll kill you!"

Joan grabbed Lisa's blouse. Buttons popped as the material tore away, exposing Lisa's bra. Still holding on to Joan's hair, Lisa slapped her again. Joan whirled and twisted, trying to break the grip on her hair. His hands came up like claws with vermilion tips. She raked them down Lisa's chest, tearing at her flimsy bra until it was in shreds.

Lisa gasped in pain and released her hold. They separated, and each assumed a wrestler's crouch, ready to go at it again.

F.T. and I moved in to stop it, but before we could, they

came together again in a snarling mass, like two angry bull-dogs.

Each clawed and tore for advantage, fingernails flashing and teeth bared. Lisa tore away Joan's blouse as if it were tissue paper, and ripped at her breasts with her nails, leaving deep scratches that filled immediately with blood.

F.T. and I moved in again to break them up, and for our trouble I got my glasses knocked off and a set of scratches from fingernails that almost put out my eyes. F.T. received a spike heel on the instep and let go of his girl like a hot potato.

Joan tried to kick Lisa, but she was too slow. Lisa grabbed her foot and down they went.

F.T. started to move in again, but this time I stopped him.

"Let them go. They deserve each other."

He nodded in agreement and went back to the bar. I closed the hall door so we wouldn't be disturbed.

Joan's dress was up around her waist, and Lisa was tearing her panties. Victory was not enough to satisfy either. Nothing short of total humiliation would do.

Joan finally got her fingers in Lisa's hair and snapped her head back so hard that she was able to free herself and go to her knees.

Lisa was also on her knees. Neither was in shape for this kind of action, and they were starting to tire. Both were breathing hard, but the fire in their eyes was still dancing to the devil's tune.

I settled back and waited for the next round. It wasn't long in coming.

Joan launched herself at Lisa, her skirt catching under her knee and tearing away completely as she did.

The force of the onslaught flattened Lisa, and Joan was able to get on top, pinning her to the ground. Joan slapped her over and over until the fire began to go out of her. Then she turned and began to fumble with Lisa's jeans, first unbutton-ing them and then unzipping them. She tried to pull them down, but they were too tight, so finally she had to settle for putting her hand inside.

Lisa bucked and cried and struggled as she felt the strange fingers touching her most intimate area. She growled, but it turned into more of a whimper than a growl as Joan continued to work on her.

It was the old control thing again, the give and take of pain and pleasure. Joan was hurting her more by dominating her and touching her than by punching her.

Lisa was no match for her, so Joan began to relax and enjoy the pain she was inflicting through the pleasure. That was her undoing, for Lisa gave a sharp twist and bucked her off.

The surprise kept Joan from regaining her balance, and she cracked her head on the corner of a glass coffee table. She lay motionless on the rug. Lisa crawled over on all fours. She shook her. Joan didn't move.

She looked up at us with tears streaming down her face.

"I think she's dead," she said.

F.T. shook his head. "Bullshit, that old girl is too mean to die."

"Help me with her," she said.

I looked at F.T. In view of the shellacking we had taken a couple of minutes earlier, neither of us felt any too charitable.

"Sure," said F.T. He got up from his chair and walked over and poured his beer on Joan's head.

"Goddamn you, can't you see she's hurt?" said Lisa with genuine hysteria, mental visions of a murder charge in her voice.

She smoothed the hair away from Joan's cheek and rubbed it. Joan's eyes opened and slowly regained focus. When she finally sat up, all the anger was gone, and in its place was exhaustion.

Lisa tenderly helped her to her feet and said, "Come on, let's go get cleaned up."

Joan pulled away weakly and said, "Go fuck yourself."

Lisa followed her out of the room, all full of apologies and "let's kiss and make up," but Joan wasn't having any.

In a few minutes Arcel joined us. He was clearly a man of two minds, radiating the unctiousness of a funeral director at a five-car pileup. He rubbed his hands together in that time-honored washing gesture made famous by Pontius Pilate himself, and tried to sound calm and somber. But there was larceny in his heart and dollar signs in his eyes as, one by one, his competition for Radio's affection was removed. He'd come from far back in the pack to now assume a front-running position, and he meant to play it to the hilt.

"I'm *so* sorry Radio can't see you to say good-bye," he oozed. "But you have to understand how trying all this has been for him. Ever since this Elvis business began, the man has been positively *stalked* by tragedy. It's simply been awful. I don't know how he has stood it. First there was Pam's miscarriage. Then, while she's in the hospital, his mother dies suddenly. Then there's Ace, Tom, and Marty, and all those attempts on his life. And now Pam. What can I say? The man is a rock, but even rocks wear down."

I patted him on the arm and said, "Yes, well, I'm sure it's been tough on you, too."

"If you only knew," he said.

"We won't add to your problems by sticking around any longer. We know you're busy, and there are some things we need to do, so if you'll see that our bags are loaded—"

"Oh, they already are. Everything has been done," he gushed.

"Thank you very much," I said, extending my hand. He returned my handshake with a hand soft and clammy enough that it should have been wrapped in newspaper.

As we drove through the gates, F.T. said, "Are you thinking what I'm thinking?"

"Yep, mama's raised her old sweet head, and I think she deserves a look. Point this rascal toward Clarenceberg, and let her go. Time's awasting."

Clarenceberg was a town that couldn't make up its mind whether to stay or go, but one thing was sure; without outside help, it would never grow.

The highest point in town was the Burger King sign. The town square had a couple of jewelry stores, a men's shop, a Western Auto, a movie theater, a furniture store, a café, a couple of ladies' ready-to-wear, a bank, and a Kuhn's five-

and-ten. There were more stores, but they were all vacant.

After a couple of tries we found the main drag and slowly drove down it. Near the outskirts of town we pulled into a Shell station that boasted the latest state-of-the-art in gas station design. Even the display of steel-belted radials looked space age. It was the sort of fieldstone-and-glass place a Malibu film producer would give up his escargot quiches to live in, grease racks and all.

The attendant was a tall, lanky fellow of about thirty-five who was dressed in Levi's jeans and a T-shirt that advertised Brown's Mule Chewing Tobacco. I got out as he approached the car.

"Fill her up," I said. As he activated the digital readout on the pump, I continued my witty repartee. "Hot one today, isn't it?"

"That's the Gods-honest truth," he said. "You're not from around here." It was a statement, not a question.

"What was your first clue?"

"Your license plate," he said.

"That makes sense," I said.

"What brings you around here?"

I took out my badge and showed it to him. He gave it the once-over and looked back up at me.

"Ever hear of Radio Johnson?" I said.

"Sure. He's the world's greatest Elvis imitator. Everybody knows that."

"We're his bodyguards. If you follow the news, you know that somebody shot him last week. Since he's from here, I thought I'd come and have a look. Might turn up something that could help. You look about his age. Did you know him when he was growing up around here?"

"Known him all my life. Can't say we were best friends, but I knew him."

"What was he like when he was growing up?"

The attendant looked past me, staring off into the distance like he was dredging up some old memories. "Like I said, I knew him, but we weren't close . . ."

"Was he popular in school?"

"No, can't say that he was."

"But he did have friends—"

"Yeah, sure."

This was getting me nowhere. I tried a different line.

"Did he play any sports in school?"

"No, can't say he did."

"What did he do with his spare time?"

"Just hung around like everybody else."

"Did he always want to be a singer?"

"Beats me."

The automatic nozzle clicked off. The attendant bent down and pumped another fifty cents' worth into the tank before he replaced the gas cap.

I paid him. As he gave me my change I said, "You don't seem to want to talk about him. Anything you could give me might help."

The attendant studied on this for a moment or two before he replied.

"He was a momma's boy, pure and simple. His mother was one of those hard, fat women with a hide tough as the paint job on a bulldozer. You ever read that comic strip in the paper—'Dondi'—the one about the orphan kid the Korean War vets bring home?"

"Yeah," I said, searching back through my memory.

"Well, that old woman in the comic strip, that was his mother to a T. Only she wasn't rich.

"Anyway," he continued, "she kept him tied to her apron strings long as she could. Didn't want him hanging around with the boys, going fishing, playing sports, anything like that. She always wanted him right where she could get her hands on him when she wanted him. This was all right when he was little, but when he got to be a teen-ager, he didn't like it too well. And the sparks started to fly between them. He'd be over at the school watching us practice football or whatever, and she'd come over, yelling and screaming, and drag him home. It'd embarrass him to death. His skin wasn't too clear in those days. He had pimples and long greasy hair. Well, when she'd come over and get on one of her tirades, it'd embarrass him so bad he'd break out worse and worse, till the poor guy's face would be one oozing sore. He'd get so mad at her that he'd just start to cry. Couldn't help himself, he'd get so frustrated. Used to embarrass everybody when he'd do that. But he got her back for it—"

"How's that?" I said.

"She owned M'Lady, the dress shop on the square. One fall she had some big people coming in from Nashville to show some clothes. She arranged this fashion show for all the ladies, and naturally she wanted her 'little boy' standing around acting like a gentleman. Well, it gets closer and closer to show time, and he's not there. Then finally at the last minute he showed up—"

He had me sucked in. "What happened?"

"He had dyed his hair green."

The sheriff's office and county jail was discreetly located on a side street. Architecturally, as jails always do, the place bespoke misery, plain and simple. Even the grass hurt.

We parked at a meter a half block away and walked. At the door we were greeted by a blast of frigid air-conditioned air and the smell of Pine-Sol so thick it could have been mustard gas on Flanders Field.

Off the hallway and to the right was the squad room. Inside was a grizzled old veteran of about fifty and a good-looking woman of about thirty-five. He was the standard issue Tennessee country sheriff, with a face so battered that it looked like somebody had set it on fire and then stomped it out with a golf shoe.

His uniform was as crisp and freshly pressed as a Greyhound bus driver's. Like so many victims of occupations filled with long periods of boredom, he had developed a monstrous belly so large that the next burst of excitement he received threatened to pop the buttons.

The woman, on the other hand, had button problems too. But her problems were located a bit higher than her belly. It gave me a warm feeling to gaze at all that proud flesh fighting to free itself of its khaki confines. As I looked at her I wondered if I should put her in touch with Radio Free Europe. Just the knowledge that such a struggle was ongoing would give hope and succor to millions of people trapped behind the Iron Curtain.

Her tiny waist was encircled with a wide black belt that supported a holster filled to the brim with Smith & Wesson. Her hair was a wild, untamed blond mane whose premeditated carelessness took an extra hour each day to arrange.

When she saw me, she walked over to the counter and leaned on it, resting both elbows and both breasts on its surface. She clasped her hands in front of her, which served to accentuate her cleavage even more, looked up at me with an innocent look, and said, "Can I help you?"

I forced myself to be all business. "We just need a minute or two of the sheriff's time," I said, nodding in the man's direction.

She flashed me a smile that would curdle milk and said, "He's not the sheriff. He's the radio dispatcher. *I'm* the sheriff."

As my old grandmother used to say, you could have knocked me over with a feather, but I made a quick recovery. "Oh, really," I said.

"Yes, really," she said in a tone that indicated she had been through this routine at least a thousand times.

I showed her my badge and introduced myself. At this point she interrupted me to say, "You're new to the game, aren't you?"

That embarrassed me. "How could you tell?"

"I was watching through the window when you parked your car. You parked it at a meter instead of the No Parking zone in front. No self-respecting cop would ever be caught dead doing that. Cops don't obey laws. They enforce laws. Or didn't you know that?"

I grinned sheepishly. "At least I didn't put any money in the meter."

"You're learning, Kirlin," she said. "Now, why don't we go into my office and see what we can do for you?"

Her office was a standard issue full of beat-up furniture and file cabinets, but colorful curtains, some pictures, and a couple of plants softened the image considerably.

She motioned to the guest chairs. We sat down.

"Want a Coke?" she asked.

F.T. and I settled on Dr Pepper. While she was gone, I got up to look at the pictures. One was a man in a sheriff's uniform. I was still looking at it when she came back.

She had her hands full, so she kicked the door closed with her heel. "That's my daddy," she said.

I turned back to look at the picture again. There wasn't much family resemblance. He looked more like the father of the radio dispatcher.

"He's the reason I'm the sheriff," she said.

"Grew up in the business, did you?" I said.

"That's right. After Mama died, Daddy would keep me here at the jail with him. You might say I grew up almost behind bars."

I let that remark pass, and she continued. "When I got grown, I headed off to Nashville to be a policewoman. Then one night I got a call that Daddy had been killed when he tried to arrest three drunks at a roadhouse. So I came back, and here I am."

"Did you ever catch the men that killed him?"

"Oh, yeah," she said.

I let it drop, then quickly outlined the situation concerning Radio.

"I stopped at the Shell station, and the attendant told me about Radio dying his hair green. Is there any truth to it?"

She leaned back in the chair and laughed out loud, covering her mouth with her hand. It was then that I noticed she had a very slight case of buck teeth, and the gesture had probably developed during childhood when she wore braces.

"Lordy, yes, it's true, and it was the funniest thing you ever saw, too. With my mama dead, Miss Louise, Radio's mama, took it as her personal mission to see to it that I received my fair share of mothering, so every time she had a tea or a fashion show for the ladies, I had to go. And I hated it as much as Radio, but there wasn't much either of us could do about it.

"As the years went by, and we got to be teen-agers, Radio resented her more and more, because she was always embarrassing him, until that night when he paid her back by walking into the party with his hair dyed green."

"What happened then?"

"Miss Louise grabbed him by the arm and tried to drag him out, but he broke free and walked around shaking hands and saying hello to everybody just like nothing was wrong. Didn't take long for the place to empty out, and there was nobody left but the three of us. By this time, his mama was ready to explode. She slapped him so hard I thought she'd torn his head off, and she said, 'What do you have to say for yourself after the way you embarrassed me tonight?' and he just looked at her like she'd crawled out from under a rock and said, 'Now you know how it feels. You've *always* embarrassed me,' and with that he walked out and never came back."

"Never?" I said.

"Nope, never, not as far as I know," she said.

"Not even to his mother's funeral—"

"Well, now that you mention it, he was back a couple of times after her death, selling the business, settling up things. That sort of stuff. But the bad blood was still there, because even after she was dead, he wanted to sell everything as quickly as possible, so he could put distance between him and here."

"When did his mother die?"

"Late last winter or early this spring, same thing around here."

"What was the cause of death?" I asked.

"An accident, pure and simple. She was a high-strung woman with a lot of health problems. One night she took too much medicine and didn't wake up."

"What was it she took?"

"It was belladonna, I believe."

"Did she have any close friends?"

"There was Roberta who worked at the shop. I guess she was the best."

We got directions and said good-bye.

It wasn't hard to find the house. A turn here, a turn there. A drive down a tree-lined street flanked with small tight houses of brick or board built during the Eisenhower years.

We stopped in front of a small white house, identifiable only by its lack of identifying features—unless you count neatness as a feature. The grass had recently been mowed, and it smelled good to me as we walked to the front door. There was no front porch. We climbed the two steps to the door and rang the bell. In a moment, a pleasant woman of about sixty opened the door. She was wearing an apron over her dress, and she was drying her hands on it. We had interrupted supper preparation.

I introduced F.T. and myself, and she invited us in. We took iced tea with her in the kitchen, where I explained that we were bodyguards for Radio even though it was no longer true. And we were trying to piece together enough evidence to convict the killer. What I didn't tell her was that Pam had already been arrested.

"We've been over talking to the sheriff, and she tells us you were close to Miss Louise, Radio's mother."

"That's right. I worked for her at the shop, and we were close friends for many years."

"This could be very important. I know Radio left here years ago, but did he or anyone associated with him have any contact with Miss Louise just before her death?"

"Why, yes—Radio did. About a month before she died, he began calling her, and just before she died he even came around."

"Do you know what he wanted?"

"No, she didn't want to talk about it. The way Radio had lived his life was a great disappointment to her. All along she had wanted him to make something of himself. She wanted him to own a business—maybe a hardware store—and raise a family, not be a musician, much less an Elvis imitator."

"So she knew about him."

"Lord, yes. Everybody around here knows about him. You can't walk down the street without someone saying something about him."

"But you would have to say there was still bad blood between them," I said.

"Yes, I suppose so. At least you could say they never saw eye to eye."

"If they didn't get along, then why did he come back here to visit her?"

"I don't know. She didn't tell me."

"But he did come around just before her death—"

"That's right. In fact I think it was the same week."

"Did she have much of an estate?" I asked.

"She wasn't rich, but she'd been careful, so there was her savings, some insurance, her house, the business, and her personal effects. Maybe the whole thing totaled a hundred and fifty thousand. I'm really not sure."

"What happened to the business and the house?"

"Oh, he sold them as quick as possible. I thought he could have gotten more, but he took the first offer from a couple from Memphis—the man is disabled, and his wife runs the store. They bought the house, too."

"You don't happen to know the date of the sale, do you?"

"Certainly," she said. "It was the day I retired. A person never forgets that day."

I wrote the date down to make sure I didn't mess it up.

"One last question. Do you happen to know why he chose the name Radio?" I said.

She blushed. "Yes, I do. He didn't choose it; that's his real name. You see, his mother was the sort of woman who didn't like men. His father was the only man she ever went out with, and he didn't stay around long. And she always said she wouldn't have let him that night if the car radio hadn't been playing such sweet music."

"And she named him Radio," I said.

"That's right," she said.

There it was, the beginning of all that woman-hate. He was a bastard, and she named him that so he could never forget.

Just like the town never let her forget by always calling her "Miss Louise."

It was nightfall when we pulled off the interstate. We bought a bagful of hamburgers and a case of beer, and checked into a motel.

F.T. turned on the television and we sat down.

"All right, let's talk about it," I said. "We have two main motives for a killing—sex or money. Since we thought the killer was a woman, all along we've been trying to figure it out from the sex angle. Pam didn't want Radio to leave her, so she decided to kill him, only each time something went wrong. Four times it went wrong, and each time someone else died by mistake."

"Not four times, three times. Nobody died when he was hit on the head and locked in the cooler," said F.T.

"Right, except one," I said. "Now, what if sex wasn't the motive, and money was? That would clear Pam, but it would make Radio the killer. Let's see how that plays."

"Let's start with Tom and Marty," said F.T.

"Right. We know they had a contract with Radio, calling for equal shares when they split up the money. That meant Radio would be giving up two-thirds of his income. In his tax bracket, that's a reason for murder.

"We know that while Pam put cleaning fluid on the suit, it was Radio who loaned Tom the suit."

"Remember, the seam in Tom's suit was split," said F.T. "It would have been simple enough to sneak into his room and cut it."

"However, if it *was* done by Radio, he got away with that one. All we can ever prove is that Pam put the cleaning fluid on it, and even in her case, they're not going to be able to make a murder charge out of it," I said.

"But it could have been Radio. There's nothing to eliminate him," said F.T.

"Right. Now, in Marty's case, we know Pam made the fatal drink, but we also know Radio handled the glass. He would have had more opportunity to poison the drink than Pam. But we did find the poison in her purse," I said.

"That bothers me," said F.T. "For somebody who was as smart all along as Pam, it would have been dumb as hell to leave that bottle in her purse."

"Do you remember when we told Radio that we couldn't arrest Pam after Tom's death? He said that he would have to do something. Maybe that's the something he did—poisoned Marty, then put the bottle in her purse for us to find. Only here he made a slip and used the same method that was used for his mother. If we assume that she was also murdered, Pam couldn't have done it. She was in the hospital."

"And his motive was the inheritance. He needed money," said F.T.

"It ties in. We've both heard him say he put money into the record company. Tomorrow let's check it out. Maybe we can tie the two together now that we have the dates."

"Speaking of the record company, what are your thoughts about Ace?" said F.T.

"From what we've been able to learn about Ace, there are plenty of reasons why Radio could possibly want to kill him. Maybe Ace conned him into putting up the money, but he was going to rip him off. Maybe he found out about Radio and Lisa. I don't know."

"What about Pam's story?"

"Nope. Like Radio said, she thinks every man in the world wants to get into her pants. It just ain't so. But it could have happened like she described. Radio shot Ace, and then shot himself to throw everyone off the track."

"There were powder burns on the wounds," agreed F.T. "Radio could have shot Ace as he came down the hall, and then went back to his chair, sat down, and shot himself. All the rest of the stuff he could have done earlier—the note, the mask, the door."

I didn't say anything for a few minutes as I tried to visualize the scene in the trailer. Then it started to come to me.

"It makes sense. If Radio was shot first and Ace second, we would have found the gun in front of Ace's body, but it wasn't. It was in front of Radio."

Now F.T. was thinking back too. "Radio's wound was on

his extreme right side, as far away from any vital area as possible, but where a left-handed man would shoot himself. Radio is left-handed.''

That brought it into focus and cleared up what had been bothering me about the angles.

"That explains why his head wound was on the same side when we found him in the cooler. Remember? I mentioned it before," I said.

"But it doesn't explain one thing—How did Radio get in and out of a cooler with walls a foot thick and the door locked from the outside? It can't be done."

Sixteen

 Pyrite Records was located in a one-story professional center with parking in front. It could have been a real estate office, a doctor's office, or an insurance office just as easily.

The waiting room had couches, chairs, magazines, a desk, and a receptionist. None of it was remarkable. In fact all of it—including the receptionist—looked like it had been picked up at a warehouse sale.

I asked for Lisa, and we went through the usual business about "Who may I say is calling?" I was in no mood for civilities, so I flashed the badge and cut through the red tape.

Lisa was seated behind a kidney-shaped desk in what had obviously been her father's office. She didn't appear too thrilled to see us.

She flashed us the old painted-on smile and said, "Snake and F.T., how nice to see you."

We sat down, and I explained that I wanted to check the dates that Radio had loaned Ace money.

"What money? What makes you think he loaned Daddy any money?" she said in a confused tone.

"Because he told me so," I said.

"If he did, I don't know anything about it," she said.

That seemed likely. Ace was not the kind of man to discuss finances with his daughter. I asked to see the record of deposits and checks for the year.

"If he did loan Daddy money, what makes you think it would be there?" she said.

"It's too large an amount to be anywhere else. He couldn't launder it, and it wasn't cash, so it has to be there."

We went through her natural reluctance as a business person to open her books to outsiders, until I finally got tired of it, and yelled some and flashed my badge.

It scared her enough to do what I wanted. I sat down with the ledgers and turned to the period immediately following Miss Louise's death. There they were: three separate entries. Probably one was from her savings, one from insurance, and one from the sale of the business. Together they totaled a little over a hundred thousand.

Ace had not tried to hide them in any way. There was no need to. He simply listed them as unsecured loans made to Pyrite Records by Radio Johnson. Everything was perfectly legal—on his side at least.

On Radio's side, I now had no doubts that he was the murderer. A man who had killed his business associate, his two oldest friends, his mother, and framed his wife, too. All to win a contest. But it was more than a contest. It was a million dollars and a shot at rock and roll immortality. If he needed a reason to turn himself into Ground Zero and kill everyone close to him, a million dollars and rock and roll immortality were two great reasons.

Now the only thing that remained to be solved was the mystery of the locked cooler.

The drive to the auditorium was much easier than when we had arrived for the festival. The parking lot was empty. As we drove across the painted yellow lines of the parking spaces, I thought about how they looked like the neat, orderly rows of a well-kept garden. I wondered what sort of a crop would grow best through asphalt.

The building gleamed in the sun, empty and waiting for the evening crowds that would throng to see Radio once again strut his stuff on the eve of his tour. We drove around to the rear. A Ryder tractor-trailer was parked near the loading dock. The roadies for the tour had already unloaded the sound equipment and instruments for the evening show.

We parked the Caddy and went to the door near the loading dock. F.T. tried it. It was unlocked. We quietly made our way to the edge of the stage where the crew was busy hooking up the myriad cords that make electric music possible. We stayed only long enough to look things over, then slipped away without being seen.

We worked our way to the basement. Everything was quiet. The dressing rooms were empty and dark. Still, we made as little noise as possible moving down the hall.

The door to the storage room that housed the cooler was locked. I took out my only credit card, an expired Sunoco card, and worked it into the crack between the door and the doorframe as I've seen television private eyes do a thousand times. When I felt I had the right contact, I gave it a snap, and the card broke in half.

F.T. shook his head and opened it with one of the pieces.

The small light bulbs cast dim pools of light, barely cutting their way through the darkness. Ahead of us, the motor for the cooler hummed like an asthmatic iron lung. It was a worrisome sound.

We moved cautiously toward the cooler, but caution wasn't necessary with the noise of the motor. We could have danced to it without being heard. However, something in the dark, in the heart of the room, made us move as if we were in a hostile rice paddy.

The door to the cooler was locked by a padlock that went through the hole in the handle and kept it from being opened without its removal.

I gave the lock a flip with my finger and said, "Damn. How are we going to see how this thing locks when some inconsiderate bastard has already locked it?''

F.T. moved into the darkness and looked around until he found a short length of pipe with which he banged the lock until it gave way. With a final twist, he opened the lock and removed it from the handle. ''Nothing to it,'' he said.

''I hope you understand that what you've just done is a criminal offense, and as a duly appointed deputy sheriff, it's my duty to arrest you,'' I said.

''It would never stand up in court. No jury in the world would believe a nearsighted, sunglasses-wearing excuse of a Wyatt Earp like you. No, they'd take my side. I've got an honest face and a decent tan instead of the prison pallor that *one* of us has.''

He knelt and looked the handle over carefully. It worked like a standard door handle, except instead of a knob, it had a lever bolted to the outside of the door. To open the door, you simply pulled the lever. If you were inside the freezer, you pushed a rod that went through the door and moved the lever exactly as if you were standing outside, opening it with your hand.

To lock it, you put a padlock through a hole in the lever. When it was in place, you could not open the door from inside or out.

This much determined, we addressed ourselves to the question of how Radio could lock himself in the cooler and still get out.

F.T. opened and closed the door a few times before I said, ''Well?''

''Let's give it a try,'' he said as he picked up the broken padlock and put it back into place. Then he swung the door shut, and it was locked. The first part of the question was answered.

''There you are. He put the lock in place and then closed the door, locking himself in. There's nothing to it. We thought the door wouldn't close with the lock in place, but it will. It's like any other door you lock and then close after you.''

''Good. Now open it up, and let's see if we can figure out his escape route.''

F.T. swung the foot-thick door open and switched on the light from the outside.

The cooler was a beer drinker's paradise. One side was stacked high with cases. The other was taken up by kegs, which supplied draft beer to the bar upstairs.

The ceiling was a little too low for us, and we had to duck our heads as we entered. I looked around. The walls were all as thick as the door, and there was no other exit.

"How did he do it? We know he couldn't open the door from the inside when it was locked. And we know it was locked because we found it—remember?"

"There's got to be another way out, but I don't see where it is," said F.T.

"You're wrong. There isn't another way out," a voice behind us said.

The voice belonged to Radio.

"Put your hands up and don't turn around," he said.

We did as we were told.

"Now kneel down," he said. "It was lucky I happened to be arriving at Pyrite just as you were leaving, and followed you here .

"One at a time, I want you to take off your guns, holster and all. You first, Snake."

I shed my shoulder holster with all the dexterity of a stripper ridding herself of a Cross-Your-Heart bra filled with fire ants. F.T. did the same. When we finished we pushed the rigs behind us. I heard Radio enter the cooler and pick them up. I turned my head slightly to see if he were close enough for us to jump him, but today Radio was making no mistakes.

He backed out of the cooler and said, "All right, you can make yourselves comfortable."

We turned, and I did my best to replace my look of fear with a look of relief at the sight of him. I clasped both hands to my chest in the general area of my heart. "Whew, Radio, don't sneak up on me like that. You nearly gave me a heart attack." As I moved to stand I said, "Do us a favor, and don't mention it at the house. It wouldn't look good if everybody knew you got the drop on us so easy."

Radio smiled with his mouth, but his eyes were drug-bright mean. "Hold it right there. I didn't say you could get up."

F.T. followed my lead and started to stand. "Enough is enough. This place is too cold to hang around in."

Radio cocked the pearl-handled .38 in his hand. "I guess you didn't hear me. I said to sit down."

We sat back down, our backs against the stacked cases.

"What finally gave me away?"

I did my best to look puzzled. "Your little secret? What are you talking about?"

"Snake, you're a fool, but don't try to make me think you're a bigger one than you are."

This time I did my best to look hurt. My face was beginning to tire from changing expressions so often, but our only hope was to act ignorant and try to talk our way out.

"You really know how to hurt a person. There's no reason to play high and mighty with us. Remember, we knew you when somebody was trying to kill you."

"I'm only going to ask you once more. What gave me away?"

I looked at him. He was standing ramrod straight and cold as ice. He had run out of patience. He had no intention of tormenting us; he intended to kill us and get on about his business, so I told him.

"Nothing really gave you away. In fact the killing with the Roman candles was so slick that I don't think a jury would ever be able to convict you for that one.

"Anyway, when we sat down and thought about it, we figured that most killings are for one of two reasons: sex or money. From the very beginning, with Ace's death, you steered us toward sex. You made it look like a woman was out to get you, and fortunately for you, other people were the victims. It worked fine until we found out about your mother.

"Her death, by itself, appears to be nothing more than another unfortunate tragedy in a string of unfortunate tragedies and, as such, would have no link to the murders except for one thing: the method. You got ahead of yourself and used the same method—belladonna poisoning—twice. There was no way Pam could have killed her. She was in the hospital when your mother died. But her death was part of the whole package, so we went back to the beginning and tried a new motive: money. We don't know all the details, but so far everything points to the fact that you were cleaning up some financial problems."

"That's an interesting theory."

"And it's right, too."

"More or less," he said with a shrug of his shoulders.

"You killed the musicians because they wouldn't let you out of your contract with them. They were very happy that they were each going to get a third of your income for the rest of their lives, weren't they?"

"Yeah, my two best friends," he said with more than a trace of bitterness in his voice. "We'd been together since the beginning, and once things got rolling, they decided to hold me up. There was no way I could give away two-thirds of my income, even after expenses, and still make it. The problems of becoming a star, and staying a star, are a lot more expensive than being a fucking dime-a-dozen drummer or guitar player. I tried to get through to them on that score, but they wouldn't listen. They were along for the ride, so I had no choice. They made me do it, and it hurt me, but there was no other way."

"That explains that, but why did you kill Ace?"

"Ace was a con man, pure and simple. After he heard me sing, he came up with the idea of the Elvis contest. Naturally, I was going to win it. Then, a little later, Ace started to run short of money, so I put up some money to give him enough working cash.

"About that time, I started seeing Lisa on the sly. Just to protect my investment. Then I decided to marry her. Ace found out and hit the ceiling. He told me I wasn't going to date her, I wasn't going to marry her, and I wasn't going to win the contest.

"There was no way I was going to let some two-bit punk like Ace Feldman keep me from my destiny, from my dreams. I had no choice. So I killed him. That's where you two come in."

"Speaking of us, why did you keep us around?" I said.

"To catch the killer, of course. Pam would never give me a divorce. There was just no way. You see, Pam is crazy. She calls it being a loving wife, but the truth is, she *is* crazy.

"It's the 'control' thing. She has to have it. She just can't leave it alone. And it was her undoing. You see, I told her that I killed Ace. I told her he wanted to go to bed with her, and if I didn't let him, he would stop me from winning the contest, and I wouldn't let him, so I had to kill him.

"She loved it. What woman wouldn't? A man who would choose her over a million dollars, and kill for her, too."

"Weren't you afraid she might turn you in?" I said.

"Never in a million years. When I told her about Ace, I gave her the thing she wanted most in life—absolute control over me. Then I just took my time framing her. Again, that's where you two come in.

"I had to have somebody to catch the killer. If I let the sheriff give me a couple of deputies, they might just be smart enough to figure out what was really going on. I didn't need that, but I did need somebody, and who comes along but a couple of hayseed reporters for a jerkwater skin magazine who would give their eyeteeth to be star fuckers. You were perfect all the way down the line, good-hearted but dumb enough to make Laurel and Hardy look like brain surgeons. Until now, that is. Like the man said, all good things must come to an end."

A chill ran up my spine. I knew those were his final words. Our only chance lay in somebody finding us. I had to keep him talking.

"You killed your mother for money, right?" I said.

He took a minute to answer. It was as if he were deciding whether or not to unburden himself. Then, sensing that we wouldn't be around much longer, he decided to say it, to get that awful load off his chest, for this was the only time he would ever be able to say it until Judgment Day.

"Yeah, it was for the money. I always hated her. God, how I hated her, but never enough to kill her. She wasn't worth that much to me. Anyway, when the Elvis thing started with

Ace, I went to her for money. It was the first time I had been to see her since I left home, and she turned me down. Her own son. She turned me down flat. The Bible teaches us that there comes a time for the old to make way for the new. This was her time. It was her destiny, and she wasn't willing to face it, so I helped her."

"How?" I said.

"I fixed her a drink and made her drink it."

"How did you make her drink it?"

"I willed it, and for the first time in my life she looked at me with respect. She didn't argue or try to get out of it. She just asked if I was sure that was what I wanted. I told her it was. Then she drank it."

"What did you do then?"

"I sat with her while we waited, and I told her about all my plans. For once in my life, she sat quietly and listened while I talked. You see, there were a lot of things that had happened to me since I left home. Things I needed to tell her. This time she sat and listened. I told her about my dreams, and my failures, and now my big chance. She listened quietly, sitting there in the chair with her hands folded in her lap, until the time came, and she went to sleep. There were still many things I had to tell her, so I sat there talking till the morning came. Then I left, knowing she loved me and approved of me."

His tears had cut great muddy gullies through the layer of makeup he wore to cover his deathlike pallor. His mouth was twisted in a clown's grimace of grief. His whole body shook with sobs. Even in this last hour, he had not lost the magic touch to make all, from the smallest to the largest, share and feel his grief, confusion, and disillusionment.

As he swung the great door shut, curiously I felt little anger, only sadness—partly for F.T. and me, and our death, partly for Radio and his life.

We heard the whine of the motor as the compressor kicked on. This meant Radio had lowered the temperature to make things happen more quickly. And it wouldn't be long. The temperature was just above freezing before he turned on the compressor. Now the blower was starting to circulate the icy

Art Bourgeau

air. In only a short time the temperature would be around zero, with the movement of the air by the blower making the windchill factor even colder. Dressed for summer as we were, we couldn't expect to live more than a few hours in the extreme cold.

F.T. got to his feet and tried the door. It was locked from the outside. The door and walls were at least a foot thick and solid in construction. The thickness of the walls made escape impossible. The heavy insulation made the freezer virtually soundproof. If Radio had locked us in a bank vault, he couldn't have done a better job. There was no way we were going anywhere—except to meet our Maker.

But we didn't panic; there was no need to. Death is an inevitable part of life, the certainty of which we become increasingly aware with the passage of each day. As a child you know you will never die; in your prime you hope you will never die; and after that, you know you *will* die. The only questions that remain to be answered are when and how. Like most people, when confronted with the fact that "when and how" is here and now, we accepted it stoically. It would be over quickly. We wouldn't linger. There would be no pain. And we were in good company. Maybe, God willing, we would go at the same time so we could cross that great chasm to the darkness together.

There was no need to yell and scream or to claw our fingernails bloody on the door, because it wouldn't do any good. Our fate was out of our hands.

I reached behind me and opened a case of Old Blue. I popped the top on one for F.T. and one for me. Satisfied there was no way out, he sat down beside me, with his back to the cases, and took a long pull on his beer. Staring off into space, he said, "Looks like this is it, partner. I don't see any way out of this one."

I didn't look at him either. "Yeah, we've had some good times together. We've been on the short end of the stick, and the long end. We've seen sunrises and sunsets. We've drunk beer and made love to women. We've laughed, cried, sung, lied, and howled at the moon. When it comes to dying, I can't

206

think of a better way to go than locked inside a walk-in cooler full of beer in the company of F.T. Zevich, the greatest sonofabitch that ever lived," I said as I held my can up in a toast.

F.T. wiped the corner of his eye with the back of his hand and in a choked voice said, "My only regret is that we were never able to have children."

I was taking a sip when he said it. The beer shot up through my nose, cauterizing my sinuses in the process. When I finally stopped coughing I said, "Don't lay that on me. You know the doctor said I was all right."

F.T. harrumphed. "Some doctor. You're talking about that old quack you went to in New Orleans when you caught the crabs and thought you'd developed an allergy to your soap."

I wasn't able to continue because I was laughing too hard. All of the tension of the situation came rushing out as we literally went into hysterics and couldn't stop laughing. After what seemed like hours, we sat there limp and teary-eyed.

"The old routines are the best, but I didn't expect you to use *that* one at the end of my death speech."

F.T. took a swig. "You were starting to take yourself too seriously. You know it ain't exactly Hamlet when you freeze to death in a walk-in cooler."

"That fucking Radio—"

"Quiet," said F.T. "I don't want to hear his name again. The place you die should be sacred, and I don't want this place to be dirtied by even the *mention* of his name."

"What do you suggest we do?"

"There's nothing we can do but wait. If nobody comes, then we die—simple as that."

"At least we can tear up some of these cartons and wrap them around us to keep warm," I said.

"Good idea," said F.T. We got busy and in a few minutes we both looked like we were from *The Wizard of Oz*. The cardboard helped a little, but I was starting to shiver.

"Christ, I'm cold," I said.

"Drink more beer," said F.T.

"Won't that waste your body heat?" I said.

"Would you rather die drunk or sober?"

"Point well taken," I said.

"Let's see if we can drink up everything in the cooler before we go."

Even the beer didn't help, and in a little while my feet were starting to get numb. I recognized the end was getting closer but shrugged it off and continued drinking.

"You know, we ought to leave a note or something so they'll know Radio did this. Maybe we can use one of these cases to scratch it on the wall," I said.

"Forget it," said F.T. "Graffiti is inadmissible in a court of law."

Time moved slowly. We huddled together for warmth, Because of his size, F.T. wasn't as cold as I was, but he wasn't far behind.

I was starting to doze off from the beer and the cold. F.T. would catch me and slap me awake.

"Don't go to sleep yet. If you do, it's all over, and I ain't ready to say good-bye yet."

But the cold relentlessly took us over, an inch at a time. The tingle had all turned to numbness, and my brain was ready to give in.

Through the haze of half sleep I kept hearing a sound. A sound like water running under pressure. It was an irritating sound that kept waking me. I tried to figure where it was coming from, then it would stop, and I'd forget it. This went on until I located the source. It was coming from the beer kegs as the bartenders upstairs drew drafts for the concert crowd.

"Sounds like they're selling a lot of beer upstairs," I said.

"Yeah," said F.T. "Looks like we'll have to give up on our idea of drinking the place dry. We'd never be able to drink all that draft, even if we could get it out of the kegs."

That started a germ of an idea, but my mind was so cloudy that I couldn't hold on to it. I started to nod off again, but the noise from the kegs woke me. Then it dawned on me: disconnect the hoses from the kegs. It would stop the beer at the bar, and one of the bartenders would have to come down to see what was the matter.

F.T. and I struggled to get the couplings loose so we could disconnect the hoses. Our cold hands didn't want to work, and each move seemed as if our fingers would break off with the effort. Finally they came free, one at a time, until all the kegs were disconnected.

Then we waited.

Help was not long in coming.

The look on the bartender's face when he opened the cooler door was a look composed of many different elements. Chief among them was surprise. It was a look that defies description but one that a great artist could spend a lifetime trying to record on canvas and still go to his grave having been unsuccessful in his attempts.

The element of surprise was quickly replaced by irritation as he took in the whole scene at a glance and jumped to the wrong conclusion. He was thinking we were a couple of thieves who had broken into the cooler and, in the midst of our good time, had accidentally locked ourselves in. A flash of my badge put that notion to rest.

F.T. and I hobbled to the door on the sort of numb feet that spelled the end for Hitler's armies in Russia. The warm humid outside air made us go into uncontrollable shivers as our metabolisms struggled to readjust. I hugged myself in pain as flashes of heat raced through my cold nerves.

The return of sensation to my hands, feet, nose, and ears was torture. It was the sort of pain you feel when your foot goes to sleep, but it was much worse.

The bartender reconnected the draft hoses to the kegs and stayed with us until we were able to move around. When at last the pain had quieted enough for me to be able to think and speak, I said, "Has the show started yet? Has Radio gone on?"

"Yeah, he went on about fifteen minutes ago," said the bartender. "Look, if you're all right, I'd better get back. We're busy as hell up there."

"Sure, go ahead. We're fine," I said.

After he had gone, F.T. looked around in the darkness near the cooler until he found the short length of pipe he had used to break the lock. As he stood there, smacking the pipe into his palm, his eyes developed a strange gleam.

"Let's go drag him off the stage. I know he'll resist arrest, and when he does I'm going to hurt him. So that he'll never be whole again. So that he'll never get another full night's sleep as long as he lives, because every time he closes his eyes, he'll see Zevich and Kirlin, and remember."

"No, you're not, F.T.—you just settle down. No deputy of mine is going to go around talking crazy like that."

Standing in the doorway was Sheriff McDuff. He ambled into the room. "The bartender told me about finding y'all down here. What happened?"

I gave him a quick rundown of our discoveries leading up to and including our imprisonment in the cooler. When I finished he let out a low whistle and said, "There's our case. With y'all to testify, we'll put him away for good. Let's go get him."

We climbed the steps and made our way to the wings. The sheriff sent a couple of deputies around to the other side to stop Radio if he tried to escape.

Radio was dressed in black: black leather jacket, black satin shirt, black trousers. There were metal studs on the pants and jacket. They picked up the star lights and reflected them back, making him look, for all the world, like a black leather Christmas tree.

The show was drawing to a close. Radio was singing "American Trilogy," Mickey Newbury's beautiful blend of traditional Southern songs. There was the wistful lonesomeness of "Dixie," sung as it should be, slow and homesick. It blended into "Hush, Little Baby," a slave song filled with the resignation and condemnation of status quo, and the inability to change. And finally, the stirring strains of Julia Ward Howe's "Battle Hymn of the Republic."

It was the story of America, but more particularly the South, our *War and Peace*, covering a hundred years in four minutes. It spanned the emotions of a century from Tom Sawyer to the death of Elvis, from Becky Thatcher to the death of Janis Joplin, and from ol' nigger Jim to the death of Martin Luther King, Jr. A century in which North and South alike achieved the American dream, as long as you didn't try to cash it.

Radio was hot and singing his heart out. As his powerful voice hit the crescendo to the "Battle Hymn," he looked to the wings where we stood. In that moment he saw the gold ring he so desperately wanted once again pull away, this time gone forever from his reach.

A look of sadness and resignation crossed his face. It was the look of the competitor, whom distance and time has robbed of his legs, as he turns into the home stretch and sees the finish line, and knows that his nipples will never again harden with the soft, silky, seductive feel of the tape as, like a beautiful woman, it surrenders to his power and speed.

It was the look of the old fighter whose once deadly hook whistles harmlessly over the bobbing head of his younger opponent, and whose own neck muscles will no longer respond to move him safely and beautifully out of the way as the thud and thunder of the younger man's gloves land again and again, until the very skin of his face tears like a cheap pair of shoes.

It was the face of a man robbed, in spite of all he could do, by the relentless passing of time—his time once passed, never to return again. The aging beauty who stayed for one dance too long, only to have the harsh lights of closing time show up what the makeup and darkness had hidden till then.

With this realization comes an emptiness, an aloneness, a sadness that nobody can comfort, for to experience it is to shake hands with death. And like all death, it cannot be shared. To those who see it, it is beyond comprehension. They say, "How can he be sad? He had so much." And they resent, rather than appreciate, the humanity of his struggle. All they can see is that as he—the Great One—passes, so pass they, the lonely piss-ants of the world, and they hate, revile, and ridicule him for it, stripping him of his robes and glory until at last he who was worshipped is less than the least of those who worship.

But like all the Great Ones, Radio knew these facts. He knew that the love of the worshippers was a love built on envy and hate. He knew that merely by their coming, each broke one of the sacred commandments as they sat safely in the darkness, coveting all, not only all that he had, but all that he be. And killer, bastard, whoremonger that he be, there was no Quit in him. He was one dog who would not turn belly-up in defeat.

We stood watching and waiting as he turned back to the audience, his hand clutching the scepter of his microphone, the lights twinkling on the stainless steel jewels of his regal leather robes. With his world in flames around him, he stood straight and tall, heir for one single moment to the vacant throne of the King of Rock and Roll.

He drew the microphone to his lips and said, "Tonight you came here hoping against hope that you would find Elvis instead of me. But you were wrong. Elvis is dead! He has been dead these five long years. I've sung his songs, worn his clothes, lived his life, and in those things found pleasure. But one thing doesn't change. Elvis is dead! The time has come for me to put him to rest. Even kings deserve that.

"What you have in his place is me. I've sung my last Elvis song. Tonight I'll close with my own stuff. I hope you like it . . ."

I could feel the hate pouring out of F.T. as he stood next to me. He wanted to get his hands on Radio, to hurt him, to humiliate him, to grind him under his heel, to make him pay for all the deaths and hurt he had caused in his pursuit of his dream.

Radio stepped away from the mike for two counts, and then stepped back to it and said, "If you don't like it, you can go straight to hell, 'cause you're dealing with a man who all his life has been 'Doing Eighty in a Forty-Mile Zone.' "

With that the band surged ahead with a train-wheel-driving blues beat as Radio danced and pranced, this time part Mick Jagger, part Johnny Winter, part James Brown, part Joe Tex, part Tina Turner, and true to his word—no Elvis.

When it was over he stood tall and silent, looking into the darkness—waiting.

The applause came slowly, like the first drips of summer

rain smacking the concrete as they hit. Then building until it reached thunderstorm proportions as the curtain came down.

It had come to pass. He had ascended to the heavens and become a star. He, Radio Johnson, bastard child of Miss Louise, the boy with the green hair. The ungainly combination of bad skin, blood, and bone from whom love, happiness, and popularity had fled like animals before a fire. But no more. No longer was he condemned to live in hindsight, only thinking of himself in terms of past failures. Now he was a star.

While he stood there listening, his hand reached inside his leather jacket and brought out his derringer. Before we could reach him, he had pressed it against his temple and pulled the trigger. As he crumpled to the stage, the last sound he heard was the sound of applause ringing in his ears.

The sheriff cleared the stage while the audience filed out. When the hall was empty, I walked out on the stage alone and looked down at Radio's body.

The few days we had spent with him had affected me like no others. For to know Radio Johnson was to know dreams. The night he had called himself the dream maker and the dream taker, the center of light and motion, the focus, he had been right.

And he had been bold as he reached out to mold and shape these dreams into clay, and flesh, and cash. For him ambition was a verb never at rest, constantly moving forward toward the light. Onward . . . onward . . . forever onward. Damn the torpedoes, full speed ahead, take what you want and leave the rest, to hell with the cost. Christmas could come twice a year if you only believed.

Even though he had just tried to kill me, I couldn't hate him. For to hate him was to live in the past and not learn from it. It was as useless as damning the wind, howling at the moon, raging at the rain, and—oh yes, cursing the light.

I heard a sound behind me and turned to look. There, in the near darkness of the empty hall, sat Elvis's true bride: Greatness. She was far back, but I knew her by her long shining hair and her gown. She beckoned, and I walked to the edge of the stage for a better look. She beckoned again, and I started to come to her, but then I saw her face.

It was the toothless, wrinkled face of a thousand-year-old hag, with bright shining eyeballs sunk in her skull. When she realized that I had seen through her, she started to laugh and cackle. I stepped back, shaking my head in wonder at those who would marry with her. Then, in turning away, I saw Radio's face.

Where peace should have been was a look of pure torment, and I realized beauty is in the eye of the beholder.

Bestselling Books

☐ 52867-8	**METZGER'S DOG** Thomas Perry	$3.50
☐ 08954-2	**THE BUTCHER'S BOY** Thomas Perry	$3.95
☐ 65366-9	**THE PATRIARCH** Chaim Bermant	$3.25
☐ 02574-9	**THE APOCALYPSE BRIGADE** Alfred Coppel	$3.50
☐ 75886-X	**SENSEI** David Charney	$3.95
☐ 79265-0	**SENSEI II: SWORD MASTER** David Charney	$3.95
☐ 05285-1	**BED REST** Rita Kashner	$3.25
☐ 11726-0	**A CONTROLLING INTEREST** Peter Engel	$3.50
☐ 02884-5	**ARCHANGEL** Gerald Seymour	$3.50

Prices may be slightly higher in Canada.

Bestselling Books from Berkley – action-packed for a great read

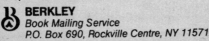